The Lance

By

Alex Lukeman

http://www.alexlukeman.com

Copyright © 2011 by Alex Lukeman

The Project Series:

White Jade
The Lance
The Seventh Pillar
Black Harvest
The Tesla Secret
The Nostradamus File
The Ajax Protocol
The Eye of Shiva
Black Rose
The Solomon Scroll
The Russian Deception
The Atlantis Stone

"*The best political weapon is the weapon of terror. Cruelty commands respect.*
Men may hate us. But, we don't ask for their love; only for their fear."

Heinrich Himmler, Reichsfuehrer, SS

Prologue: Antarctica
February 19, 1945

The Fenris Mountains reared stark and black against the dazzling white of the Antarctic plain. SS General Dieter Reinhardt watched two crewmen from U-886 clear ice and snow from steel doors set into the side of one of the nameless peaks. A motorized sled waited nearby. Reinhardt was tall and thin, his face almost a mirror of the death's head emblem on his high, peaked hat. In his long greatcoat and dark, round snow goggles he looked like a malevolent insect.

The doors swung open. The crewmen picked up a wooden crate from the sled and followed Reinhardt down a dark corridor into the heart of the mountain. The corridor ended at a steel vault. Reinhardt worked a numbered combination dial, turned a large, spoked wheel and pulled open the heavy door.

Metal boxes lined one side of the vault. On the opposite wall, gold bars stamped with the eagle and swastika shone in the bright light of Reinhardt's electric torch.

"Put it there, against the back." His breath formed clouds in the frigid air as he spoke.

The crewmen set the box down. Reinhardt drew his pistol and stepped up behind one of the men, placed the muzzle at the base of his skull and fired. The report was deafening in the enclosed, metal space. His mate turned, eyes wide in shock. Reinhardt fired again. Blood sprayed across the stacks of gold.

Reinhardt holstered the pistol, stepped around the bodies and went back into the corridor.

He closed the vault door and locked it in place, retraced his steps and came out into the polar glare. Taking his time, he placed charges around the entrance to the bunker. The explosion brought down an avalanche of ice and snow over the doors. No one would ever find the entrance again, unless they knew exactly where it was.

Reinhardt got on the sled and headed back toward the distant edge of the ice shelf and the submarine. He thought of the night he'd been summoned from Berlin.

20MM twin anti-aircraft guns at the front and rear of Himmler's private train pointed at the moonless sky. Not far away, on the other side of the Rhine, flashes of light and the distant rumble of artillery signaled the advance of the Allied armies. A faint glow hinted at fires banked in the boilers of two huge locomotives. The quiet hiss of escaping steam gave notice the train was ready to move.

Frosted globes lit the interior of the command car, the light held prisoner by blackout curtains drawn tight over the windows. SS Reichsfuehrer Heinrich Himmler sat halfway down the car behind a desk. He looked up as Reinhardt entered.

The yellow lamplight reflected from Himmler's round, flat glasses. In civilian clothes, with his receding, thin hair and sandy mustache, he could have been mistaken for a mild mannered grocery clerk. In his SS uniform with the silver wreath and oak leaves on his collar, he looked like what he was; the most dangerous man in Nazi Germany. Only Hitler had more power.

Reinhardt raised his arm and snapped his heels together.

"Come with me, General." Himmler stood. Reinhardt followed him to the baggage car. Four hard-looking SS guards armed with Schmeisser sub machine guns sprang to attention.

"Leave us."

Himmler waved them away. On a table at the side of the car was an open crate. Inside the crate was a polished box of black walnut. The lid of the box bore a swastika and victory wreath of solid gold, set with diamonds. The stones glittered in the lamplight.

Himmler lifted the cover. The Holy Lance lay within on lay on a bed of blood red silk, the spear that had pierced Christ's side. Reinhardt laid his hand on the ancient blade. It felt warm, even in the chill of the unheated railroad car.

It was said that whoever possessed the Lance controlled the destiny of the world. The legend had been written by centuries of blood and conquest. All the great conquerors of Europe had carried the Lance before their armies. Only Napoleon had failed to secure it.

Some thought the power of the Lance came from the Antichrist. Reinhardt and Himmler didn't care where the power came from. They knew it was real. That was the only thing that mattered. Only the Knights of the Grand Council knew Himmler had the Lance. Only Himmler and the Council knew it was the Lance that had brought victory in the early years of the war.

Himmler handed Dieter a thick packet.

"Your orders. Take the Lance to Antarctica and conceal it, then proceed to Argentina."

"Base 211?"

Himmler nodded. Few people who knew of the hidden research complex in the Antarctic wastes were still alive. No one had been there since '42.

"We will regroup in Argentina. In time we will retrieve the Lance and continue."

Himmler laid his hand on Reinhardt's shoulder, a rare gesture of comradeship.

"Dieter. It is possible I will not survive this war."

He held up his hand to silence Reinhardt's protest. The light glinted from Himmler's glasses and the death's head ring on his finger.

"If I fall, there will be a new Grand Master. Aid him in every way you can."

"As you command, Riechsfuehrer."

That Grand Master will be me, Reinhardt thought.

Both men looked down at the Holy Lance. It seemed to glow with faint blood light.

"We have lost for now," Himmler said. "But as long as the Lance is ours, we will never be defeated."

A patch of rough ice under the sled jolted Reinhardt out of his memories and back to the present. He could see the submarine waiting in the distance, dark as Jonah's whale in the open water past the edge of the gleaming ice.

He would tell the Captain of U-886 his crewmen had been buried by a fall of ice. It was of no importance. When they reached Argentina, the Captain and the others would soon join their dead comrades. It was all arranged.

Three days later, British depth charges found U-886 as she approached the Argentine coast. She breached the surface long enough for the officer of the watch to record her badge and type before she vanished beneath the waves.

In the lightless vault under the mountain, the Lance waited beneath the diamond swastika. One day, someone would come. It was only a matter of time.

CHAPTER ONE

The sweet scent of Jasmine vines climbing the wall of the crumbling tenement in the Old City of Damascus wafted through an open window. A man bent over a wooden table with a soldering iron. He wiped sweat away from his forehead with the frayed sleeve of his shirt and concentrated on his task.

Another man watched from a sagging couch pushed against one of the stained yellow walls. He wore a dark suit of European cut. His crisp, white shirt was open at the collar.

The man on the couch had a face that was blank, forgettable. His features were smooth and calm, as if life had never quite reached the surface. It was hot in the apartment, but the man was not sweating. His eyebrows were unnoticeable above his colorless eyes. His nose seemed to disappear into the vagueness of his features. His lips were a thin, invisible line.

The man at the table was called Ibrahim. The man on the couch was called the Visitor, but Ibrahim didn't know that. It was better that way.

The bomb was almost finished. It was a very fine bomb, perhaps the best Ibrahim had ever made, and he had made many. He was well known throughout the terrorist network. If you wanted something unusual, reliable and easily concealed, with the most destructive result, you sought out the Syrian.

Anyone with a simple knowledge of electronics could build a suicide vest or a roadside device, but few could do what Ibrahim did. The truth of his skill was easy to see. He still owned almost all of his fingers and both eyes, no mean feat for an old bomb maker.

He soldered the final connection. He set the iron down and allowed himself to relax.

"It is ready?"

The man in the suit spoke in Arabic, his voice quiet, pleasant. He got off the couch, looked over the bomb maker's shoulder. Ibrahim tried to place the accent. German, perhaps.

Ibrahim took an unfiltered cigarette from a crumpled yellow pack, held it in nicotine stained fingers and lit it. The harsh tobacco smoke formed a blue cloud as he exhaled. The man in the suit concealed his disapproval.

"Yes, ready. When you place the charge, set and activate the timer. There is a twenty-four hour window."

Ibrahim showed his guest the arming device, small like a woman's wrist watch. A red arrow was etched on the bezel surrounding the dial. The face was marked for twenty four hours. A second, smaller ring within the first was divided into twelve five minute increments.

"Set the hour by rotating the outer ring clockwise. Then, set the inner ring counter clockwise for fine adjustment. You can reset until you press this button. After that, no. The timer will run until your mark is reached. The bomb is safe until the time chosen. Then, boom."

The Visitor nodded.

"Give me the pack."

The Visitor handed Ibrahim a backpack. Bright yellow letters over a yellow and green ram's head imprint spelled out Colorado State University on the flap. Inside were socks, two tee shirts, a teaspoon or two of beach sand, a pair of hiking shorts, postcards, dirty underwear, a pair of Dockers, a package of condoms, sandals and a water bottle.

There were also two books. One was a popular paperback listing hostels and restaurants in Israel. The other was a hardbound travel guide to the holy sites of Jerusalem.

Ibrahim opened the guide to a hollowed out space where the bomb would be concealed. The new compound his guest had provided was a marvel of technology, fifty times more powerful than conventional Semtex or C-4. It had a color like sand or old, yellowed limestone and could be molded and shaped as needed. It seemed small, but the explosive force it yielded was devastating. It was also undetectable by current methods. Even the dogs would never sense it.

The book was well thumbed, innocent in appearance. The pages concealed shielding that blocked detection by the most sophisticated electronic equipment. Of course there was always a chance of discovery. The Jews and the Americans were good at counter terrorism. Ibrahim assumed the bomb was meant for one or the other.

Success was not Ibrahim's concern, nor was he concerned about where or how the bomb would be used. He knew it was good. His work was done. He placed the bomb in the book. He locked the pages in place that would keep a casual observer from noticing anything. He closed the cover and put the book back in the pack.

The haunting sound of the call to prayer echoed through the ancient city from speakers atop the Umayyad Mosque. Ibrahim would go to the mosque and refresh his relationship with God. The other could do as he pleased.

"You have done well, my brother." His client's voice was quiet, toneless. "Allah will reward you in the afterlife."

"There is still this life, no? You have brought payment?"

"Of course. I have it here."

The Visitor reached under his jacket and took out a silenced .22 Ruger automatic pistol and shot Ibrahim in the forehead. The bomb maker's mouth formed a soft oh. His eyes opened wide and rolled upward. The Visitor fired another round into the Syrian's left ear, a whisper soft as a baby's breath. The body toppled sideways from the chair to the floor. A trickle of blood ran out onto the worn, scarred linoleum.

The Visitor bent down and wiped a few spatters of blood from the end of one of his shiny black shoes. He took the backpack and placed it in a cloth shopping bag. He turned on a small radio set on the table. The rhythmic notes of an oud and drums filled the room with sounds of life. Ibrahim's neighbors would not notice anything amiss for some time.

The Syrian had been a good asset, but all possible trails to what was going to happen, any loose ends, must be eliminated. Ibrahim had been a loose end.

The so-called nation of Israel would soon cease to exist. All it would take to start the process was this one, small bomb. The Visitor closed the apartment door behind him and walked down the stairs to the cobbled alley below, whistling to himself.

CHAPTER TWO

Nicholas Carter looked at Elizabeth Harker and thought if there were any elves in the world, they probably looked like her. She was small boned and slim. She had milk white skin and small ears tucked under raven black hair. She had wide, green eyes. She was dressed in a black pants suit and white blouse with a Mao collar. In two years working for her he'd never seen her wear anything but black and white.

Harker ran the Project, the Presidential Official Joint Exercise in Counter Terrorism. She was Nick's boss. Her boss was the President.

On Harker's desk were a silver pen, a picture of the Twin Towers burning and a manila folder. The pen had belonged to FDR. The picture was a reminder. The folder was likely going to shape his day. Working for Harker meant he never knew if the day might leave him hanging out on the edge and wondering if he could pull himself back in.

He heard Harker say, "Someone's thinking about making trouble in the Middle East."

"Someone's always thinking about making trouble in the Middle East. What's different now?"

He fumbled in his pocket, found a crumbly antacid tablet and popped it in his mouth. Carter felt the tremor of a headache starting. Harker picked up her silver pen and began tapping it on the polished surface of her desk. Each tap vibrated inside his skull.

"The President is speaking in Jerusalem on Thursday. We have a source who says there's going to be trouble. He wants a face to face meet."

Carter tugged on the mutilated lobe of his left ear, where a Chinese bullet had taken off the lobe a few months ago. The bandage was off. It had looked better with it on.

It was the same ear that itched whenever things were about to get dicey, his very own personal early warning system. It itched now. A gift, or a curse, that he'd inherited from his Irish Grandmother, along with dreams he didn't want to have.

"Have you passed this to Langley? What do they say?"

"I'm supposed to back off and leave things up to the 'professionals'." There was an edge to her voice. "Lodge says there's no need for concern."

Wendell Lodge, Acting Director of the CIA.

"He says he and his Israeli counterparts have everything under control."

"Mossad?"

"And Shin Bet."

"What's Shin Bet?" said Selena.

Selena Connor sat next to Carter on Harker's leather couch. The ceiling lights caught the reddish blond color of her hair and turned her eyes violet. She wore a tan silk outfit and a pale blouse that went with her eyes. She was the first woman Nick had let get close since Megan died. He didn't know where it was going. Or if he wanted it to go anywhere. She was new to the team, which meant she had a lot to learn, which worried the hell out of him

Selena brushed a stray wisp of hair from her forehead.

Harker said, "Shin Bet is Israel's version of the FBI, on steroids. They handle internal security and counter-terrorism. Mossad is foreign intelligence and ops, like MI6 or CIA."

Carter looked down at his hands and picked at a broken fingernail. "Lodge is a devious bastard and a narcissist."

"Whatever he is, he's not going to brush us off. You're going to Israel. You find something that threatens Rice's security, give it to Shin Bet and the Secret Service. They've got the manpower, let them handle it. You leave today."

"I always wanted to see Jerusalem. Maybe I'll get a little sightseeing in."

She set the pen down and folded her hands. "It's not a vacation, Nick. You're booked into the same hotel as the President as part of his party, right outside the Old City. The Israelis may not let you keep your weapon. They're sensitive about guns and you're not Secret Service."

"Who's the source over there?"

"His name is Arshak Arslanian. He has a shop in the Armenian Quarter." She slid the manila folder across her desk. "His photo and info is in there."

Harker turned to Selena. "Selena, you continue with Ronnie this afternoon."

Ronnie was the third member of Nick's team. He was just back from visiting his family on the Navajo Reservation in Arizona. He'd been coaching Selena. Physical training, weapons, codes, the tricks of personal survival. All the things that might give her a chance to make it through the next year.

Harker tapped her pen and looked at Nick. "You'll need a lot of time to clear security. You'd better get going."

CHAPTER THREE

Carter sat with his back against the wall at a café in the New City, drinking espresso, watching the crowd. The night was warm. The pedestrian mall where King George and Ben-Yahuda streets and the Jaffa Road came together in Jerusalem was packed with people.

For the Jewish people, Jerusalem was the center of the world. It was where the Messiah would some day appear. It was the place where God had commanded the building of His Temple, where every stone, pebble and grain of dust on the Temple Mount was sacred ground. Devout Jews all over the world recited prayers each day for the restoration of the Temple, destroyed by the Romans in 70 CE.

The most important shrines of Christianity were here. The tomb of Christ, the room of the last supper, the Garden of Gethsemane where Christ received the Judas kiss. The place where Pontius Pilate passed sentence. The place of crucifixion. Every Christian denomination in the world had a church or shrine somewhere in the Old City.

For Muslims, the al-Aqsa Mosque on the Temple Mount was one of the holiest sites in Islam. The Mosque faced the Dome of the Rock, where they believed Muhammad had ascended to heaven on a winged horse to receive instruction from God. The Muslims had lost Jerusalem to the Israelis in the 1967 war. They wanted it back.

Armies had fought over Jerusalem for three thousand years. The narrow streets of the Old City had run ankle deep in blood more than once. Unless someone found a path to peace in the region, Carter figured the streets would run with blood again.

He'd thought he was done with all that, with the blood, when he left the Marines. Now he worked for the Project. Even though he was a civilian, he was still waking up in war zones. He did his best not to think about it. Best thing, focus on the mission. It was why he was in Jerusalem on a perfect October evening. Someone had to do it.

Carter drank his coffee and watched the crowd, tracking, reading expressions, looking for anything unusual. His eyes never stayed still. It was an old habit and it was why he was still alive. He never assumed he was safe. He never trusted appearances.

A young woman in a red dress played an accordion nearby. She had long, dark tresses and she laughed while she played. A small group of smiling people stood in front of her, tapping their feet in time to the music. Children ran through the throng. Carter smiled.

The night disappeared in violent white light.

The blast sent Nick backward into the wall and down to the pavement.

Everything went white. He was back in Afghanistan. He could smell the dust, hear the AKs firing, the explosions all around him. Then the white faded. The flashback faded. He could still hear the echoes of the AKs and smell the dry dust of the street. For a moment he didn't know where he was. Then he did.

A pall of black smoke hung over torn bodies spread in a red smear across the plaza. A flat, dead silence filled his ears. Then the screaming started.

A heavy café table lay on top of him. He pushed it to the side and got to his feet. The woman in the red dress lay crumpled and torn nearby, her accordion shattered and silent.

Broken glass and smashed furniture littered the plaza. There was blood on him, but it wasn't his. Carter took a step and tripped. He looked down at a child's foot in a blue shoe. It was just a small foot. A piece of white bone stuck out of a pink sock.

He bent over and threw up the espresso in a yellow brown stream. The acrid, coppery stench of blood poisoned the clean night air. He straightened up and wiped his lips. Something caught his eye across the way.

A man stood off to the side of the plaza. He was of medium height, with close set dark eyes, black hair, a thin black mustache and neat beard. He wore a shapeless brown jacket, baggy brown pants and a dirty yellow shirt. He was talking on a cell phone.

He was smiling.

The smile vanished when he saw Carter looking at him. He turned and walked away, holding the phone to his ear.

Who smiles at a slaughterhouse? Carter started after him.

Brown Jacket picked up his pace. He glanced back and turned into a wide alley between two buildings. Nick wished he had his .45. The Israelis had refused to let him carry it. He began running. Shouts sounded behind him as he sprinted into the alley.

The alley crossed between the buildings to the next street over. Brown Jacket and two others stood halfway down. At the far end of the passage a white Volvo waited, motor running, one man inside. Brown Jacket said something to the two men and walked toward the car. The others started toward Nick.

The larger man wore a loose blue jacket over a dingy white shirt and jeans. His head was bullet shaped and shaven. His face was dissolute, with ridges of old scar tissue over eyes that looked dead. His ears were crumpled cauliflowers and his hands were broad clubs, scarred with swollen and broken knuckles. A street fighter, a boxer.

The other man was the leader. He was small, mean looking and dark, with shiny, squinty eyes, a scruffy beard and a nasty smile that showed gaps in his teeth. The two separated, a few feet apart, Squinty to Nick's right, Boxer to his left. A flash of steel appeared in each man's hand.

Knives. He hated knives.

Words echoed inside his head.

You've got two choices in an alley fight. Run or attack. If you attack, if there's more than one man, go for the leader. Always take out the leader first.

He walked straight at them. Not what they expected. Then he sprinted at Squinty and shouted from deep in his gut, a harsh, primal scream that vibrated off the alley walls. It froze both men, just long enough.

Squinty lunged forward, the knife held straight out and low, coming up for a classic strike under the rib cage to rip the diaphragm and the aorta. Carter grasped his wrist and reached over with his left hand, levered up and out and broke Squinty's elbow, using momentum to fling him to the side. He side kicked and took out Boxer's knee.

The knee folded sideways at an impossible angle. It crunched and broke, a deep, unmistakable sound of terrible injury and unbearable pain. Boxer screamed and slashed out as he went down. A cut cold as ice opened along Nick's thigh.

Boxer tried to sit up. Carter kicked him in the throat. He clutched his neck and fell back choking. His eyes opened wide in terror as he tried to breathe. At the other end of the alley, Brown Jacket got into the Volvo. As the car drove off, he threw Nick a look of venomous hatred.

Squinty reached for his knife with his left hand. Nick kicked him hard in the head, a kick that could have got him into the NFL.

Back at the entrance of the alley two cops appeared, guns drawn, shouting. Carter raised his hands, fingers spread wide.

He guessed he was about to find out what the inside of an Israeli police station looked like.

CHAPTER FOUR

Selena and Ronnie Peete were in the basement pistol range of the Project building outside of Washington. Ronnie was Navajo, born on the Rez. He was a tough man, yet Selena had seen him reciting a sacred Navajo ritual just before the three of them were about to parachute into the highest mountains on earth.

She thought it an odd mix, a man who could hold on to something sacred or an MP-5 with equal ease. He'd been in Nick's Recon unit in Afghanistan and Iraq, and, she thought, a few other places people didn't usually hear about. Sometimes she felt a little jealous of the bond between the two men.

Ronnie was broad shouldered and narrow hipped. He had sleepy brown eyes that looked out past a large, Roman nose and strong arms that bulged under the short sleeves of his Hawaiian shirt. His skin was the color of the desert on a summer day, light brown blended with a subtle undertone of red.

She watched him lay out two Beretta nine millimeter automatics on the shooting bench.

"How was Arizona?" she said.

"It was great. You been down there?"

"Monument Valley and Four Corners. I've never seen colors like that, the way the light paints the rocks and the desert."

Ronnie nodded. "You can let your mind go in all that space. When the rains come and the clouds build up over the Sacred Mountains, it's one of the most beautiful sights in the world."

He reached in his pocket, took a picture from his wallet. He handed it to Selena. It showed a stout, older woman in front of a low building of wood capped with an earthen roof. A deep red velvet dress, almost purple, reached to her ankles. Around her neck and on her arms and hands she wore heavy jewelry of silver and turquoise.

Next to her stood a man in jeans, a plaid shirt and a flat brimmed black Stetson sporting a silver Concho hat band.

"This is my Auntie and Uncle. They're both traditional Navajo. He's a Singer."

"A singer? You mean like rock and roll?"

Ronnie laughed, a deep, belly laugh. "No, a Singer is...like a doctor. Only he's a doctor for restoring harmony, not a doctor with pills. When something bad happens, like sickness or if you break one of the traditional taboos, you call in a Singer. He helps you restore personal harmony. Then everyone feels better."

"Are you traditional?"

"No. It's mostly the old people. But I speak the language and keep the stories in my mind. So I guess I am, in some ways."

He put the picture away and picked up one of the Berettas.

"I don't like these much," he said. "You find them everywhere, so you need to be familiar with them. Our troops carry them and some of our allies."

"Why don't you like them?"

"It takes three or four rounds from one of these to put down someone doped up and ready to die for Allah. Not enough punch with nine mil. Nick likes his H-K. I like Glocks, like the one you've got. They're light, they're reliable and they'll stop anyone."

They shot for a while. Ronnie showed her how to field strip, clean and reassemble the pistol. He had her practice until it felt familiar to her. He timed her and made her increase her speed. Then he blindfolded her and had her practice some more. After another hour he began packing up.

"How long have you known Nick?" Selena asked.

"Eight years. We were in Recon together. Special Ops. He was the best officer I ever served with. Never asked us to do anything he wouldn't."

"Were you there when he got hit? With that grenade?"

Something flickered across Ronnie's face, was gone.

"Yeah, I was there. But I don't really want to talk about it."

"Sorry."

"No, it's not like that." He smiled at her. "I just don't want to talk about it."

"Neither does Nick," she said.

Ronnie picked up a pistol, set it down again.

"You serious about him?"

Selena picked up one of her targets. Round holes in the black. "He's still in love with Megan," she said.

CHAPTER FIVE

Back in her rooms at the Mayflower, Selena dressed in a yellow sport bra and workout pants. She put on a light over shirt to cover her holster and a pair of running shoes. Rule one at the Project: never go anywhere without your gun. Time to go for a run, go to the gym, clear her mind.

She exited the building and headed for DuPont Circle. She didn't see the blond man across the street taking pictures of her with a telephoto lens. She ran along the busy streets, dodging traffic, feet pounding on the pavement, the sweat building, waiting for the burn. She ran, circled back, slowed, came to the gym. She went inside.

The place was cool with air conditioning. Filters tried to take away the odors of testosterone and sweat. The A/C couldn't quite pull it off. There was a faint, sour smell of deodorant and mildew in the air. She walked over to a heavy stationary punching bag. She paused in front of the bag, closed her eyes and centered herself, as she'd been taught. She opened her eyes and began hitting it, quick jabs, picking up speed until her arms were pistons, quick blurs of motion. Like a striking cobra. Or whatever snake was so fast, the motion blurred and you were down before you knew what had happened.

She began throwing side kicks, leg straight out, heel extended, balanced so the full strength of her body traveled down the bone and into the bag. The heavy bag rocked and shuddered with each blow.

She thought about Nick. She loved his hard, scarred body, the way he took her. But he never relaxed, even after they'd made love. He always acted like he expected something to jump out at him. He never stopped watching, observing. His gray eyes were always moving. He never sat with his back to a door or window. He always walked away from walls. He always carried a pistol.

She did too, now. She felt the hard shape moving against her hip.

Damn him. The fury of her kicks increased. She forced herself to slow down, to focus. Being with Nick was like being with two or three different people. He was moody as hell. He got headaches and sometimes he had a far away look in his eyes like no one was home.

Relationship, as in a real relationship with a woman, was like a foreign concept to him. At least as far as she was concerned.

Then there were those nightmares. She'd asked him about them. He dreamed about Afghanistan, where a child threw a grenade that almost killed him.

He dreamed about things that hadn't happened yet. It was something passed down in his genes. Sometimes the dreams came true, although not always the way he thought they would. It was weird, beyond weird, spooky.

He dreamed of his dead fiancée. Sometimes when they were in bed she felt like there was a third person in there with them. Megan. All Selena really knew about her was her name.

Thirty minutes later she was back in her rooms. She stripped off her sweat stained clothes and headed for the shower. She stood under the stream and let the hot water run down. She held her face under the shower and ran her fingers through her hair while the water beat on her breasts.

She stepped out of the shower and toweled herself off. She stood naked and considered her body. Five ten, a taut hundred and forty pounds. She wasn't into the anorexic thing. She worked hard to keep herself in shape. It let her do things that made life interesting, like sky diving and scuba, her martial arts.

She looked in the mirror, touched her face, the high cheekbones, brushed a wisp of hair away from her forehead. She turned on the dryer and thought about the Project while she mussed her hair.

Before she'd met Harker, she'd consulted with NSA and worked the academic circuit. She was a world class expert on ancient and oriental languages. She was more than accomplished in martial arts. She was rich. She could jump out of airplanes and hit the center of a pistol target from fifty yards. She could run must men into the ground. She could do most anything she wanted to. And she had been bored.

Before the Project, life had been predictable. A lecture. A consulting assignment. A translation. Then she'd met Nick and Elizabeth Harker and found herself caught up in a world where people tried to kill her.

Now she was part of the team. Now she carried a Glock 10 mm in a fast draw holster instead of a pen. She was sleeping with Nick and wondering where the hell it was going, or if it would go anywhere. Her life had turned upside down.

She looked in the mirror and smiled. At least it wasn't boring.

CHAPTER SIX

Fluorescent light glared off scarred yellow walls. The cement floor was painted dull gray. The room was bare except for a metal table bolted to the floor and two plastic chairs. A camera watched from one corner. A large mirror took up a portion of one wall.

Ari Herzog, senior Shin Bet agent in Jerusalem, watched through the one way mirror. The man in the room was around six feet tall, about two hundred pounds. He had black hair and eyebrows, wolf-like eyes, and a hard, square-jawed look. He needed a shave. He sat quietly, waiting for whatever came next. There was no fidgeting, no nervousness. The medic had dressed his knife wound an hour before.

"He's a cool one."

The comment came from a tall man with black eyes and sallow skin and big ears. His face was weathered from the desert sun with lines that made him look older than his forty-eight years. He wore a short sleeved white shirt, black tie, crisp blue pants and black shoes. Silver insignia of the National Police glittered on his shoulders. A name tag on his shirt identified him as Ben Ezra.

"Eighteen stitches for that gash in his thigh, no anesthetic," he said. "He didn't even flinch. While he was being sewed up he worked with the sketch artist. We're running it through the database now. So far, no hits."

He held out the artist's rendering of the man Nick had followed into the alley. Herzog looked at the drawing, then opened a Shin Bet dossier he carried in his right hand.

"Nicholas Carter," Herzog said. "Former Major in their Marines, Force Recon. That's part of their Special Operations Command now. He's supposed to be part of an advance party for the US President's visit."

Herzog continued reading.

"Silver star, bronze star with cluster, three purple hearts, tours in South America, Persian Gulf, Iraq, Afghanistan. Redacted records. High security clearance. Part of a covert unit that answers to their President and specializes in targeted operations against terrorists."

"Sounds a little like one of yours, Ari." The policeman scratched under his armpit.

Carter's effects were in a box on a nearby table. Herzog looked through them. Airline ticket. Rental car keys. A wallet with driver's license, credit cards and two thousand dollars in currency. There was a picture in the wallet of a dark haired woman standing in front of a restaurant, blowing a kiss at the camera. Carter's passport was full of stamps from all over the globe.

There was a state of the art, encrypted satellite phone. A small pocket knife and flashlight, locally bought. A flat, black credentials holder with Carter's ID. A room key for the King David Citadel Hotel.

Carter's pistol, a Heckler and Koch .45, had been sent forward from storage at Ben Gurion airport. Herzog picked up the gun, examined it. He eyed the three fifteen round magazines and the shoulder rig.

"Big pistol. Custom hollow points. This one doesn't fool around." Herzog set the pistol down.

"You think it's a coincidence he was there when that bomb went?"

"What does he say?"

"That he was having a cup of coffee when the bomb exploded. He says he saw a man talking on a cell phone. In his opinion the man was involved with the bombing, so he went after him. When he did, two others attacked him. The one with the phone got in a white Volvo and was driven away. Then my men showed up and took this one into custody. We're on the lookout for the car, but there are a lot of white Volvos."

Ben Ezra scratched his arm. "One of the men he fought is dead. The other is in a coma. The one he killed was in our files from demonstrations in the West Bank. No ID on the other yet. When he comes out of it, if he comes out of it, we'll encourage him to answer some questions."

"Mmmm."

Ben Ezra continued. "We found two knives in the alley." He gestured through the glass. "This one was unarmed. Except for that little penknife. It was in his pocket."

"Not bad, against two with knives. We're sure he's who he says he is?"

"Confirmed."

"Their President gives his speech two days from now. Why send a covert operative here, using his own name, claiming him as part of the Presidential party?"

"Maybe we should ask him."

"Let's do that."

CHAPTER SEVEN

Carter looked up as two men entered the room. The first was about forty-five, dressed in a crumpled dark blue suit, white shirt with no tie, and black shoes. His hair was curly and black with touches of gray. Around five ten and a hundred and seventy, his eyes were dark brown, intense and bloodshot. He looked tired. Lines of stress were grooved into his cheeks and forehead. He was wearing a wedding ring and carried a folder in his left hand.

The blue logo of Shin Bet was prominent on the credentials he held up for Nick to see. Shin Bet's motto translated as "The Invisible Shield". In the covert war zone comprising all of Israel, Shin Bet was the front line.

Standing next to him was a ranking policeman with silver pips and a leaf on his shoulders. A cop in uniform entered the room, closed the door and stood by it.

The man put his credentials back in his jacket pocket. "My name is Ari Herzog."

"Nick Carter." Nick rose and held out his hand, trying not to wince at the pain in his leg. Herzog looked surprised. He hesitated, then shook. His grip was firm.

"This is Commander Ben Ezra. We'd like to talk with you." He gestured at the chair.

They sat down. The cop and Ben Ezra remained standing.

Carter looked at the folder under Herzog's arm. The only way he'd get out of here was cooperation. He decided to play it straight. "You've checked me out by now," he said. "What is it you want to know?"

Herzog and Ben Ezra looked at one another. Herzog cleared his throat.

"Many things, Mr. Carter. Beginning with what you were doing at the mall earlier this evening."

"I was having a cup of coffee."

"At the exact time and place of a terrorist attack."

"Wrong time, wrong place. But yes, having a cup of coffee. Do you think this attack had something to do with me?"

"Not necessarily." Herzog glanced at the folder. "You were sent here as part of an advance detail prior to your president's visit?"

"Yes."

"For what purpose? You're not Secret Service."

"My boss thinks there could be a terrorist attack timed to coincide with Rice's speech. We have a source in the Old City. I was sent to see if I could find specific facts to back up that intelligence. That's why I'm here."

"Armed."

"I was, until your people confiscated my weapon. If I'd had it tonight, your terrorist might be sitting here instead of me."

"Or not. One of the men you fought is dead, the other is badly injured. He's in a coma."

Nick shrugged. "I didn't have many options."

"How were you to obtain the facts needed to, as you say, back up your intelligence?"

"I was going to connect with your organization after I'd scouted around a bit. This isn't the kind of meeting I'd pictured, though." He gestured at the room.

"What had you planned to do next?"

"Meet with our source."

"When was this meeting to take place?"

"It's today at nine. I'd hoped yesterday, but no luck. My instructions were that if I discovered anything definite to let your people handle it."

"Mmm." Herzog was non-committal. "You are willing to share this source with us?"

Carter thought about it. He'd never given up a contact. But Israel was an ally and what counted was the success of the mission.

"Yes. But I think it's better if he doesn't know you're involved."

"You're proposing that you and I work together?"

"We've got a common interest. Tonight's attack could be part of some bigger terrorist scenario. I'll bet you've already had to divert manpower from Rice's visit to handle it. Put me back out there and I can help."

Herzog gave him a long look. He turned to Ben Ezra. "What do you think?"

The policeman let out a long breath. Scratched under his arm.

"It's your call, Ari. We're stretched thin right now. If you trust him, maybe he can help, but we need him on a tight leash."

"Mmm. Mr. Carter, if we do this you must remain under my operational supervision. No 'cowboy' stuff, yes?"

"Agreed. One thing, though."

"Yes?"

"I'd like my weapon back."

"You think you need it?"

"If you trust me, there's no reason not to return it. I'd take it as a sign of good faith on your part."

"That's a lot of faith."

"Isn't that what Jerusalem is all about?"

Herzog smiled.

"All right, Mr. Carter." Ben Ezra didn't look happy about that.

"Please. Nick."

"Nick. Tell me, what is the name of your contact?"

Now it was his turn to demonstrate faith.

"Arslanian, Arshak Arslanian. He has a shop in the Armenian Quarter." He gave Herzog the address.

Herzog took a card from his jacket, wrote on the back of it. "My number. I suggest you return to your hotel and get some sleep. A car will pick you up at 0700. We will start our joint effort then, beginning with your contact."

"Understood."

It felt good to stand up after hours of sitting. The stitches hurt. Outside the interrogation room, Herzog gave him his possessions and his pistol. Nick strapped it on and breathed easier. He was spattered with blood from the mall, his head hurt and he needed a shower and about ten hours of sleep he wasn't going to get.

A police car took him back to the hotel.

CHAPTER EIGHT

It was after two in the morning on Wednesday in Jerusalem. It was seven in the evening on Tuesday in Washington. Nick called Harker. He told her about the attack on the mall, his new alliance with Shin Bet.

"Give me a minute."

Carter heard her coughing in the background. He rubbed the back of his head where he'd hit the pavement. He had a hell of a headache and he was dizzy. Probably a mild concussion. He'd sleep it off.

After a brief pause Harker came back. "I've got a file on Herzog on my screen now."

"How far should I go with him?"

"He's a serious player. You don't get Jerusalem as your job in Shin Bet without a great track record. Wounded twice in the field, commendations from his superiors, a medal from the Prime Minister. He's a good man to have on our side."

"So, full cooperation?"

"Yes. Let Herzog run the show, but keep your ear to the ground and keep me informed."

"Roger that."

"Get some sleep. You'll need it."

Carter signed off. He thought for a moment and decided to call Selena. He wasn't sure why.

"Hey."

"Hey, yourself. How's Jerusalem?"

"Not what I expected." Her voice made him realize he missed her. It was an odd feeling, something he'd forgotten. He told her what had happened.

"Are you okay?"

"I'm fine, just tired."

Her voice was tense. "You were almost killed by a bomb, two thugs went after you with knives, you were arrested and you're just tired? That's it? How do you feel?"

"Like I said, tired. What am I supposed to feel?"

"I don't know. Upset, maybe?"

"What good would that do? What did you do today?"

Carter felt his head getting tight, like it always did when someone pushed him for feelings. After Afghanistan some shrink was always asking how he felt. It was a stupid question. He'd always answered it the same way. How would you feel, if you'd blown the head off a kid? There wasn't any point in talking about it. Probing it. He'd had to do it, that's all. He didn't want to think about it. Feelings just got in the way.

Selena took a deep breath. "I worked out with Ronnie. He's something, isn't he?"

That was better. "You bet. He'll run you under if you let him."

"I got even, though. We practiced some hand to hand combat. After that he decided we'd go to the range."

Nick laughed. Selena had a 7th degree black belt in Kuk Sool Won. Ronnie was outmatched.

"I miss you," he said. It surprised him. It was true. "I wanted to hear your voice."

"When are you coming back?"

"I don't know. After Rice's speech."

"When you get back, let's go someplace and drink too much wine."

"A date? You're on."

A few more words and Carter hung up.

On the other end, Selena set the phone down. She let out a long breath. Talking with Nick was like talking to someone who lived inside an armored car. As long as it was about anything except the way he felt, it was fine. Try to get in, and the doors were locked.

She knew something about armor. She'd been ten when her parents were killed. Armor kept the pain away. Hers was forged out of achievement. Perfection in everything. Academics, sports, it had worked like a dream. Maybe it intimidated some people, but it had worked.

At least it had worked until her uncle had been murdered.

Then she'd met Elizabeth Harker and been tossed into Nick's world. A violent, dangerous world, and she'd gotten hooked on it, hooked on Nick in spite of herself. She'd never be able to go back to the life she'd had before. It was gone. Gone like the wind.

It made her mad at herself. She was hooked on a man who kept the lid clamped down tight on his feelings. Who kept them locked up in the dark. Sometimes looking at him was like looking at a mirror. She wasn't sure she liked what she saw.

She went down to the workout room in the hotel and began stretching. She was almost ready to test for her next belt. At her level, there was no room for error. One mistake and it would be a year before she could test again.

For the next hour she practiced, watching herself in the big wall mirrors. She told herself that anyone who decided to mess with her would be making a big mistake. She told herself she was invulnerable.

She almost believed it.

CHAPTER NINE

Carter got out of his bloody clothes. His back was turning colors from where he'd hit the pavement. The disc injuries he'd gotten in the Himalayas sent warning shocks up his spine. He stepped into the shower and turned up the hot, trying to keep the stitches on his leg out of the stream.

He thought about Selena, how different they were from each other. It was hard to see how people as different as they were had come together. Take family, for instance.

His family was a mess, a textbook example of dysfunction. His father was an alcoholic bully. His sister was neurotic and angry and married to a total asshole. His mother had been a doormat for his father and now she had Alzheimer's. He'd never had much money and he'd worked his way through school.

Selena had been raised by a loving, wealthy uncle. She'd gone to the best private schools and when her uncle died he'd left her more money than anyone could ever spend. His death had brought her to the Project. Education, money, background, Carter and Selena might as well be from different planets.

Carter got out of the shower and dried off. He set the alarm and lay down. He fell asleep.

He dreamed the dream.

He's coming in over the ridge again, the rotors echoing from the valley walls, beating out a rhythm of death. The village is like it always is, a shitty, dust-blown cluster of flat-roofed buildings, baking in relentless heat, surrounded by sharp, brown hills. A wide, dirt street runs down the middle.

His team drops from the chopper and hits the street running, M4 up by his cheek, his Marines behind him. On the right, houses. On the left, more houses and the market. It's just a chaotic mix of ramshackle bins and hanging cloth walls. Clouds of flies swarm around dead things hanging in the butcher's stall.

They make their way past the market. He keeps away from the walls, so a round fired won't burrow down a wall and right into him. He hears a baby crying. The street is deserted.

A dozen bearded figures rise up on the rooftops like ducks popping up in a carnival shooting gallery and begin firing AKs. The market stalls disintegrate in a firestorm of splinters and plaster and rock exploding from the sides of the buildings.

He ducks into a narrow doorway. A child runs toward him, screaming about Allah. Carter hesitates, a second too long. The boy cocks his arm back and throws a grenade as Nick shoots him. The M4 kicks back, one, two, three.

The first round strikes the boy's chest, the second his throat, the third his face. The child's head disappears in a red fountain of blood and bone. The grenade drifts through the air in slow motion...everything goes white...

He woke, heart pounding, drenched in sweat.

Ghosts. Impressions from the past, his very own personal time machine.

He waited for dawn.

CHAPTER TEN

The Visitor looked out over the lights of Jerusalem.

A cell phone rang, one of several he kept for these calls.

"Yes."

"We have a problem."

The caller spoke in German, with a slight American accent. The voice was husky, a rasp of cigarettes or whiskey. He might have been in the next block or across the Atlantic. There was no way to tell.

"Yes?"

"Our business strategy requires modification. A representative of a rival consortium based in America has arrived. He intends to interfere with our negotiations. Perhaps you could resolve this with him?"

"His name?"

"Carter."

"You wish me to visit him?"

"Yes, please do. I am sure you can make a satisfactory arrangement. Your usual consulting fee will be doubled for this assignment."

"Where is he staying?"

"At the King David Citadel Hotel. He is one of their best negotiators."

A pause.

The Visitor asked, "Is the meeting still on schedule?"

"It is. Continue supervising the arrangements. An update has been sent to you. Negotiate with our competition."

"I understand."

The call ended. The Visitor placed the phone on the floor and crushed it with his heel.

It was an unexpected assignment, but it shouldn't take long. The Visitor went to his laptop. He opened a program that had never been certified by Microsoft or anyone else and tapped into the reservations computer at the King David Citadel. He noted Carter's room number and the fact that he was in the hotel.

He tapped another key and brought up an encrypted message, the "update" his caller had mentioned.

Carter was going to meet with an Armenian merchant in the Old City. The instructions were clear. Eliminate the Armenian and the possibility of that meeting ever happening. A picture of Carter, his contact and the address where the meeting was to take place were provided.

Perfect. The Visitor was efficient. When Carter came to meet the Armenian, opportunity might present itself to take care of two problems at the same time.

He thought about the day ahead. He went over the assignment in his mind's eye, a professional working through his game plan, visualizing the steps, the terrain, possible complications or obstacles.

The Visitor shut down his laptop. He took out the silenced Ruger .22 he preferred for his work. Quiet, effective, with little chance of rounds penetrating places they shouldn't go, it was his favorite weapon. He got a kit and laid everything out in a precise row and began cleaning the gun. The smell of solvent and gun oil and the sheen of the deep bluing on the metal provided a peaceful, ordered sense of purpose, an existential meditation focused on the instrument of death in his hands.

The Visitor thought of his home in Germany, in the mountains of Bavaria. It was so different from the barren, desert land of this Jew nation. Green trees and black earth, snow capped peaks rising like gods to the pure, blue skies. The smell of pine and the glory of alpine flowers blooming in the high country in the spring. Warm summer days. Fair women with rosy cheeks and wide hips.

But his beloved Bavaria was corrupted, diseased.

Poisoned by Jews and foreigners, mongrel races swarming like cockroaches over his beloved Fatherland, Germany's patrimony traded for a mess of porridge by spineless politicians catering to the Zionist Americans and their ilk.

It wasn't too late to reverse the damage. Soon, the Jews would be brought down. A long delayed completion of the final solution was coming to this nation of sub-humans called Israel.

The Visitor hummed to himself as he wiped excess oil off the pistol.

CHAPTER ELEVEN

At the German research station on the Princess Martha Coast in Antarctica, spring was in full swing. For the last four weeks the thermometer had soared above freezing. Global warming and the hole in the ozone layer were hot topics of conversation in the dining hall.

The thinning ozone layer was Hans Schmidt's field of expertise. Thirty years old, he was a rising star in the expanding science of environmental studies. Hans had an engaging, open face, hazel eyes and fair hair. He'd let his beard grow over the last few months, the reddish color hinting at his Viking ancestry. In a month he was going back to Germany to marry his childhood sweetheart, Heidi. Life was good for Hans.

He'd dressed in high brown laced boots, sturdy pants over insulated underwear, two shirts and an open red jacket. He wore a fur lined hat with flap ears tied up on top. Antarctic weather could change to fury in an instant, even in the warmer months.

He'd checked out a Sno-Cat and persuaded Otto Bremen, the head of the station and the chief geophysicist, to go inland with him to the mountains of the *Fenriskjeften*, the "Jaw of Fenris", named for the giant, ravenous wolf of Norse myth. It was still largely unexplored territory.

Bremen was older, in his early fifties. He was stocky, shorter than Hans. His face was round and jolly, which made him a favorite for playing Kris Kringle at Christmas time. He had tufted eyebrows turning white over blue eyes and silver-rimmed bifocals set slightly askew on his large ears. He wore an insulated yellow parka with a German flag stitched on the shoulder and sturdy boots and pants.

They pulled out of the garage cavern hollowed from the ice beneath the station and headed toward the mountains. The heater in the high cab of the Tucker Sno-Cat was on low in the fine weather. Hans cracked a window for fresh air. The Tucker was one of three identical vehicles donated to the station by Eric Reinhardt, a wealthy American businessman of German descent.

The big Allison diesel engine rumbled in a contented drone. They headed over the snow and ice toward the mountains an hour away. With two 60 gallon tanks, a closed cab and plenty of storage, the Tucker was like a Rolls Royce in this part of the world.

Bremen tinkered with another Reinhardt gift, an experimental device using ultra sound technology to detect mineral deposits. The Fenris Mountains would provide a good field test. No one had ever found much in the Antarctic ice, only a little iron and some copper. None of it promised commercial development. Besides, the Antarctic treaties prevented any kind of serious mining operations.

The big Sno-Cat closed on the mountains and Hans turned parallel to the front of the range, looking for anything unusual in the melting ice and snow. After ten minutes the mineral seeking device began to beep.

"Something ahead," Otto said. "According to this, no more than three of four hundred meters." He consulted a chart. "High density iron, copper, the readings are going crazy."

"Look there!" Hans pointed through the windshield.

He slowed and brought the Tucker to a halt. On the side of one of the jagged peaks, ice and snow had broken loose in the spring thaw. A gray, regular outline was visible against the dark rock.

"What the hell is that?" Hans let the engine idle.

"I don't know. It looks man made. That's where the readings come from."

"I don't remember anything about a station or camp here."

Stations were often abandoned in the Antarctic. Both men were familiar with the history of the region. Neither had ever heard of anything in this area.

They climbed down from the cab and walked to the mountain wall. Two wide doors of rusting steel, each twelve feet high, were set into the rock. Ice and snow blocked the lower part of the doors.

Excitement filled both men.

"What do you think?" Otto said. "Can we get in?"

"Maybe we can push the debris aside."

"Let's try it."

The Sno-Cat was equipped with a heavy blade used to groom the station runway for supply planes. Otto and Hans climbed back into the cab. Hans engaged the four speed transmission and brought the Tucker around to the doors. He lowered the blade and began working. In twenty minutes, the way was clear.

The two men stood before the doors. There was a large, U-shaped handle on each one.

"They have to open in." Hans rubbed his glove across his face. "No one would have doors that opened out. They'd get blocked by snow."

"I wonder if they're locked?"

"Against what? Penguins? Let's push and see."

They pushed against one of the doors. Grunting, they pushed harder. With a rusted squeal, the steel door opened. They pushed at the other door and swung it inward. The interior lay in darkness.

Hans went back to the idling cat, backed it around and pointed it straight at the open entrance. He switched on the six halogen headlamps and hit high beam. The interior lit up with brilliant white light. He took two hand held torches from the cab and joined Otto.

A high roofed tunnel ran straight as an arrow into the mountain. Bare electric light bulbs, long dark, were spaced down the center of the ceiling.

"Whoever built this bored right into the mountain."

"What could it have been for?" Otto said. "This is huge. It would take a lot of equipment. I never heard of anything like this down here."

A little way in, Hans paused at a room on the right.

"This could have been a guardroom." He pointed at a frost covered stove in the corner. "That looks like something from sixty or seventy years ago."

"A military base? For what? Who built it?"

On the other side of the corridor was a kitchen and eating area, big enough for a hundred men. They passed two barracks rooms with gray wooden lockers still in place at the ends of the bunks. Hans opened one. Empty.

They walked down the corridor, past what might have been officer's quarters with two bunks to a room. They came upon a radio room. A microphone and telegraph key still sat on top of a metal desk, next to a large transmitter console tied with snaking cables to a tall rack of receivers and test equipment. Next to the transmitter was a wooden box. Otto opened the box. Inside was something like a typewriter, with a complex keyboard arrangement of letters and buttons.

Everything was covered by a thick layer of white frost. Otto wiped off the face plate of the silent transmitter. The switches were marked in German. Both men saw the swastika at the same time.

"Holy shit! This must be Doenitz's secret base!"

Grand Admiral Karl Doenitz, head of Nazi Germany's naval forces, had once referred to "an invincible fortress in the Antarctic", but no one had ever found evidence of its existence. Now Otto and Hans were standing in it.

Hans picked up a logbook lying on the desk. He thumbed through it without absorbing the words, set it down again.

"This short wave stuff was state of the art in the forties," Otto said. "Look at the size of that transmitter. Must be two kilowatts at least. There've been rumors of this place since the war, but no one ever knew where it was, or if it was real."

"Berlin isn't going to be happy about this."

"No one wants to think about that Nazi crap anymore. What they do with this is their business. But we have to report it."

They left the radio room and continued down the passage. The next room contained two large diesel generators, silent and cold. Exhaust tubes disappeared into the ceiling.

Down the tunnel a series of four rooms opened to the sides. Three were empty. The fourth held six large wooden crates, each stenciled in black with an eagle and swastika. Hans rubbed frost away from a label.

He looked at Otto. "It says 'kitchen supplies'."

"That's a lot of supplies."

In the corner Otto spied a long crowbar, set against the icy wall. He picked it up and pried away the lid of a crate. He shone his light inside.

"Not kitchen supplies. Look at this!"

The crate was filled with paintings. They peered in.

"That's a Vermeer!" Hans said. "I recognize the style. Or it's a damn good copy."

"No one would stash a copy here." Otto pushed the lid back in place. "That painting is worth a fortune. It must have been stolen during the war. I'll bet all these crates are full of things stolen by the Nazis."

They walked down the tunnel and passed two large closed doors on their left. The doors didn't budge when Otto tried to open them. At the end of the corridor they came to a steel door with a spoked wheel and a combination dial.

Hans tried to turn the wheel, but it was locked in place.

"If they left paintings worth millions outside this vault, what could be in here?"

Otto shrugged. "Who knows? We'd better get back and tell the others. It's going to play hell with our research time once Berlin sends people to check it out."

"Look on the bright side. There has to be a finder's fee for that art work. Maybe we'll get some real funding out of it. Publicity, too. That never hurts."

In the scientific world, fame was a good thing. Both men thought that the future had just gotten brighter.

Back at the station, Otto contacted Berlin by satellite with news of the find. It never occurred to him that someone else might be listening.

CHAPTER TWELVE

In a secluded enclave outside of Washington, the Grand Master of the Council sat behind his desk. He took a deep breath of the heady aroma rising from a crystal snifter of Louis XIII cognac in his hand.

The light was fading. The French doors of the library were open. It was warm even though October was more than half gone. The sound of a fountain came from somewhere in the garden behind the house. The library was filled with books, many in German. Nietzsche, Heidegger, Marx, Engles, all were there. There was even a well-worn, autographed copy of Mein Kampf.

A glassed gun case of rifles and shotguns stood in one corner. Antique prints of European hunting scenes hung nearby. A painting of Frederick Barbarossa, the Holy Roman Emperor, stared out from the wall behind the desk. His expression was stern.

Photographs of the Grand Master with congressional figures, business leaders and Presidents covered one wall. In one photo a blond haired young man stood in cap and gown before the entrance to Yale University. A tall, brittle woman in a blue dress stood next to him.

The floor of the library was covered with thick Persian carpeting. A maroon Chesterfield couch with two matching chairs was placed near the garden doors. In the far corner, a mounted set of antique armor stood guard.

The Grand Master had the kind of face people trusted. No one could have guessed his real thoughts. No one would have believed them possible.

His encrypted phone rang.

"Yes?"

The voice on the other end spoke in German. It was exultant.

"The Spear has been found!"

The Grand Master felt a surge of adrenaline. *At last! With the Lance recovered, success was certain*

"Secured?"

"Not yet, but a unit has been activated."

"When will they arrive?"

"ETA six hours. Further transport tomorrow afternoon."

"Excellent. Arrange a conference for nine tomorrow evening."

"As you command."

The Grand Master set the phone down. He could barely contain his excitement. He went to the painting of Frederick Barbarossa, swung the picture away from the wall and opened a safe. He took out a cracked black leather binder embossed in gold with an eagle and swastika. The binder contained SS Reichsfuehrer Heinrich Himmler's long term plan for after the war.

PARSIFAL.

The Grand Master knew the contents by heart, but it always inspired him to read the vision of the Reichsfuehrer. He opened the binder. The pages were foxed and turning brown. The neat, ordered lines of type were still legible. He read for a few moments. He set the PARSIFAL documents aside and rested his hand on a thin booklet. The cover page was inscribed with the runic letters of the old Germanic tribes.

ᚠᚢᚱᚢᚠ ᚹᛟᛗ ᚠᛚᛏᛗᚾ

His father had been one of Himmler's inner circle. All through his childhood and early years, his father had taught him. Prepared him for the day when his father had shown him the binder and told him of PARSIFAL. Of the Grand Council. Then he'd talked about the ritual that had brought German success after success early in the war.

"I was having dinner with Himmler and Heydrich in the North Tower of the Reichsfuehrer's castle." His father had sighed, remembering when the swastika had flown over three continents.

"Heydrich said he had written down the words of the invocation. Himmler was Grand Master of the Council but it was always Heydrich who invoked the power of the Spear. After he was assassinated in '42, things turned against us."

"But the Fuehrer, father. Surely he could have carried it on, or the Reichsfuehrer."

His father had snorted in contempt. "The Fuehrer! In the beginning, he understood. He believed. He had learned. He did what was necessary. He followed the ritual. But he turned his back on the old ways. He forgot where his power came from and became caught in the illusion of his own will. You must never make that mistake.

"Himmler tried to continue, but the power is…difficult…to control. It will not respond unless conditions are perfect. The right day and time. The right setting. Everything must be exact."

His father had held up the booklet with the runes on the cover. "We will study this together. One day we will retrieve the Spear. On that day the Reich will be reborn. If I am gone, it will be your duty to speak these words. If your honor is pure, if your loyalty is true, you will prevail."

"Yes, Father."

He had never forgotten.

The final stages of PARSIFAL were unfolding. It couldn't be coincidence that the Holy Spear had been found just as the forces he'd set in motion were coming together. It was a sign from the gods, a sign he was favored. It was only right, his just due. The Grand Master raised his glass toward the painting of Barbarossa and smiled.

CHAPTER THIRTEEN

Carter found Arslanian's store on a narrow side street of the Armenian quarter. The metal gate that protected the shop was rolled up. The entrance was stacked with hand crafted Sabbath trays, candlestick holders, plates and ceramics decorated with vivid colors, flowers and animals.

The shop stretched back from the street through the entire block. The walls were lined with goods. The interior was in shadow. A sliver of daylight came from a door cracked open at the far end.

Halfway down, someone sat in a swiveled wooden office chair at a desk piled high with papers and pots. The chair was turned away from the entrance. The figure wasn't moving.

Carter's ear began itching. The darkness of the shop didn't feel right. He slipped his pistol out and held it down by his right side. He moved away from the light at the entrance, toward the figure in the chair, scanning the shadows.

He reached the desk and turned the chair around. Arslanian's body slumped over and slid to the floor. Something fell from his right hand.

There was a small hole in his forehead. Blood trickled from his ear and into his beard. His eyes were open. They told nothing about whoever had killed him. The only messages Carter had ever seen in dead men's eyes were reminders of his own mortality.

Arslanian's cheek was warm, the blood not yet dry. The killer had been here a few minutes before. Probably right after Arslanian opened up for the day.

Nick bent down to pick up whatever had dropped from Arslanian's dead fingers. A soft sound like a sneeze came from somewhere in the darkness of the shop. A stinging wind passed the back of his skull and a vase exploded behind him. He ducked and fired three quick shots over the desk at the back.

Pottery shattered along the wall where the rounds hit. The .45 sounded like cannon fire in the narrow confines of the shop. A rapid patter of silenced shots sent broken plates raining down on his head. There was a burst of daylight and the sound of the back door slamming shut. Nick got up and ran to the back. He stood on the side and pulled open the door.

The door opened onto a walled garden. A small fountain trickled under a tree shading a rickety table and two chairs. There was an ashtray on the table. A vase held wilted red flowers. In the far wall was a closed wooden gate.

Nick ran across the garden and swung the gate open. He glanced into the street on the other side of the wall. Two Armenian priests were walking toward the entrance to the quarter and St. James Cathedral. Another priest in an odd hat and black ankle-length robe walked in the opposite direction. Across the way a stout couple looked at postcards. There were shopkeepers, food vendors, strollers. Everything looked normal. There was no way to identify the assassin.

He holstered the .45, closed the gate and bolted it. He went back into the shop and closed the rear door. A crowd began to gather in front, drawn by the gunfire.

Rivka Stern, Nick's Shin Bet watcher, came in through the entrance. She had a Baby Eagle nine mil out and held by her side. Her dark, thick hair was pinned up under a pale yellow scarf. She wore an olive green skirt that came to her knees, sturdy sandals tied with thongs on her lower legs and a loose tan shirt of cotton under a light tan jacket. She had wide hips and full breasts bound close under her shirt. Her skin was dusky with the legacy of the Middle East. Sunglasses hid her eyes.

"What happened?" Her voice was low, tense.

"I found Arslanian dead. Someone took a shot at me. I shot back. He got away through the rear."

Rivka holstered her pistol, took out a phone, dialed, and began talking. Nick looked at what had fallen from Arslanian's hand. It was a flash drive. He dropped it in his jacket pocket.

He looked at his watch. It was only 2:30 in the morning in Washington, but Harker needed to know about this.

"Yes, Nick." Her voice was full of sleep. She cleared her throat. "What's happening?" She coughed.

"Arslanian's dead. Someone put a hit on him before we could meet. The shooter was waiting for me but he missed. He got away."

"You're sure he was after you as well?"

"Had to be. Arslanian had only been dead a few minutes. The shop was open to anyone and the killer was still inside. When he missed me he got out fast."

"Who knew you were going there this morning?"

"No one except Shin Bet and you."

"That's a short list."

There was a brief silence while Harker thought about that.

"What's your plan?" She coughed.

"I don't have one. Herzog will think of something. I'm following his lead right now."

"You'd better watch your step. All right, I'll see what I can uncover at this end."

"I'll be sending something to you." He fingered the drive in his pocket.

"Keep me posted." She ended the call.

Rivka stood near. He caught her scent, a subtle combination of musk and Judean flowers.

"Calling your mother?"

"Yes. Someone knew I was coming. The timing's too much of a coincidence."

"You could be right. We'll talk it over with Ari."

Police showed up and cordoned off the shop. Two more Shin Bet agents arrived. Carter took another look around. He knew the cops would do a better job of finding anything useful than he would. They left to meet with Ari.

CHAPTER FOURTEEN

Elizabeth Harker leaned back in her black leather chair. She took a tissue from a box on the desk and coughed into it. She folded it and dropped it into the wastebasket. She tapped her pen on the desk and thought about Nick.

Two days on the ground and he was already up to his neck in the madness of the Middle East. It was uncanny how much trouble he drew to himself. She sipped from the cup of coffee she'd brewed and added more sugar. She broke into a fit of coughing, almost spilling the coffee. She waited for it to pass, blotted her lips with a tissue. She excavated an inhaler from her purse and took in a labored breath.

Elizabeth had been up since Nick's call, running through possibilities. She'd had no reason to think someone would kill Arslanian. She'd had no reason to think someone would try to take Nick off the board. Someone didn't want Arslanian talking to Nick or anyone else.

Her intuition bugged her, demanding attention. It was something she didn't talk about, intuition. Her male peers would have rolled their eyes if they knew how she operated. Sometimes it made her feel like a modern day Cassandra, warning of disaster and trouble to come.

Something was very wrong.

Her phone rang.

"Director, it's Stephanie. General Hood is in Walter Reed. He went down with a stroke last night."

Stephanie Willits was Elizabeth's deputy and right arm. General Hood was the Director of the National Security Agency and Elizabeth's ally.

"What's the prognosis?"

"It doesn't look good. He's not going to be able to run the agency. My sources say his successor will be General Dysart."

"Where are you now, Steph?" Elizabeth heard the sound of traffic in the background.

"On the Beltway, on my way in. Traffic's bad, like always. Maybe thirty minutes."

"Thanks for the heads up. Better plan on a long day."

"Roger that, Director. See you in a bit."

Elizabeth hung up the phone.

The Director of NSA was one of the few who knew about the Project. Part of Elizabeth's job was to review NSA CRITIC briefs sent to the President. She'd had a good working relationship with General Hood. It had made things a lot easier. Now he was out of the picture.

Elizabeth knew Dysart and she didn't like him. He was a Pentagon power player, conservative and hawkish, allied with several important congressional figures. He was smart, she'd give him that. He was also controlling and patronizing, dismissive of women and others he considered his inferiors. The largest and most secretive intelligence agency in the world was about to come under his sway. The day had just gotten worse.

Her secured desk phone rang. She picked up and covered her surprise at the voice on the other end of the line.

"Director Harker, this is General Dysart. General Hood has been taken seriously ill and I have been ordered to assume his responsibilities. I've been reviewing his files and I wanted to give you a call. You seem to have enjoyed an unusual relationship with him."

Elizabeth kept her voice neutral. "I'm sorry to hear he's ill. General Hood has always been supportive."

"I'm calling to offer a bit of friendly advice. You are currently running a mission in Israel." It wasn't a question.

Her intuition sounded an alarm. How did Dysart find out Nick was in Jerusalem? No one was supposed to know that, outside of the team. Hood hadn't known. Even the President didn't know yet. Dysart continued.

"I believe it's in your best interest to recall your agent. I've been talking to Lodge over at Langley. I realize you have the President's interests to consider, but there is more than enough security in place. You're treading on toes, Director. I just thought I'd let you know."

Director Central Intelligence was another on the short list of those who knew about her unit. Elizabeth trusted Lodge about as far as she could throw the Pentagon across the Potomac.

Dysart had been in charge of NSA for only a few hours at most. He should have more important things to do. Yet here he was, "advising" her to end a sensitive intelligence operation that might affect the President's safety and security. Her intuition waved a red flag.

"I certainly don't want to tread on any toes," she said, in her best "little lady" voice. The voice worked almost every time. She only used it when she wanted someone to think she was compliant, but compliant wasn't an important word in Elizabeth's vocabulary. She wasn't about to let Dysart know what she was thinking.

"I appreciate the call, General. I'll take your advice under consideration."

"Good. You've done some excellent work for NSA in the past, Director. I'm sure we'll be able to work well together in the future."

Dysart sounded conciliatory, but Elizabeth knew better. She hadn't gotten where she was without developing a fine sense of when she was being conned. Dysart had no intention of working well with her. He ended the call.

She replaced the phone. Why did Dysart want Nick out of Israel? She didn't believe for a moment it was because of ruffled feathers over at Langley.

At odd times Elizabeth would remember something her father, the Judge, had told her. Now she remembered an incident that had happened when she was seventeen. She'd been accused of cheating by one of her teachers. Sent home in disgrace.

The Judge had sat across from her at the kitchen table, a tall glass of bourbon and ice nearby, dressed in an old sweater and jeans. Her mother had been off shopping in town. The Judge was taking a rare day away from his offices in the County Courthouse.

Outside, the snow was almost gone. Spring had arrived on the western slope of the Rockies and color was everywhere. Purple crocuses, yellow daffodils and green shoots lifted through the remaining patches of snow. Green leaves had appeared on the aspens in the front yard. But for Elizabeth, spring had been colored by anger.

"It's not fair," she'd said.

"No, it's not. What do you think you should do about it?"

"Can't you do something?"

"Not really. It has to be worked out between your teacher and you."

"But she doesn't want to work anything out. She's mean and she's stupid."

"If that's true, you have to rethink your relationship with her. She's the teacher, she's got the power. But only if you give it away to her. You're the one who really has the power over yourself. You know you weren't cheating, whatever she thinks. Who's right, her or you?"

Elizabeth had smiled, in spite of herself. "I am."

"If I were you, I'd put it down to the experience of people, how they can be difficult and unfair, wrong headed sometimes. You'll be graduating in a couple of months. You'll be gone on to college and there won't be anything she can do or say to affect you. Plan your next steps, put her in the past. You can't change people. They are the way they are."

They are the way they are. You can't change them. Plan your next steps. The Judge's words echoed in her head. He was right. She'd have to wait and see what Dysart was going to do. She needed to prepare in case he turned out to be a problem.

However he'd found out Nick was in Israel, the Project was compromised. Elizabeth had a contingency plan for that possibility. She'd never had to use it.

She took out her sat phone and sent a short, pre-programmed burst. A classified encryption chip broke the message into indecipherable scrambled pieces that were reassembled by a matching chip at the receiving end. Even if intercepted, the message would mean nothing in the wrong hands.

Alpha Red. 3P.FC.XG.E5.

CHAPTER FIFTEEN

Carter looked at the message on his satellite phone.
Alpha Red. 3P.FC.XG.E5.
Jesus, what now? Alpha Red was the equivalent of the Titanic sending up flares. He sent a burst acknowledging the message. He decided to keep Arslanian's flash drive to himself for the moment.

He and Rivka were in Herzog's office, watching the arrival of President Rice on television. Air Force One taxied to a precise halt at the end of a long red carpet. The carpet was lined on both sides by a platoon of honor guards in white and blue uniforms. Daniel Ascher, the Prime Minister of Israel, waited with key members of his cabinet at the end of the red pathway.

The President appeared at the door of the plane and waved. He descended the steps with his security detail, followed by the Secretary of State and the National Security Advisor. He stopped to speak with one of the soldiers standing at attention, then continued on to the welcoming party. The two leaders shook hands.

Rice was here to try and get agreement for establishing a Palestinian capitol in East Jerusalem, captured during the 1967 War. East Jerusalem was the Old City, the heart of three religions. Most people in the region, Muslim, Jew and Christian alike, were opposed to any solution that gave up any part of Jerusalem to anyone. There were large protests planned and threats of violence. The Prime Minister and the President had their work cut out for them.

Ari turned off the monitor. He leaned back and steepled his fingers in front of him.

"So. Tomorrow your President speaks to the world from in front of the al-Aqsa Mosque, to call for peace."

Nick tugged on his ear. "You don't sound enthusiastic."

"I think it will create trouble, not peace."

"You must have serious security issues."

"Security will be maximum. We're placing armored vehicles and troops around the Temple Mount. Only one hundred people are invited for the speech, all fully vetted. Rice and the Prime Minister will be surrounded by security people from half a dozen agencies. The *Waqf* has been difficult, but they have decided to cooperate."

"The Waqf?"

"That's the Muslim authority for the Mount," Rivka broke in. "*Waqf* means *holding* in Arabic."

Ari sighed. "There will be many problems because of this speech. As usual, politics gets in the way of common sense."

"Any luck on the mall bombing?"

"The bomb was in a backpack. One hundred and thirty-seven dead and over two hundred more wounded. We're still counting. No one has yet claimed responsibility."

Ari clenched his hand into a fist, made an effort to straighten his fingers. He picked up a glossy 8 X 10 photograph and handed it to Nick. It was a picture of the white Volvo, taken from one of the omnipresent cameras monitoring the streets and highways of Israel.

Nick tapped the picture. "That's him. The one in the passenger seat had the phone."

"The car was stolen. We found it five kilometers from the alley where you were attacked. The occupants are unknown to us."

"A dead end."

"So far. We are a patient people, Nick. We'll find them."

Rivka took off her scarf and shook down her hair, ran her fingers through it. It was a rich, deep brown, almost black, with a long, flowing wave.

"Let's talk about Arslanian," Ari said. "The fact he was killed tells us there must be substance to whatever he wanted to tell you. His assassin knew you were coming and tried to kill you as well. There's no purpose to that unless you are a threat to whatever is being planned."

"That makes sense. But no one is supposed to know I'm here or why. Just a few people on my end and now your people here in Israel. There aren't many, in either case. On top of that, I haven't learned squat."

"Squat?"

"Anything of value."

"Ah, but you have. Someone is worried you will find out something, therefore there is something to be found out. It seems someone has betrayed you. The question is who?"

Nick thought of Harker's signal.

Alpha Red.

Ari leaned back in his chair. "Arslanian was researching the Holocaust, particularly the criminal SS and Himmler's role in the so called final solution. He visited Germany two weeks ago."

"Do you think that has something to do with his death?"

"With Nazis, anything is possible," Ari said. "In Israel, the Holocaust was not so long ago."

Rivka tossed her head and pushed her hair back over her shoulder. "What's next, Ari?"

"We keep looking for the men in the Volvo. We watch everything around the President. Nick, you're seen as a threat to the opposition. Perhaps we can turn that to our advantage."

"Why do I get a feeling you're thinking advantage as in bait?"

Ari shrugged, held up his hands, palms up. "I wouldn't put it quite like that. But someone wants you out of the picture. They might try again. If they do, we have a chance to grab them."

"Not if they're sitting on a roof somewhere with a rifle and a nice, big scope." Carter felt a headache beginning.

"Then you should stay away from places where a sniper might have a good shot." He smiled. "No, I think if they come after you it will be, as you Americans say, up close and personal. Rivka will walk you around the Old City and I'll assign backup. It's possible we can draw them out."

Carter couldn't think of a better plan. If painting a target on his chest would flush out the people who had killed Arslanian, it was worth it.

CHAPTER SIXTEEN

Carter and Rivka sat in the Quarter Café, overlooking the Western Wall and the Temple Mount. The golden Dome of the Rock glowed in the late afternoon light. The view was fantastic, the food less so, but the strong *katzar* coffee was just what he needed. Nick's legs ached from wandering the maze of Old Jerusalem. His back felt like it was in a vise. The knife wound throbbed. His headache was constant.

Getting old, he thought. Maybe it's time to pack it up.

"One more sight." Rivka set down her empty cup. She was enjoying it, showing him around her city. Even waiting for something to happen.

Nick groaned.

"Let's go see the tunnels."

"Tunnels?"

"You can't see Jerusalem without seeing the tunnels. They're right over there." Rivka nodded at an arched entrance below the Mount. "There are old cisterns, chambers, dead ends. It's a maze. Where people pray is just a small portion of the Wall. There's a tunnel that follows the wall for several hundred meters under the Mount."

They walked down into Kotel Plaza, the large square where people prayed in front of the Wall. At the entrance to the tunnels, signs in Hebrew and English proclaimed "The Western Wall Heritage."

An open gate of black iron led to an arched chamber of grayish stone. They walked through the next arch and entered a long corridor. Walls of stone formed a long, narrow passageway lit by pools of yellow light at regular intervals. Far down the tunnel a group of sightseers chattered as they moved along.

Behind them a middle aged couple gawked, the man pointing his video camera everywhere. The woman was dressed in a yellow polyester dress with pink accents, her lipstick too red, her hair a damaged bottle blonde. The man was about forty, broad shouldered and red cheeked. He wore a Cincinnati Reds baseball cap. There was no mistaking American tourists.

Nick and Rivka moved along the tunnel. They came to a side passage opening onto another stone chamber. Far ahead, the group of sightseers paid no attention. Perhaps it was the long day or not enough sleep, but when it happened Nick wasn't ready.

He felt the hard barrel of a pistol in the small of his back and wasn't tired anymore. The tourist couple had come up behind, quiet as cats. The peroxide blonde slipped alongside Rivka, her left hand concealed under a shawl. She placed her right hand on Rivka's shoulder and gripped her on the pressure point. Rivka gasped with pain.

"Just step right in there," Blondie said. "No moves. You won't make it before you're dead."

The four of them stepped down into a small room of ancient, fitted stone. Another narrow tunnel led away into darkness. It was unlit. A large sign in three languages warned that the passage was unsafe and closed to tours.

"Let's see what's down there, shall we?" Blondie's companion pressed his pistol harder into Carter's back. He smelled of cigarettes.

"What do you want?" Nick said. "All I've got is traveler's checks. They won't do you any good."

"Shut up, asshole."

They moved past the sign and into the unlit passage.

Rivka said, "If you kill us, you'll never leave Israel alive. You know that, don't you?"

The woman sneered. "Shut your mouth, you Jewish bitch. You have no idea."

Nick glanced over at Rivka. She tipped her head, a tiny movement.

The couple were too close. It was a mistake to get too close. It cut down the advantage of a gun. Close was for instant killing strikes, or incapacitating an opponent.

Nick knocked the man's gun arm away with his elbow and drove stiffened fingers into the soft area below the sternum. His fingers slammed into a rigid surface and pain exploded in his hand. The man was wearing a Kevlar vest.

The gun went off. Nick felt the bullet tug at his jacket. His attacker staggered back, raised the gun. Nick's left hand was useless, his arm numb to the elbow. He threw a forearm strike to the throat. The man went down.

Rivka whirled and landed a vicious hit with her elbow to Blondie's kidney. The woman arched backward in pain and Rivka kicked the gun from her hand. It bounced along the stone floor. Nick pulled out his .45.

It should have been enough. The paralyzing blows should have ended it. The man brought up another pistol, his second mistake. Nick shot him in the face. The back of his head disintegrated in a thick spray of blood and bone that plastered the rock behind him. The round whined away down the passage.

"Jew bitch!"

The woman grabbed a snub nosed pistol from under her dress. Rivka fired twice and the yellow dress bloomed with red.

The shots echoed from the ancient stones.

Someone began yelling in the main tunnel outside. Waves of pain ran up Nick's arm. Ripples of light moved just behind his eyes. He held his left hand against his chest and bent over the man's body. He went through the pockets, looking for identification. Nothing. Rivka searched the woman's purse. She looked up, shook her head.

"Nothing here."

"Not here, either."

Nick felt where the bullet had grazed him. A rip in his shirt, a little blood, another ruined jacket. The pain began to subside in his arm.

"You all right?" Rivka looked at Nick.

"Yeah. They're dead."

Rivka's eyebrows went up. "You think? What gave you that impression?"

"I mean, they're not going to tell us much, are they?"

"Not in words. But they had to come from somewhere. We'll track them down." Rivka looked down at the woman and the blood pooling under the yellow dress.

"Somebody really doesn't like you, Nick."

CHAPTER SEVENTEEN

A mixed tour group of college students waited to enter Solomon's Stables, at the south eastern corner of the Temple Mount. Security was tight. Students were allowed to carry only tourist guides and literature. Cameras were forbidden. Backpacks were forbidden. A pile of them was stacked outside the entrance under the watchful eye of a security guard.

A tall, blond man in his mid-twenties waited for the tour to begin. He was absorbed in a travel guide he held in his hand, reading about the Stables.

King Herod had built the chambers to support the southeastern corner of the Temple Mount, back in the first century, before the Temple had been destroyed by the Romans. The Stables covered an area of 5000 square feet. It was formed from a series of high, vaulted passages lined with eighty-eight rows of pillars and arches, some of the arches thirty feet wide. A thousand years after Herod, the Crusaders had stabled their horses there and left the name. Holes in the rock could still be seen where the Templar knights had tied the animals' reins. Now the Stables housed the el-Marwani mosque, open to tours except during prayers.

Thirteen meters above the floor of the cavernous space, preparations for President Rice's speech were under way. The halls and arches of the stables extended beneath the spot where Rice would stand and partway under the al-Aqsa Mosque.

The tour guide led his charges into the famous chambers and began his commentary. The students straggled in spite of the guide's admonitions. The tall young man drifted further behind the group, then ducked into one of the side passages.

He knew where to go. He stopped in a dim recess. He opened the book and removed the bomb. He checked his watch. He set the timer and molded the explosive against the stone, in the exact place where aerial sonar scans had shown a serious fracture in the bedrock supporting the mosque above.

It took only a minute. His father was going to be proud of him.

CHAPTER EIGHTEEN

Ronnie and Selena were on the rifle range at Quantico. Time to get Selena familiar with M4A1 rifles. Their sat phones signaled. Ronnie grunted when he read the message. Selena looked at her display.

Alpha Red.3P.FC.XG.E5.

"What…," Selena started to say. Ronnie placed his finger on her lips, shook his head. He tore a page from his pocket notepad and wrote on it.

Talk about the weapons. Act normal. Trouble.

Selena began loading magazines for the rifles. She asked him about the laser range finder.

"We'll get to it in a bit," Ronnie said. He rummaged around in his bag and took out a black metal box about eight inches square. He set it on the shooting bench and pressed a button. A green light began blinking on top of the box.

"We can talk now. This will scramble any electronic surveillance aimed at us. I'll fill you in, then we'll turn it off and get on with the guns. Don't say anything important unless this box is on."

"Ronnie, what's up? What's 'Alpha Red'?"

"I don't know what's up. Alpha Red is an emergency code. It means the shit has hit the fan."

"Nice choice of words. What's the rest of it?"

"3P means we meet the Director at three o'clock this afternoon. FC means change our sat phones to a shifting frequency. It's not much used."

"What about the rest?"

"XG means deactivate the GPS locator in the phones."

Ronnie took Selena's phone and entered the new frequency. He showed her how to shut down the signal that told anyone with access to the Global Positioning System where she was.

"E5 is something Stephanie set up," Ronnie said. "It routes email and the internet through so many countries and servers no one can find the point of origin."

"Where do we meet Harker?"

"At the Marine Corps War Memorial."

"What about Nick?"

"He'll get the message. He'll be all right."

Selena waited.

"We shoot for a while, like we planned." Ronnie gestured at the weapons. "We get back to the car, I'll run a sweep. It's all part of Alpha Red. Clear?"

Selena nodded. Ronnie turned off the box and put it back in his kit. He picked up a rifle. They'd been blacked out from eavesdroppers for less than a minute.

"You're familiar with the MP-5," Ronnie said, "so you know how to control rate of climb and get off a three round burst."

The Heckler and Koch MP-5 in its many variations was a favorite weapon of SOCOM units all over the world. Selena knew how to use it. It had been part of her baptism in blood.

"The M4A1 is different from the H-K, but the principles are the same. This is what most of our troops carry. It fires a 5.65 by 45 millimeter NATO round, high velocity, good penetration. After five or six hundred rounds it can heat up and jam in a bad firefight. That's why we use the MP-5. But you should get familiar with this weapon."

He handed it to her. "It's not much good beyond 300 yards. It's meant for close combat. Let's get you set up at a hundred and we'll try it out."

He showed her the attachments, scope adjustments, stock configurations. They began shooting. After two hours they packed up and headed back to Ronnie's Hummer. He took a detector from his bag and walked around the car. He reached down and found a tiny device the size of a grain of rice, covered with grease. He made walking movements with his fingers.

Selena nodded. A bug.

Ronnie put the bug back where he'd found it. He completed the sweep outside, then covered the inside of the car.

"Hop in," he said.

They drove out through the main gate and headed toward the city.

Ronnie said, "Let's get something to eat. There's a joint along here that's pretty good. Slow service, but we're done for the day. Let's grab a beer and a steak."

"Sounds good."

Ten minutes later they pulled into the restaurant parking lot. Ronnie got out and removed the bug. A green BMW with Virginia plates was parked two cars down. Ronnie sauntered near, stooped down and planted the bug underneath.

They headed for Washington.

CHAPTER NINETEEN

The DC-3 turbo prop conversion came in low in the dark Antarctic night. The plane's landing lights glared bright white on the hard packed ice and snow of the runway. The throaty growl of modified Pratt & Whitney engines shook the room as the plane passed over the research station.

Hans had been unable to sleep, his mind filled with thoughts of the Nazi bunker. Now he was charting observations made during the last month. He heard the plane. He put down his pen and went to a window.

He watched the DC-3 make a smooth landing, turn at the end of the runway and taxi to a stop a hundred feet away. A large cargo hatch in the port side of the plane opened. Armed men in black spilled from the aircraft and ran toward the station. Hans thought for a second. Then he reached out and hit the fire alarm.

A hundred and twenty decibel klaxon began blaring. Lights came on all over the station. Doors slammed as people roused themselves and made for the assembly area near the main stairs leading down to the outside.

The station rested six meters above the ground on hydraulic legs. It looked almost exactly like a large ferry perched on narrow piers, a wide rectangle two hundred feet long with two levels and two long rows of windows along the angled sides. Entrance was through an enclosure that reached down to the ice from the middle of the structure.

Hard boots pounded up from below. Nervous voices called out as people streamed from all over the station to the central area near the stairs.

"Where's the fire?" It was Otto Bremen. He was flushed and annoyed, wearing unlaced boots and a thick jacket over his pajamas.

"No fire. Soldiers coming toward us. They look like a SWAT team."

Hans cut the blaring klaxon. The door burst open. Helmeted men dressed in black fanned out through the room. They pointed assault rifles at the confused scientists. An officer wearing embroidered silver oak leaves on his collar entered the room. Hans thought the insignia looked familiar. Where had he seen it?

The officer barked orders in perfect German and sent men into the maze of station passages to find any stragglers still in their rooms or laboratories. Then he looked over the assembled scientists. He was tall, his hair the color of bleached sun under his helmet, his face chiseled from stone. His blue eyes were empty, as if no one lived behind them.

"Who is in charge?"

Bremen stepped forward. "I am. I'm the chief geophysicist. Who are you? How dare you break in here?"

"If you cooperate, no one will be harmed. I will ask the questions, *chief geophysicist*. You discovered something today. We are here to examine your find. Where, exactly, is it?"

Hans remembered where he'd seen an insignia like the one the man was wearing. In pictures of Nazi SS officers from the war. This was like something out of the American television series, "The Twilight Zone".

Except for the fact that the guns were real.

"I won't tell you," Bremen said.

The officer pointed his rifle at Otto and shot him. The burst nearly cut him in half. It drove Bremen back against a table and spun him to the floor, splashing blood over the table and Hans's careful notes. A stunned silence filled the room. The station personnel stared at their chief's broken body.

"You." He turned toward Hans. "The one with the beard. Where is it?"

Hans looked at the blood pooling under his dead friend. Let them have the damn stuff. Old paintings weren't worth more lives.

"An hour and a half from here. You can follow the tracks we made. In the *Fenriskjeften*. Follow the tracks to the range, turn right and not long after, you'll see it on the left."

"In the Jaw of the Wolf. How fitting. Where are the Sno-Cats?"

"In a cavern under the station. You'll see the doors outside. That end. The keys are in the ignitions." Hans gestured toward the south end of the station.

The officer gave his orders. Most of the soldiers left the station, leaving three behind to stand guard. The man who had shot Bremen in cold blood walked over to Hans. He took his black-gloved hand and grabbed Hans by the jaw, pulled him close. Hans could smell his breath, foul like overripe cheese. Looking into his eyes, Hans thought it was like looking into a lightless pit.

"If you have lied to me, you will die. If there is any trouble while I am gone, you will die. So will all the others. Understand?"

Hans nodded, fighting the pain of the grip.

"Good."

He gave a final squeeze, patted Hans hard on the cheek, then turned and left after the others.

One of the soldiers ordered everyone to sit on the floor, hands over their heads. When one of the biologists protested, the soldier clubbed him to the floor with the butt of his rifle. After that there was no more talking.

Four hours later, the officer returned. He smiled a cold smile at Hans.

"Thank you. Your directions were accurate."

He stepped back and gestured. "Kill them."

Like a well oiled machine, the guards raised their weapons in one smooth motion and began firing at the helpless people on the floor. *It's not fair,* Hans thought. *I'm going to be married.* Then his thoughts were gone.

The officer walked among the bodies, rifle in hand. Twice, he fired.

"All right. Let's go."

At the top of the stairs, the last man out tossed two incendiary grenades into the station. He pulled the door closed and ran down the steps. Orange and yellow flame exploded through the windows and shot skyward.

Someone pulled the cargo hatch closed. The engines of the DC-3 rose to a full-throttled roar. A thousand feet later, the plane lifted away and disappeared into the night. On the desolate, frozen ice shelf below, the flames from the burning station soared skyward like a beacon of warning from some dark and ancient Nordic myth.

CHAPTER TWENTY

Elizabeth wanted the latest NSA information on President Rice's trip. She had full access to the NSA database. The kind of details NSA had on the trip were highly classified, but Elizabeth's clearance was UMBRA, as high as it got. She entered her password.

Except the computer screen displayed a curt message.

Access Denied.

She tried again, with the same result. An unpleasant thought occurred to her. She entered a different search, unrelated to the President but still restricted.

Access Denied.

She buzzed Stephanie. "Steph, can you come in for a sec?"

Stephanie had on one of her favorite red and black color combinations. A tailored blouse and jacket hid the Glock tucked into the waist of her black skirt. She came into Elizabeth's office.

Stephanie was one of the secrets of Elizabeth's success. If necessary, she could take over the Project. More, there was nothing Stephanie couldn't do with a computer. Elizabeth sometimes thought Steph had binary bits and electrons running through her veins along with her blood.

There was no need to talk about Alpha Red. Stephanie knew the drill.

"Let's have lunch," Elizabeth said. She pointed at the screen with its infuriating message and put a finger on her lips. "We can sit out back in the shade garden."

The back of the Project building sheltered an enclosed garden with high walls and a pleasant, shaded fountain. In good weather it was a favorite spot for lunch and impromptu meetings.

"My pleasure." Stephanie twirled the gold bracelets on her wrist.

Harker shut down her computer. She had Stephanie. That was all she would need.

The two women rode down to the first floor and went out past the security station into the parking lot. They walked in silence to Elizabeth's Audi. Stephanie used a detector to make a sweep. She found a bug near the driver's side door and placed it on the curb.

They headed for the highway.

In a darkened room lined with monitors, the technicians manning the audio surveillance and tracking equipment noticed nothing amiss. They were multi-tasking, monitoring a stream of audio and video transmissions from multiple sources. The locator showed Harker's car parked outside her building. The bug transmitted normal background sounds. The subject had given no sign she knew she was being surveilled. There was no reason to be suspicious.

The GPS readouts indicated the vehicle belonging to Ronnie Peete was parked in Virginia at a well known restaurant. Selena Connor's car was still in the parking lot next to Harker's and she was with Peete anyway. Everything looked good. Just another routine job.

Elizabeth drove toward the city. She told Stephanie of the morning call from the new head of NSA.

"Dysart is the only one who could have blocked my clearance."

"Do you think it's personal?"

"I hardly know him, Steph. He's got no reason to do this." She paused. "He's moved fast. General Hood only went down last night."

Her intuition sent vibes all over her body, raising goose bumps.

"Do you think he had anything to do with that? Dysart?"

"With General Hood's illness? Elizabeth, that's a terrible thought."

"Dysart wants me to pull Nick out right away. A decorated, effective agent in place when the President is in a high risk security situation and Dysart wants him gone. Then he knocks out my classified access. I don't like what I'm thinking."

"You think Dysart is setting something up. Something about the President."

Stephanie shifted in her seat, adjusted the pistol tucked behind her back.

Harker said, "The Middle East is a powder keg. I think someone may want to set it off. If Dysart is part of a conspiracy, he'd try to shut us down before we discovered whatever is being planned. It would explain the surveillance, everything."

Stephanie looked out the window.

Elizabeth thought about Dysart. *I hope I'm wrong and this is only some petty vendetta. But what if I'm right? Something must be set to happen in Jerusalem, or why block me? Block the Project? How do I stop something I can't pin down?*

She had no answer. There was no one outside of the team she could trust. She'd have to handle it on her own.

CHAPTER TWENTY-ONE

They skirted the Capitol and crossed the Arlington Memorial Bridge. Elizabeth turned right onto Memorial Parkway. In a short time they came to the Marine Corps War Memorial. The thirty foot high bronze figures were frozen in time as they struggled to raise the flag on Iwo Jima. The flag flew overhead in a brisk autumn breeze. In the distance the Washington Monument thrust white and shining into the blue sky.

America.

Ronnie and Selena came across the grass. The four stood facing each other next to the polished granite base of the memorial. Ronnie set his black box down on the ground between them.

"Hell of a thing," said Ronnie. "Someone bugged my Hummer, high end stuff, government issue."

"My car, too, Ronnie. We have to assume Selena's car is tagged also."

"What's going on, Director?" Selena brushed a wisp of hair away from her forehead. It was a habit Elizabeth had noted.

"Nick is blown. He found our contact in Jerusalem dead. Someone was waiting and tried to kill him, too. NSA has a new boss, General Dysart. I've got a bad feeling about him."

Selena's voice was strained. "Is Nick all right?"

"Yes."

"Dysart is bad news." Ronnie looked up at the flag. "He's one of those Pentagon desk jockeys who thinks paper work is more important than body armor. Why is Hood gone?"

"He's in Walter Reed, supposedly with a stroke."

"Supposedly?"

"Maybe Hood's stroke wasn't an accident. Hood goes down. Then Dysart calls me up and tells me I should terminate a mission he's not supposed to know about. He's blocked my classified access to NSA. We're being surveilled. Someone tries to take Nick out of the picture. I think we've stumbled into something."

Ronnie looked down and scuffed his shoe against the grass. "You think someone's going after Rice? You sound like you think there's a conspiracy to take over the NSA. Who could set that up?"

"Dysart said he'd been talking to Lodge, so CIA may be in on this, too."

"What's our next move?"

"I think we'd better be damn careful. Whoever's behind this may try to take us out of circulation. If Dysart or Lodge are involved, we're in trouble."

Elizabeth looked around. The only people in sight were an older couple some distance away. The man was taking pictures of the Memorial.

"I think we go to ground," Elizabeth said.

Stephanie said, "The safe house?"

"Yes. We've got everything we need there. No one at NSA or Langley knows about it."

The safe house was in the rural Virginia countryside, an hour and a half from Alexandria. Elizabeth had set it up two years ago. Not even the President knew about it.

"We'll leave now for the house. Then we decide our next moves. If I'm right, it won't be long before people will be looking for us."

Elizabeth looked up at the flag, then back at the others. "Agreed?"

The four got back in their vehicles. In a short time it was as if they had disappeared from the face of the earth.

CHAPTER TWENTY-TWO

Carter and Rivka were in the sushi bar at Nick's hotel. It was evening. Two of the president's entourage sat at the end of the counter, watched by a Secret Service agent loitering near a tall, potted palm.

Nick's headache was gone. The fingers of his hand were swollen and stiff, but aside from that he felt pretty good. He downed a cup of sake, to help his fingers.

"So, now you've seen Old Jerusalem." Rivka sipped her sake and set it down. She lifted a piece of *maguro* with her chopsticks. "I'm curious. What do you think?"

"It's like a schizophrenic's dream. Like three or four different worlds."

"They are different worlds. Jerusalem puts on a face of diversity but it's a time bomb. Jews, Christians and Arabs are all crammed into sections of the city side by side. They don't like each other."

"Religion doesn't have much to do with reason."

"That's the problem."

"You're not religious?"

"I love my religion, but I'm what they call a secular Jew. The Orthodox disapprove of people like me. Those kinds of divisions in Israel make it hard to get any real consensus."

"Like peace with the Palestinians."

"Like that." She nodded and dipped a tuna roll into soy sauce. "It's an impossible situation. Too much blood's been spilled. There's too much anger."

"You sound like Ari." He poured another cup of sake. It was good, light and dry, not too sweet.

"Ari's right. All that's likely to come out of this trip by your President is trouble."

Carter looked at his watch and signaled for the check.

They walked out to the lobby and the elevator.

"I'd better ride up with you," she said. They got out on the fifth floor and walked along the deserted corridor. At Carter's door, he stopped short. He held up his damaged hand and slipped his pistol out. The tell-tale he'd placed on the door was out of place. Rivka drew her pistol. She held it pointed toward the ceiling in both hands.

Maid service? She mouthed the words. Nick shook his head, pointed at the Do Not Disturb sign hanging on the handle.

He took the plastic room key out of his pocket, stepped to the side of the door and inserted it into the slot. A green light came on with a loud click. The lock released. He pushed the handle down. Like most modern hotel doors, it was designed to close by itself. No way to throw the door open and have it stay that way.

Maybe this was nothing. Maybe the maid had come in and left chocolates on the pillow.

He pushed the door in hard and went in fast and low, gun held out in front. The room was dark. The glass balcony doors were halfway open. He'd left them closed. Across the way, the illuminated fortress walls of the Old City crowned the ancient hills. A cool desert breeze bearing the clean smell of Jerusalem pine and fading heat came in from the terrace.

To the right, the bathroom door was open. There was no one inside. A short wall blocked the part of the main room with the bed. Rivka was right behind him, silhouetted against the hallway lights outside the room.

A black figure appeared on the terrace and fired. His gun spit hard, raw coughs and bright flashes from the muzzle. Nick fired three quick shots. Blooms of light lit the room as he pulled the trigger. Rivka's pistol barked next to him, crisp, flat explosions.

The glass doors to the terrace disintegrated. The bullets drove the shooter back over the balcony railing. His scream lasted past all five floors to the courtyard below. It stopped suddenly with a sound like someone dropping a sack of wet cement.

Rivka went down to her knees and folded forward onto the carpet. There was a bloody hole on her back.

She moaned, her face contorted with pain. Nick grabbed towels from the bathroom and pressed them against the wound. The bleeding slowed.

"You're okay, you're okay. Don't move. I've got the bleeding stopped."

Rivka was chalk white, clenching her jaw.

"You got him, he went over the balcony. The bullet missed your lung. Don't worry."

Nick was pumped from the adrenaline and he was angry. He'd blown it. He should have made sure she stayed outside. He told himself Rivka was an experienced agent who knew the drill. It didn't make him feel any better.

Running footsteps and shouts in the hall told him they'd have help soon.

CHAPTER TWENTY-THREE

The safe house sat back from the road on ten acres of rolling Virginia countryside, shielded by a spread of giant oaks planted fifty years before the first shots fired in the Civil War.

The house was a classic ante-bellum southern home, two stories of weathered brick with a slate roof, paned windows and a wide chimney rising at each end. A railed gallery painted white ran along the second story and formed a columned porch along the front of the house. The gallery looked out over fields where Bobby Lee's boys in butternut and gray had passed in a vanished time. A low wall of fieldstone marked the boundaries of the property. Signs warned trespassers away.

The trees and landscaping hid cameras and sensors. It would take a rocket propelled grenade to get through the innocent looking front door. The windows were authentic in style, but they were made of bullet proof glass.

Elizabeth believed that a safe house needed to be *safe*. There was even an emergency escape tunnel. Maybe it was overkill, but it was satisfying to anyone with reason to be cautious or paranoid.

Elizabeth's paranoia was in full bloom.

Stephanie had hacked into NSA and was probing for anything to hint at what was going on in Dysart's mind. The security monitors on the wall above her in the darkened room showed nothing except serene countryside straight from a realtor's dream book. The ground alarms were active and silent.

Ronnie and Selena were in the kitchen cooking up spaghetti and meatballs. Except for the weapons on the kitchen table it could have passed for a normal dinner hour in America.

Elizabeth's white silk blouse was limp, stained with dark rings under her armpits. She wrinkled her nose at the sour smell of her own stress. Stephanie's fingers moved across the keyboard, entering a steady stream of commands.

Elizabeth began coughing, trying to catch her breath. Sharp pain spread through her chest. *Not now!*

"Are you all right, Director?"

"Yes." She coughed. "Excuse me. I'll be right back."

She got to her feet and went into the bathroom and closed the door. Coughing, she reached into her purse for a small black case. She opened it and took out a syringe and glass vial. She fitted a needle, punched through the rubber seal on the bottle and drew 5cc of clear liquid into the syringe. Her fine, thin boned hands trembled. She pushed air out of the syringe, sat on the toilet, exposed her thigh and injected the liquid.

She waited for the symptoms to pass. In a moment, she began to feel better. She found the inhaler in her purse and took a deep breath into her lungs.

The doctors had said the attacks would come more often, but she hadn't expected it so soon. She looked in the mirror, at the dark shadows under her eyes. She flushed the unused toilet, patted water on her face and went back to the computer room.

"What have you got, Steph?"

Lines of code streamed across the monitor. Stephanie's fingers flew over the keyboard. "I'm into the main servers and past the firewalls. Now I'm after Dysart's emails. He's got sophisticated encryption, something I haven't seen before, but I think I'm close."

"Will anyone know if you get in?"

"Yes. But they won't know who did it or where it came from. I won't have much time once I crack it, but I'll download everything as fast as possible. We should get most of it before the system shuts me out."

The screen cleared and a list of files appeared.

"I'm in!"

Stephanie tapped a key. A window appeared with a moving bar marking progress of the download. Elizabeth watched. Ten per cent downloaded. Fifteen. Twenty-five. She realized she was holding her breath, exhaled. Fifty-six per cent. Seventy. Seventy-eight. Ninety-three. The screen went blank. Stephanie tapped a key, disconnected.

"We got almost all of it. Right now they're going nuts over at Fort Meade, but there's no way they can trace it back here. It will look like someone in Uzbekistan was playing games."

Ronnie called from the kitchen. "Chow's up! Come eat."

Elizabeth's stomach growled. Dysart's files could wait another ten minutes. As she sat down her phone signaled a call from Nick. She turned on the speaker.

"Director, what the hell's going on?"

"General Dysart took over NSA this morning. He knew you were in Jerusalem and wanted me to recall you. He's not supposed to know you're there. Nobody is. Then someone bugged our vehicles, high tech. Our security is compromised. I don't know what's happening, but it smells rotten. We're all at the safe house."

"Someone came after me again. Twice. The first time it was a couple posing as tourists. They're dead. Then someone tried when I went to my hotel room. He's dead too, but he got one of Shin Bet's agents. She's in bad shape."

She? In his hotel room? Who was Nick hanging out with? Selena felt flushed, then guilty. *Someone tried to kill him and you're jealous. What's the matter with you?*

"Are you all right?" Harker said.

"Yes."

"Nick, I think Dysart is setting up the President. Maybe an assassination."

"The Director of NSA? Are you serious?" Nick's voice faded in and out. It sounded like someone talking from the bottom of a well filled with electronic gargling, but Selena could hear the shock in his voice.

"Yes."

"Can you prove it?"

"Not yet, but my gut tells me I'm right. I want you to get close to Rice. I'll call him and set it up."

Elizabeth looked at her spaghetti cooling on the table. Ronnie wasn't waiting. He twirled pasta on his plate with his fork while he listened to the conversation.

"Arslanian had a flash drive in his hand when he was killed," Nick said. "I'm going to upload it to you now."

Elizabeth watched the download progress on her phone until it was done.

"Got it."

"Director, I'm blown. I should get out of here."

"Rice needs you there. Tell him there may be a plot to assassinate him and that I'm working on proving it."

"I don't like it." He paused. "When will you call Rice?"

"Now. As soon as this conversation is over."

"Then I'm gone." Nick broke the connection.

CHAPTER TWENTY-FOUR

Elizabeth sat at the kitchen table with a cup of coffee, watching Selena load the dishwasher. Something was bothering her, and it wasn't whether the forks should point up or down. Ronnie and Stephanie were in the computer room. Selena closed the appliance door. The machine began to cycle.

"Tell me about you and Nick," Elizabeth said.

Selena brushed hair away from her forehead. "What about Nick?"

"How serious are you?"

"That's the second time someone's asked me. Ronnie wanted to know."

"Does it bother you that I ask?"

Selena didn't answer.

"Because it's important. I have to know that whatever there is between you isn't going to get in the way."

"In the way?"

"Of what we do. Of what Nick has to do. Of what you have to do. Don't misunderstand me. You've been fine and I'm thrilled you're part of the team. I just need to know emotions aren't going to affect your judgment."

Selena sat down and sighed. "I don't know what to tell you. You asked how serious it is. He's the first man I've met in a long time that doesn't run the other way because he thinks I'm smarter than he is or too independent. So, yes, it's serious enough that I want to give it a shot. Is that what you want to know?"

"Part of it."

Selena got up, got coffee, sat down again.

"Can I talk to you as a friend, instead of a boss?"

Elizabeth looked at her. "Of course you can."

"I can handle the emotional part. What I'm having trouble with isn't Nick." She paused. "My uncle was the only family I had. When he was killed, I felt lost. Alone."

Elizabeth nodded.

"Since then everything's changed. You and Ronnie and Steph and Nick, you're my family now. Except we all carry guns and now the good guys may turn out to be bad guys. It's all upside down.

People keep trying to kill my lover. I'm staying in a house with bullet proof windows. I don't know what's happening, I'm not in control and I can't do anything except react. It's making me crazy."

"It does take some getting used to," Elizabeth said. The way she said it made Selena laugh.

"Do you ever get used to it?"

"Sort of."

"I feel...vulnerable. If something happens to Nick, or any of us. I'm not sure how I'd handle that."

"That's honest, what you just said. I used the wrong word, earlier. It's not about emotions, it's about feelings. You have them, you deal with them, you keep going. You take it as it comes. You'll handle it, I'm sure, no matter what. You did that in Tibet. I made the right choice when I let you on the team."

"How do you handle it?"

"I compartmentalize. One thing at a time, more or less. If you think about everything at once it can overwhelm you. I don't let personal feelings get in the way."

"Yes, but you have them."

"Sure. But I've learned to put them away. So has Nick. So has Ronnie. And so have you."

"What do you mean?"

"How did you feel in Tibet? You killed people."

The words hung like a bright neon sign in the air between them. Selena said nothing.

"We see the worst side of things," Elizabeth said. "We never know what's going to happen and we have to keep a clear head"

"I can't pretend I don't have feelings. About Nick."

"I know. But if they get in the way you could make a mistake. It could kill you. Or Nick. There is something that balances things out a little."

Selena looked at Elizabeth.

"We can trust each other and channel our feelings into that. It's what makes any team work."

"Who else do we trust?"

"No one."

"That's cynical."

"That's reality."

"What keeps you doing this?" Selena asked.

Elizabeth thought about it. "I think everyone deserves a chance at some kind of justice. The people we go after don't believe that. Somebody's got to try and stop them."

Selena looked away, out the kitchen window. It was night. There wasn't much to see.

"I wonder what Nick's doing now?" she said.

CHAPTER TWENTY-FIVE

People milled about in the corridor. Nick watched a medical team load Rivka onto a gurney. They'd given her a shot of something and she was out of it, her dusky skin the color of milk. He called Ari.

"Is she all right?"

"She's badly wounded. The medics are here, she's on her way to Hadassah."

"How did it happen?"

"We went through the door of my room and someone started shooting from the balcony. We fired and he went over the edge. She took one all the way through."

"You?"

"He missed." Nick thought of Rivka taking a bullet meant for him. It wasn't a good thought.

"Stay where you are," Ari said. "I'll be there in ten minutes."

Down the hall, three men and a woman in dark suits and earpieces made their way toward him.

"I may not be here. I see Secret Service coming. They're going to want some answers."

"Ten minutes." Ari hung up.

The four agents stopped in front of Nick. They didn't look friendly.

The lead man was over six feet tall and purposeful, with a face that had serious all over it. His eyes were like ice. He was around forty, clean-shaven even this late in the day. He had a high forehead and a combination of green eyes and red hair that said Ireland in the background somewhere.

"You're Carter?"

It wouldn't take a rocket scientist to know who he was. They'd only needed to check the hotel register.

"Yes."

"Calloway." He flashed his ID and gave a pointed look at Nick's holstered H-K. "Hand over your weapon, please."

The other agents waited to see what he would do. The hallway was filling up with police, Secret Service, spies and who knew what. It reminded him of a scene from a Bogart movie. The only thing missing was Sydney Greenstreet.

A large Israeli police officer wearing the insignia of a Sergeant Major stepped in front of Calloway.

"Just a minute. We are in charge, here." His English was heavily accented. He turned to Nick, said, "Give me your pistol, please." He had his right hand on his holstered weapon, the strap snapped back and the hammer cocked, his left hand held out for the gun.

Agent Calloway was cool before, but now he turned glacial. "The President's security takes precedence here. This man will come with us."

"I don't think so. You are on Israeli sovereign territory. This is our country, not yours. Your President is upstairs and quite safe. This man is in our custody." He turned back to Nick. "Your weapon, please."

Nick carefully lifted his .45 out of the holster, using a thumb and one finger on the grip, and held it out to the Israeli. He took it, nodded once in satisfaction. Calloway's expression looked like he'd been forced to drink vinegar.

The agents crowded in and the tension level in the hall went up. Several Israeli policemen moved closer. Then a commanding voice cut through the noise in the hall.

"That's enough!"

President James Rice was coming down the corridor, thirty feet away. He wore tan slippers and an unbuttoned gray cardigan vest over a blue shirt and casual slacks. Three more grim faced agents were with him. Calloway straightened. All sound died away. Down the hall, a woman in a pink robe and hair curlers peered out of her room.

The President had the kind of presence people expect of the single most powerful politician in the world. With Rice, it was more than political practice. He radiated command and confidence. An intense energy belied his sixty-seven years. He was just under six feet tall, with silver hair still showing a few strands of black. His penetrating, hazel eyes didn't miss anything.

Calloway stepped forward. "Mr. President. Sir, you shouldn't be here."

"It's all right, John, I know who this man is. He is not a threat."

Rice looked at Nick. "A short time ago I received a phone call from Director Harker. When I heard what happened down here, I decided to see for myself."

The President was known for hands-on involvement with anything he deemed important. It drove his advisors and his security details crazy.

"Mr. President," Nick said. "Sir, if I could have a few moments, I need to speak with you."

"All in good time, Carter, all in good time. Sergeant." He nodded at the police officer. "It is Sergeant, isn't it? Please return Mr. Carter's weapon to him."

The Israeli policeman was at a loss as to what he should do. He opened his mouth to speak, closed it. Just then Ari came down the hall, his Shin Bet ID held high in front of him. The crowd parted before him like the red sea before Moses. He stopped in front of the policeman.

"Sergeant Major, I think you had better do as the American President suggests."

The Israeli cop started to say something, thought better of it and gave the pistol back, butt first. The woman agent had moved to the side of the President and was talking into her microphone, holding one hand against her earpiece, the other on her holstered Glock, watching Nick the way a cat watches a mouse.

"You are…?" Rice looked at Ari.

"Ari Herzog, Mr. President, Shin Bet. Mr. Carter and I have been working together. One of my operatives was with him and injured when they were attacked. It's an unfortunate incident. We'll pursue it. "

"Shin Bet. You believe this was a terrorist operation of some sort?"

"Mr. President. We—Mr. Carter and I—have been concerned about your safety. It's possible this attack has something to do with your presence here in my country."

Rice sighed. "Thank you, Mr. Herzog. I regret the trouble my visit causes you. I hope your agent recovers quickly." Rice paused. "Perhaps you would allow me to take charge of Mr. Carter. I'm sure you have much to attend to."

It was a gracious dismissal and an order at the same time.

"Of course, Mr. President. Nick, please contact me."

"As soon as possible, Ari."

Rice said, "This way, Carter." He turned and headed for the elevators, his detail flanked around him. Nick caught a hard look from Calloway, but the agent said nothing. Rice was the boss. There was no doubt about who was in charge.

The ride up to the ninth floor was made in silence. Rice looked preoccupied. Calloway and his agents looked unhappy. Nick didn't know how he looked but decided to keep his mouth shut and work at getting the sake under control. He had a vivid picture in his mind of Rivka lying on the floor of his room.

CHAPTER TWENTY-SIX

Touted as the most exclusive accommodations in Jerusalem, the Royal Suite where Rice was staying was twelve hundred square feet of carpeted luxury. Kings, Premiers and Presidents had all stayed here.

The main room featured a grouping of white brocade chairs placed before a fireplace at one end. Sideboards, tables and elegant side chairs of polished hardwoods were arranged throughout. A windowed terrace swept the length of the entire suite, with a million dollar view of the Old City and its spotlighted battlements. Above the ancient walls, the deep black of the Judean night sky glowed with stars.

The suite had separate reception rooms and a full kitchen. A large bedroom opened off a study furnished with a Chippendale style desk. Paintings in earth tones and grays dotted the walls. The room reeked of privileged elegance and money.

Rice led the way into the study. He took a seat by the desk and gestured Nick to a chair. Calloway stood by the door, hands clasped in front of him. Nick half expected him to put on sunglasses, even though it was nighttime and indoors.

"At ease, Carter, for God's sake. You're making me nervous."

"Yes, sir." Nick made an effort to relax.

Now that they were in the quiet privacy of the President's rooms, Nick could see how tired he was. Rice's eyes were fringed with red and there were deep shadows under them. The President was a man who needed sleep.

"John," Rice said to Calloway, "we may have a situation."

"Yes, Mr. President."

"Carter." Rice took a sip of water from a bottle on his desk. "I don't think Director Harker is the kind of person who makes unfounded accusations or gets pulled into conspiracy fantasies. Would you agree?"

"Yes, sir."

"Are you aware of her concerns?"

"Yes, sir. She believes General Dysart may be part of a conspiracy and that there may be a plot to assassinate you."

For an instant Calloway lost his mask of composure. Good, Nick thought. The guy's human after all.

"Mr. President, someone tried to kill me three times today and a deep cover source of ours was murdered before I could talk with him. Someone breached our security. No one was supposed to know I was here, but Dysart found out. Now he's running NSA and he tried to get Harker to call me off. It adds up to a lot of suspicion."

"General Dysart took over General Hood's duties because he's in Walter Reed after suffering a stroke."

"Sir, he'd just completed his annual physical and he was in fine health. How could he have a stroke?"

"We're going to find out. I've directed his medical team to pursue detailed toxicology studies as well as the usual regimens. In any event, Director Harker was adamant that I am in danger. She said she is working on getting evidence Dysart is involved in a conspiracy."

"If something is there Harker will find it, Mr. President."

"As of now, Carter, you are part of my immediate security detail until I leave Israel. I'm sure the Director can take care of herself. I want you close by and I want you armed."

There was only one possible response. "Yes, sir."

Rice glanced at Calloway. "Okay with you, John?"

It wasn't really a request, but it was typical of Rice to include others in decisions he had already made. Calloway was in a tough spot.

"Of course, sir."

"Good. Find a place for him to sleep. Put him up with our people. I want him with us tomorrow on the Temple Mount."

"Yes, sir."

"Mr. President, may I call Director Harker and tell her of our conversation? I also need to contact Shin Bet."

"Use your discretion and get some sleep. You'll need it."

Time to call Harker and Ari and then try to grab a few hours. Maybe he wouldn't dream.

CHAPTER TWENTY-SEVEN

Morning in Jerusalem, and the sky was a luminous blue that went on forever. It reminded Nick of New Mexico, the only other place he'd ever seen that kind of unearthly color.

The President rode with Prime Minister Ascher in the third of five identical armored, black limousines. Flags of Israel and America flew from the front fenders. Nick rode in the car behind the President. It was cool and insulated inside and smelled of new leather and stress. Nick felt trapped. The car was an easy target, armored or not. He looked out through tinted windows at the hostile faces passing by.

The motorcade rolled between a solid line of Israeli soldiers, through checkpoints manned with armored vehicles and troops carrying the latest Tavor Tar-21 assault rifles. It was a security nightmare, a scene of barely controlled chaos.

Thousands of protesters pushed against crowd control barriers keeping them from the Mount and from each other. Muslims, Jews, and Christians shouted and waved signs in Hebrew, Arabic and English. The noise was deafening. The crowd moved in a constant, seething motion, a coiled, restless serpent.

The *Waqf* had refused to let Rice drop in by helicopter. He would have to walk to the Mount like everyone else. Once out of the vehicles, the President's party was surrounded three deep by a phalanx of Secret Service and Shin Bet. They entered a covered walkway over a wooden bridge that stretched above the Western Wall. The large plaza in front of the Wall was packed with people praying.

The walkway was lined with more Israeli troops. It led to the Moors Gate, the only entrance for non-Muslims onto the Temple Mount. Carter walked a few steps behind Rice and Prime Minister Ascher. He couldn't help thinking it was heady company for a beat up former Marine. What the hell was he doing here?

Rice wanted to staunch wounds bleeding since the time of the Crusades. He was going to appeal for reason and new peace negotiations between the Palestinians and Israel. He'd chosen the Temple Mount to make his speech as an acknowledgement of Islam. Many saw it as a political gimmick at best and defilement at the worst. Nick thought it would have to be a damn good speech, if the uproar around the Mount was any indication of things.

They entered the Mount and were met by a delegation from the *Waqf*. A contingent of uniformed Muslim guards assigned to the Muslim Authority stood at attention along the sides of the broad square in front of the Mosque. They wore dark khaki colored uniforms with green flashes and green berets and were unarmed except for batons. The Israeli soldiers kept to the perimeter and were armed to the teeth. Overhead, Israeli military helicopters circled in the distance.

Thousands of square feet of carpets had been laid everywhere people would sit and walk, to keep their shoes from touching the sacred surface of the Mount. Guns and cell phones were never allowed on the Mount, but there were plenty here today.

The air was electric with tension. Nick's ear itched like hell. It felt like anything could set off a confrontation. If it went bad there was no telling what would happen.

The golden Dome of the Rock dominated the Mount. It was reached through a set of steps and an arched colonnade. The building was octagon shaped, the huge dome sheltering the Rock of Abraham rising from the center. Arabic inscriptions in green and gold ran along the eight sides of the shrine below the dome, over arched openings protected by carved grillwork. On the peak of the dome, the crescent and star of Islam gleamed in the bright morning sun.

The al-Aqsa Mosque was across from the Dome at the southern end of the Mount. Seven tall, strong arches lined the front of the Mosque, forming a sheltered porch and colonnade. In front of the Mosque was a large, square fountain for ablutions.

Unlike the golden Dome of the Rock, the smaller dome of al-Aqsa was sheathed in grayish lead. Four ancient minarets graced the building, the newest seven hundred years old.

It was here that Muhammad had arrived on the Night Journey. Muslims believed that from al-Aqsa the Prophet had gone to the rock of Abraham across the way and ascended on a winged horse to paradise, to talk with God. To the Muslim world, al-Aqsa was only a shade less important than Mecca itself.

In Islam the Temple Mount was called Haram-al-Sharif, the Noble Sanctuary. In the West the nearest equivalent was perhaps St. Peter's Basilica, but the religious fervor and sacred devotion directed at the Noble Sanctuary by Muslims had no real counterpart in the Christian world.

The news networks had set up cameras and satellite links for the event. Nick saw logos for CNN, Al-Jazeera, Israeli television, BBC. There were others he couldn't identify. The entire world was watching.

A speaking stage had been erected. Two rows of chairs for dignitaries lined the back of the stage. Secret Service and Shin Bet agents were stationed on the stage and around it. A raised podium bristled with microphones. It was armored and big enough for Rice to get behind if someone was stupid enough to start shooting. Bullet-proof deflectors were attached front and sides. It seemed an odd way to bring a message of peace and reconciliation to the world.

Calloway positioned Nick on the square in front of the stage, to the right of the podium. He gave him one of the earpieces and mikes used by the Secret Service. With his wrap around shades and cord curling away from his ear, Nick felt like he fit right in, even if his suit was gray instead of black.

In front of the stage, seats for the invited guests were arranged in a semicircular pattern. It was meant to create a friendly atmosphere. Nick couldn't help thinking it was going to take more than seating arrangements to get these people to agree on anything. The seats were filled, buzzing with speculation about what the President was going to say.

At five minutes before ten, Rice positioned himself at the podium.

Someone made last minute adjustments to his makeup. Someone else moved a microphone. The cameras fired up.

It was showtime.

CHAPTER TWENTY-EIGHT

The cell in the basement of Shin Bet Headquarters was damp and cool. It had a bare cement floor and a drain in the middle of the room. It smelled of something unpleasant, old and dark. A single bright light glared down on the prisoner.

The prisoner sat in a battered wooden chair, his arms and feet bound with stained leather straps. He had been sitting there for more than three hours, waiting. A black, coiled hose was hooked to a rusty water faucet on one wall. The walls were unpainted gray cement, stained with dark streaks and splatters that might have been anything, but might have been dried tissue and blood.

The room was far underground. No sound could penetrate the building above. The door was of steel. It was not the kind of room anyone would want to be in. It was a room heavy with anticipation.

Ari Herzog observed the man Carter had seen at the mall bombing, two days and what seemed a lifetime ago. He'd been beaten when he was captured. His face was bruised and one eye was blackened and puffed shut, but he'd suffered no real damage. Two silent interrogators stood to the side of the room, dressed in black jeans and tee shirts. They waited for Ari to begin.

In the hard and secretive world of Shin Bet, Ari was legendary for getting results in interrogations. The old school methods were not his style. Ari detested violence and torture. He believed it debased prisoner and jailer alike. He was sure there was a better way.

Over the years Ari had perfected the art of deception. The cell in which the prisoner sat was part of that deception, a prop created to prepare the subject's mind. No one who found himself in a room like that could doubt that he was about to enter a world defined by agony.

Ari stood outside the room. Like an actor about to go on stage, he took time to find the part of himself that would convince the bomber he was at the mercy of a serious and ruthless man. It wasn't far from the truth. If Ari believed it, so would the man in the chair.

He was ready. He entered the room. He stood in front of the prisoner and addressed him in Arabic.

"You are Achmed al-Khalid. We know who you are. We know where you live." Ari's voice was flat, almost bored.

Khalid watched him.

"This man," Ari pointed to one of the interrogators, "wishes to hurt you. His sister was killed at the mall the night you set off your bomb."

It wasn't true, but Khalid didn't know that.

"I set off no bomb." Khalid looked defiant, but Ari could see the fear. Khalid gave off a faint sour odor, an almost visible mist that surrounded him like primal fog. He licked his lips.

Once Khalid's identity was known, Shin Bet had discovered the rest. He lived with his wife and sons and his extended family in the West Bank area controlled by Hamas. Khalid was also Hamas. He was dedicated to the eradication of Israel.

Khalid was more than a suicide bomber. He was one of the few with operational control over the bombers as they went about their murderous work. That made him important. He could be difficult to break, but Ari knew that family, above all else, was one of the keys that might unlock a terrorist's psyche. To gain anything of value, Ari would have to trick him.

Khalid was Palestinian. In the culture of Palestine nothing was more important than family. Along with Islam, family was the center around which life revolved.

"I set off no bomb," Khalid said again.

"Oh, but you did." Ari spat on the floor. "Your denials mean nothing to me. Let me tell you what will happen if you don't cooperate."

Ari bent low and whispered for a long time in Khalid's ear. He knew how to think like a terrorist. He knew what they were capable of doing. Color drained from Khalid's face.

"My family is innocent!"

"It doesn't matter to me if they are innocent or not. If you do not tell me what I want to know before I leave this room, they will pay for your crime."

Ari spat again. "You are not innocent. An insult in blood must be atoned for in blood. Honor must be upheld."

Honor. The ancient tribal concepts of honor had fueled thousands of years of murder and war in the Middle East. They were little different today than in the time of Abraham. Both Ari and Khalid understood them well.

"Allah will throw you into hell!"

"Perhaps, but not before your family pays the price. You will be kept alive to think about what you have done." Ari paused. "Although you will not be as—healthy—as you are at this moment."

Tears ran down Khalid's cheeks. "You cannot do this."

"I can," Ari said. He smiled a terrible smile at Khalid. "I will. This is your only chance. I will not ask again."

He waited. Khalid said nothing. Ari nodded at the men dressed in black. "Begin," he said. He turned as if to leave the room. Would Khalid break? He had his hand on the door when Khalid called out.

"Wait! Wait! I will tell you what I know."

Ari turned back, his face dark. "If you lie, your family will suffer."

"No lies, no lies, I swear by Allah!"

"Did you plant the bomb?"

"Yes! It was Jibril, who now resides in Paradise, who set it off."

"Who else is involved?"

"There are others, I don't know all of them. There is another bomb." Khalid stopped. He had said too much. Now, he was trapped.

"Another bomb?"

Khalid nodded, shame-faced at his cowardice.

Ari looked at the other men in the room, then Khalid. "Where?"

"I don't know, I swear by Allah, I don't know. I was told it would be used against the American President."

Ari's heart skipped a beat. "When?"

"My family, you must protect them."

"I will, if you tell me the truth. When?"

"Today. While he speaks. I don't know."

Ari was out of the room and on the phone.

CHAPTER TWENTY-NINE

Elizabeth and Stephanie were looking at an exchange of encrypted emails between Dysart and an unidentified person earlier that day.

Unidentified Sender: *The key to Parsifal has been found.*
Dysart: *Antarctica?*
Unidentified Sender: *Yes.*
"What's Parsifal? What does it have to do with Antarctica?" Stephanie asked.
"I've got no idea, Steph. Must be a code name."
Unidentified Sender: *Status Valkyrie?*
Dysart: *On schedule. Minor problems.*
Unidentified Sender: *Resolve them.*
Dysart: *As you command.*

"That's interesting," Elizabeth said. "Who commands Dysart?"
"Valkyrie," Stephanie said. "Parsifal. These guys are into Wagner, or some kind of operatic fantasy."
"I don't think it's a fantasy. It looks like Dysart's part of one op and running another."

Unidentified Sender: *Council 9 tonite. Sec protocol 7.*
Dysart: *Yes.*
Unidentified Sender: *Prepare for transition.*
Dysart: *As you command.*

The exchange terminated there.
"Transition? Transition to what? Director, I don't like this."
Elizabeth shook in a brief, involuntary movement that traveled from her head and shoulders to her feet. Her intuition had woken up.
"I think it's an assassination attempt. We have to find out who was on the other end of that email. It looks like there was a meeting last night. If it was a conference call we might be able to back trace."
"There's always a way," Stephanie said. "If it was a call and I can isolate it, we can find out who else was on the line. Do you think we're the 'minor problems' Dysart is talking about?"

Elizabeth was tight lipped. "Maybe."

Nick had called again, to tell her she was now under Rice's direct orders. So far there hadn't been any orders to follow. This was something outside of her experience. She'd have to let things play out while she pursued the slippery threads of conspiracy and hope they led somewhere.

"Time for Rice's speech," Stephanie said.

Elizabeth was tired. The seven and a half hour time difference from Jerusalem made for early viewing and it was after two in the morning. The team sat in front of the television and waited for Rice to begin. Ronnie and Selena had caught a couple of hours sleep, but Elizabeth and Stephanie hadn't been that lucky.

The camera panned across the Temple Mount, then switched to shots of the angry mobs below and the troops and police holding them at bay. It moved back to the stage and podium. President Rice was visible behind his shield of bodyguards, getting ready to speak.

"There's Nick!" Selena pointed at a tense figure in sunglasses and a gray suit standing in front of the stage, almost in front of the podium. The stage came up shoulder high behind him. The al-Aqsa Mosque loomed in the background of the shot, behind and to the right of the stage.

Ronnie said, "Son of a gun looks ready for trouble and he's tugging on his ear. I've seen that look before. He thinks things are about to go south."

"I hope you're wrong about that." Elizabeth pulled at her skirt. "I'm beginning to wonder if Rice knew what he was doing when he set this up."

"Sometimes things look different when it gets real. Anyway, it's set to go. Rice is ready to start."

Rice stepped up and the cameras zeroed in. He placed his hands on the sides of the podium. Behind him, the Prime Minister of Israel, the Secretary of State and the National Security Advisor sat stage center, bordered by their security guards.

Rice began with thanks to the Israeli Government and the Muslim Authority for the honor of speaking from a place sacred to three of the world's great religions. He spoke of the history and the conflict that had always surrounded the Mount and the city of Jerusalem.

A few minutes into the speech Selena said, "What's Nick doing?"

On screen, Nick took his phone from his pocket and placed it against his ear. His body tensed. He stepped over to a tall agent standing a few feet away and said something to him.

Later, when people went over the many tapes of the explosion, no one could quite agree on the exact sequence of events. It depended on the viewer's perspective and religion. But all agreed that things began when the man in the gray suit answered his cell phone in front of an estimated two hundred and fifty million viewers watching around the globe.

CHAPTER THIRTY

"Calloway, there's a bomb."

Agent Calloway didn't ask where, or how. He moved fast, yelling into his microphone. He leapt onto the stage as agents began to converge on the President. Rice stopped mid sentence, his eyes narrowing as he took in the sudden flurry of frantic activity around him. Behind him, the Prime Minister rose from his chair, a look of confusion on his face. Ascher's personal bodyguard moved toward him.

Carter stood rooted to the spot, not sure what to do next. Two agents grabbed Rice by the arms, lifted him up off his feet and ran with him toward the end of the stage.

Rice and the Secret Service had reached the edge when the ground shook and rumbled. A geyser of yellow earth and rock and black smoke erupted with an ear-shattering roar and shot into the morning air. The stage rose upward, hurling chairs, people and debris in every direction. Nick was thrown backward into the group of guests sitting before the platform.

The seven-arched porch on the al-Aqsa mosque swayed and fell in on itself in a crazed jumble of moving stone. The walls of the Mosque rippled in kaleidoscopic motion like falling dominoes, collapsing backward from the façade to the dome, sinking into a gaping maw opening in the ground. Two of the ancient minarets leaned sideways and fell. Huge blocks of stone caromed off the Mount and down into the packed crowds.

In the Stables of Solomon, excavations for the el-Marwani Mosque had weakened the southeastern corner of the Mount. The explosion blew through the shoring erected to stabilize the area and the corner collapsed in an avalanche of dirt and stone. Tons of earth and rock cascaded onto the streets and buildings at the foot of the Mount.

The rumbling died away. A third minaret toppled in a grinding mass of stone. The huge stones tumbled together like giant dice, down onto the helpless, screaming crowd below.

Carter stumbled to his feet. Thick clouds of dust hung over the square. A broad, deep pit had opened over Solomon's Stables. The

President, Calloway and the others were somewhere in that pit. Nick ran to the edge and peered over.

Rice lay half buried in dirt thirty feet down. One of his agents lay next to him, head twisted in an unnatural position. Calloway was nowhere in sight. Someone's arm extended from under a mound of rock. The edge of the Mount had disappeared and the fabled Stables were now open to the sky. Dirt and stone sloped down like a ramp to the President. Nick jumped into the pit and slid down, feet first.

He placed his hand on the President's neck and felt a strong pulse. There was a long gash on Rice's forehead. Rice's eyes fluttered. Nick began pulling rocks and dirt away from him, all the time looking around. Where were the others? Why was he the only one here with Rice?

He pulled the President free. Rice was coming to.

"Mr. President. Are you all right? Can you hear me?"

Rice opened his eyes. Suddenly they cleared.

"Carter. What happened?"

"A bomb. We'll get you out of here, sir."

Up above, on what was left of the surface, there were shouts and screams, cries, confusion, the beat of helicopter blades coming close. Someone pointed a camera over the edge of the pit. Another figure appeared. It was one of the Muslim honor guards. His beret was gone, his uniform torn and streaked with dust. His eyes were wild. Tears ran down his face. He had a gun in his hand. He was screaming.

"Allah hu Akbar! Allah hu Akbar!"

The last time Carter had heard that cry was in Afghanistan, right before his unit was almost overrun by two hundred Taliban. He'd never wanted to hear it again.

The man started shooting at them, sending chips of rock flying. Carter threw his body over Rice, drew his pistol and fired. The first two rounds took the shooter in the abdomen. He tumbled over the edge. Nick kept firing as he rolled down the slope. More faces appeared at the rim, this time, Israeli soldiers.

In a few minutes they were surrounded by a cordon of soldiers and enough firepower to hold off an average army. The soldiers got them out of the pit.

The square in front of the Mosque was strewn with fragments of stone, the remains of the stage and broken chairs. Dead and injured lay scattered across the bloody carpets. The surface of the Temple

Mount had collapsed all the way to the southeastern corner, fallen away into the open chambers of the Stables and the streets below.

The al-Aqsa Mosque was in ruins.

The roof was gone. The walls were broken down all the way back to the dome. The dome was reduced to a gray, shapeless mass on a heap of rubble and stone. One of the minarets still stood, but not for much longer. A thick cloud of yellow-white dust drifted lazily up from the ruins and across the Mount. The sound of the crowds below spiraled up in a swelling chorus of grief and rage, the cry of a great, wounded beast.

An Israeli military helicopter settled hard onto the Mount. Soldiers fanned out around Nick and the President, weapons ready. Nick supported Rice under his arm. He was limping. They were hustled on board in a storm of dust and debris kicked up by the spinning blades. Calloway was nowhere in sight. Angry soldiers took up posts at the doors of the chopper.

Rice turned to the hard faced captain sitting next to him. He shouted to be heard above the sound of the big rotors as the chopper lifted away toward Mount Scopus and Hadassah Hospital.

"The Prime Minister?"

The soldier shook his head. "Dead."

"The others, the Secretary of State?"

The soldier shook his head. No one said anything the rest of the way in.

At Hadassah, a delegation of worried doctors waited on the helipad. Rice turned to Nick before he was whisked into the hospital.

"Carter. I want you with me when I fly out of here today. We're going back to Washington. Someone has started a war and I'm going to have to try and stop it. Get Harker. Get her on this. Tell her to find out who's behind it. This isn't a Muslim attack. Al-Qaeda and the others wouldn't go after me at the Mount or blow up al-Aqsa."

"Yes, sir."

Rice turned to the Israeli Captain. "Captain I want this man protected like you would protect me. Coordinate our return to Air Force One immediately with your superiors. I can't say it's been a pleasure meeting you, but thank you. You must come visit me in America when this has passed."

It was typical of Rice. Someone had tried to kill him and he was taking time to acknowledge a soldier who had just been doing his duty.

The Israeli saluted. "Yes, Mr. President. Thank you, sir."
Nick followed the President inside.

CHAPTER THIRTY-ONE

The team watched the explosion in disbelief.

"Oh, my God!" Selena put her hand to her mouth.

They watched the stage lift, the people flying into the air. They watched the Mosque collapse in a deep rumble of falling stone. The camera shook and swayed. The sound of the detonation died away. Screams came from the television speakers.

"Holy shit!" Ronnie said. "The President! And the Mosque! It's gone!"

Elizabeth put her hand out, gripped Stephanie's shoulder. "There's Nick!"

On screen, the camera steadied. They watched Nick scramble to his feet and run to the edge of the pit. He disappeared into the hole. Fragmented, shaky images of the destruction filled the screen as the cameraman ran forward. The picture steadied. The camera looked over the edge of the pit.

Nick was helping the President sit up. The camera zoomed in on their faces. Rice was bleeding from a wound on his forehead. Nick's sunglasses were gone and his suit was torn and dirty. The camera swung toward a man in the uniform of the Muslim honor guard. He was standing on the edge of the pit and brandishing a pistol.

He was screaming, distraught. He began firing into the pit. The camera moved again and the team watched Nick cover the President with his body, draw and fire. His face was closed and angry. He kept firing while the shooter rolled down into the hole. The camera followed him down. They watched the slide lock back on Nick's .45.

"The whole magazine," Ronnie said. "He gave him the whole magazine."

The camera swung round to a jittery shot of running Israeli soldiers. The screen went black. A few seconds later a studio shot with a famous anchor appeared. The live feed from Jerusalem was down. Ronnie went to the set and turned off the sound.

They looked at each other. No one knew what to say.

Stephanie took a deep breath. "What shall we do, Director?"

"This will start a war. We've got to get evidence to take Dysart down. So far we've got nothing. For all we know Valkyrie and Parsifal are part of a school play for his teen age daughter."

"Sure they are," said Ronnie. "That bastard is in this all the way. Can he find out where we are?"

"I don't know. We'll stand watch. Four hour shifts in front of the monitors. Ronnie, you and Selena take the first one. You got a little sleep earlier. Steph and I are beat. We're too tired to do much good. Wake us in four and Steph and I will get back on the computers."

In her room, Elizabeth stripped off her crumpled clothes and headed for the shower. She stood for a long time with the hot water streaming down the front of her body. It washed away some of the stress and tiredness of the day, but she was exhausted. She turned around and let the water soak her hair and back, feeling some of the tightness go out of her shoulders.

She dried off and pulled an old shirt and pair of jeans from the closet. She dressed and lay down on the bed. She was drifting off when the phone signaled. It was Nick.

"Director. You know about the bomb?"

"We watched it live. Good work with the President."

"They broadcast it all?"

"Yes. You've got your fifteen minutes of fame."

"Director, Rice wants you to find out who did this. He told me to 'get her on it'. I'm flying back with him today."

"We're already doing that. Tell the President he'll be first to know if I find something to nail Dysart or anyone else."

"What happens when I get to Washington?"

"That's up to Rice. Assume you'll be watched. Use the email protocol or the sat link to keep me up to speed."

"Roger that, Director."

"Good luck, Nick." But he was already gone.

Elizabeth set the phone down on the nightstand and lay back on the bed. Her eyes closed and she slept.

She dreamed she was being buried alive and woke gasping for breath.

***

The Grand Master watched a rerun of the explosion for the fourth time. For the fourth time he smiled as the Mosque crumbled into ruin. But then came the part where the President was rescued by that woman's operative. It was irritating. Now he'd have to find another way to get rid of Rice. Harker and her agents were proving to be an obstacle that needed to be eliminated.

Perhaps he could turn things to an advantage. Rice would have to be killed here in America. It could add fuel to the fire he had started. Proof could be found of Iranian involvement.

Yes, that would fit nicely. He knew just the person for the job. Nothing would stop PARSIFAL.

Nothing.

CHAPTER THIRTY-TWO

The rhythmic tramp of Nick's military escort echoed on the tiled floors of the hospital ward. The ward supervisor looked up from her station by the elevators. She was stout and dark haired. She reminded Nick of his old drill instructor at Pendleton.

"Could you tell me where Rivka Stern is?"

The nurse was pretty in a hard way, around thirty, which meant she'd done her time in the army. She gave the soldiers a once-over and studied the tall American. She ignored the weapons. Everyone in Israel saw weapons all the time. It was part of daily life, along with the random, lethal explosions marking the reality of terror. By contrast, the drive-by violence of America's inner cities looked almost peaceful.

"She's in 1438, down the hall on the right. Please have your escort wait outside the room."

"Yes, Ma'am," Nick said. "Thank you."

Ari Herzog was there. He put his phone away, ready to leave. Rivka sat propped up in bed in a blue hospital robe, her left arm strapped across her chest. She sipped something red from a clear plastic glass held in her good hand. There were dark circles under her eyes. An IV was taped to her good arm.

Ari looked haggard and tense.

"Your call saved the President, Ari."

"No, Nick, you saved him. I only gave the warning. Anyway, he's safe. But Ascher is dead. In hours Israel will be at war."

"It can't be stopped?"

"No. I just got a call. A Jewish group has claimed credit for the bombing. They've been a problem for years, calling for the demolition of the Dome of the Rock and construction of a new Temple on the Mount. They released an announcement to all the major networks, starting with Al-Jazeera."

"Is it authentic?"

"Maybe. I don't know, yet. We've already detained the leaders of the group. They deny any knowledge or participation. Even if the announcement is a phony, the damage is done. The entire Muslim world now believes a group of fanatical right-wing Jews desecrated one of the holiest sites in Islam. We're on full alert. The reserves are being called up as we speak."

"That's bad news."

"A masterpiece of understatement."

"I'm leaving with the President," Nick said. He thought for a moment. This man was a friend. "How can I help?"

"Keep an open channel for me. I'd like to know what's going on. I don't expect you to betray confidences, but..."

"I'll do what I can."

"Good enough." Ari took out a card, scribbled on it. "This number will reach me any time of the day or night." Nick took it.

Ari bent over Rivka. He gave her a light kiss on the cheek.

"*Shalom*. Get well."

The door closed behind him.

"How are you?"

"Messed up. I'll be in rehab for a few months."

"Rivka, I'm sorry."

"For what, Nick? You know better. I should have been more careful."

"Yes, but..."

"No 'buts'. There is no 'but'. I should have ducked or shot sooner, that's all."

"At least we got the son of a bitch."

She smiled, looked away, back again. "You are with somebody."

"Yes. But I haven't figured it out yet."

Rivka laughed. "Figured it out? Oh, Nick." She laughed again. "Ow, that hurts," she said, still laughing.

"Why are you laughing?"

She laughed harder. After a minute she stopped, wiping tears off her face. Nick wasn't sure what was funny. He'd never understand women, how they thought.

"Rivka, I have to go."

"Nick, when you figure it out, make sure you let her know, will you?"

"Goodbye, Rivka."

"Come over here."

He walked over to her bedside. She reached up with her good arm and pulled him down to her. Her kiss tasted like strawberries.

"*Shalom*, Nick. Keep safe."

He hoped Rivka would be safe. He hoped they all would.

CHAPTER THIRTY-THREE

Rice was leaving. The Secret Service took over escort duties. Rice and Nick boarded a helicopter on the hospital roof manned by a squad of Marines in full combat gear, detached from the Embassy. Flanked by hovering Apaches with Israeli markings, they lifted away from Hadassah's roof and headed for Tel Aviv and Air Force One.

At Tel Aviv the helicopter set down at the far end of Ben Gurion Airport where the President's plane waited. Israeli armor and heavy machine guns mounted on tracked vehicles surrounded the plane.

Air Force One was one of two Boeing 747-200B aircraft modified far beyond the civilian models. It was a beautiful plane, impressive, as it was meant to be. The white body was streamlined with blue. The American flag was painted on the tall tail section and the words *United States of America* on the sides of the fuselage left no confusion about who was on board.

Nick followed Rice up the retractable stairway to the President's entrance near the front of the plane. They began rolling down the runway as the hatch closed.

Rice sent Nick back to the cabin space reserved for senior staff, at the leading edge of the starboard wing. The aisle from the President's office and quarters ran along the port side of the plane. Heading aft, Nick passed a medical room that converted into a state of the art operating theater. He passed a gleaming galley.

He nodded at the only other person seated in the senior staff area, an Army Colonel in pressed uniform with a black leather case beside him. Nick knew what it was.   The football.

It held the electronics that could launch America's nuclear arsenal. It was never far from the president's side, no matter where he traveled.

The chairs in the senior staff area weren't like anything on a regular passenger airplane. The fittings were custom made of polished woods. The seats were of light brown fine grain leather. It was like being in someone's living room.

Everything was clean and new looking, the carpet thick underfoot, the decor muted and soft, beiges and light greens, earth tones to soothe the nervous political mind. An Air Force Steward took Nick's order for a double Irish, which is what he wanted for personal soothing. His head hurt. His ribs ached and stabbed him every time he took a deep breath. His back was tight as a steel drum.

Air Force One lifted into the air and climbed skyward. Off the starboard wing a flight of Israeli F-16s pulled alongside, armed escort until American planes could pick up the task.

The explosion on the Mount had killed the Israeli Prime Minister. The Secretary of State and the National Security Advisor were both dead. Calloway was dead, with five other agents. More injured personnel had stayed behind at Hadassah. Two key Presidential Aides were dead. Nick supposed it could have been worse.

Who was he kidding? There wasn't a doubt in his mind that war between Israel and all of Islam had begun. Someone had kicked the pot over into the fire and a lot of people were going to die. The more he thought about it, the angrier he felt.

The whiskey was doing its work and he sank deeper into the chair. The stitches on his leg felt like hot cactus needles under his skin. He set the glass down and closed his eyes and thought about Selena and wondered what she was doing. He drifted into an uneasy sleep.

He dreamed of Megan, his brown haired lover.

His dead lover.

Megan waited at the edge of the cliff, the sea wind blowing her long, brown hair out behind her.

"Hey, Baby," she said.

He knew he was dreaming, knew Megan was dead. Sadness overwhelmed him, an abiding sense of loss. When he was awake he could put it away where he didn't have to think about it. That wasn't possible here. But he'd rather see her here than not at all.

"I miss you. I miss you so much." He held her tight.

"I know."

The dreamscape changed. A gaping chasm opened at his feet. At the bottom red and orange flames flared. Dark shapes danced in demented time with the flames. A sound like cold wind whistling through razor wire came and went at the edge of hearing.

"You've got to find it, Nick."

"I don't understand. Find what? Where is it?"

The cold wind was getting stronger and Megan started shredding, bits of her flying away. He reached out to touch her, touched air.

"You have to stop it." Megan put a transparent hand on his shoulder. She gestured at the chasm. "Find it, Nick."

"Major Carter."

He jolted awake. The hand on his shoulder belonged to the steward, an Air Force Sergeant. "Sir, the President would like you to come forward."

Carter felt the dream fading. Find what? The chasm in the dream looked like someone's vision of hell. Maybe his own.

Now and then he had a dream that warned of things to come. It was called the "sight" in Ireland. It had skipped a generation and passed to him from his Irish Grandmother. Sometimes that kind of dream gave advice. Dreams like that always had a weird, intense quality and he always remembered them. This was one of those.

Megan, he understood dreaming about her. It happened a lot. But the dream made no sense.

He looked out the window. The Israeli fighter escort had been replaced with the smooth, futuristic shapes of American F-22 Raptors. He'd been asleep for a while. He got up and went forward.

CHAPTER THIRTY-FOUR

President Rice watched a television monitor on the bulkhead. A neat white bandage covered the cut on his forehead. He was wearing a blue sweatshirt with the Presidential Seal on it. His face was drawn. Dark shadows circled his eyes. He looked ten years older than he had the night before.

"Take a seat, Carter."

Nick took a seat on the couch. Sitting in the President's plane as the world slipped out of control felt like another one of his dreams, but a glance at the fighters keeping pace outside told him it was real enough.

Whatever Rice did in the next few days might make the difference between peace and world war. Mao had said that power came from the barrel of a gun. The briefcase sitting with the army colonel aft meant Rice had his finger on the trigger of a very big gun and wielded a lot of power. But there were a few other big guns out there. It might not take much to precipitate a shootout. Then everyone would lose.

"Take a look." Rice gestured at the screen.

The picture was sharp, high definition living color. Thick smoke drifted over Jerusalem. The sun shone blood-red over the shattered ruins of the Mosque. Parts of the old city were on fire. The scene switched to a live shot of Israeli armor moving in columns. Trucks full of soldiers armed with assault rifles and encased in body armor were going somewhere. At reserve call up centers all over the country, Israel's armed and trained citizen army was showing up for work.

Rice clicked his remote. Protests and riots all across the Middle East. In Tehran a mob of a hundred thousand people screamed in rage, chanting in carefully orchestrated responses. Green and white banners in Arabic and misspelled slogans in English proclaimed death to America, Israel, Zionists, Jews and Rice himself. Israeli and American flags burned in every Islamic country.

Rice turned off the set.

"That's only the beginning. Pakistan went to full alert and India followed. They're snarling at each other. North Korea has pledged its undying support for the 'victims of American and Jewish aggression'.

Saudi Arabia recalled its ambassador. Syria and Jordan have announced a joint military effort. Egypt is mobilizing. We've detected movement of Iran's mobile missile forces. They're trying to hide them."

Rice paused.

"The Gulf States withdrew their ambassadors. Yemen is calling for a regional conference and a mutual military pact against the enemies of Islam. That means us, Israel and the West in general. China and Russia have called an emergency meeting of the UN Security Council. All of this in less than six hours since the bombing."

"What about the Iraqis, sir?"

"There are indications the Shias and Sunnis are setting aside their differences for the moment and forming an alliance. That's a good one. They hate each other, but they hate us and Israel more. The enemy of my enemy is my friend and all that." Rice sounded bitter.

A steward appeared with a silver tray and coffee pot. There were two cups. The steward poured for the President, then brought the tray around to Carter. He poured. When he was gone, Rice continued.

"Turkey and the Saudis sent expressions of gratitude that I was not killed in the explosion, but at the same time they're going to war status. All of Islam thinks a Jewish group is behind this. For all I know that's true, in which case there isn't a lot I can do to head this off. It's even possible the primary target was Prime Minister Ascher, not me. There are radical elements in Israel that don't want peace unless it comes with total control of what they consider to be the biblical homeland.

"Ascher was the only one in Israel who might have gained support for a semblance of peace. Now that he's dead the right wing will take control. It's a scenario that's happened before. If someone wanted to guarantee a war, they couldn't have done anything more provocative than blow up that mosque."

Rice sipped his coffee. "Russia and China have raised their alert status and everybody is nervous as hell. Whoever did this has brought the world to the edge. There's going to be a war. I don't know yet if it can be confined to the Middle East, or how big it will get. NATO is on full alert. I've ordered our military to DEFCON3. The Navy is at DEFCON2."

The Defense Condition system could be set at different levels for different units within the armed forces. The Navy had the broadest global reach in position, with plenty of nukes and enough air and sea power to thwart most aggressive measures or initiate them if needed. DEFCON2 was one step short of war. The jump to full war status would only come under threat of imminent attack and would take few minutes to achieve. If Rice went to DEFCON1, the bombers would lift off, the silos would go hot and things would go south in a hurry. DEFCON1 would mean World War III. No wonder Rice looked stressed. Nick wasn't feeling too relaxed himself.

"Carter. Like it or not, you and Director Harker have become players in the big game. Someone tried to kill me today. They failed because of your actions and because Director Harker smelled a rat. I haven't said thank you yet. Thank you."

"Yes, sir. You're welcome."

"I'd like your advice on Dysart."

"Sir, I don't think I'm qualified to do that. I don't know what's going on or what's happened since the last time I talked with the Director."

"Then let's call her up." Rice pressed a button and spoke to the communications center on the flight deck above.

Nick heard the signal tone. Harker picked up.

"Yes." Wary, strained, ready to disconnect. Who was calling?

"Director Harker, this is the President."

"Yes, sir." Her voice became energized. "I recognize your voice. I'm glad you're all right, Mr. President."

"Director, Carter is here with me. I've put you on the speaker. This is a secure transmission. I want to talk about Dysart."

A brief pause. "Yes, sir."

"Have you established proof General Dysart is involved in these events?"

"No real proof yet, but very strong suspicions. We have emails between him and an unknown party, referring to at least two covert operations and a meeting. They don't sound right. Someone is telling Dysart what to do. Literally what to do, as in 'command'. One of those operations was coded 'Valkyrie'. I think it referred to the events of this morning, the bombing and the attempted assassination. I'm wondering who it is that commands a three star general, if it isn't you? Sir."

"In your opinion, General Dysart is part of a plot?"

"Yes, sir, I am sure he is. He was told by whoever is directing him to 'prepare for transition'. That sounds ominous to me. I think someone is trying to get you out of the way and provoke a crisis in the Middle East. They seem to have succeeded with part of their plan."

"What is your recommendation regarding Dysart?"

"You mean what do I think you should do?"

"Yes, Director."

"Sir, he can't possibly have set this up by himself. I think he should be left in place and watched. He may lead us to other conspirators. If he does anything to threaten national security you could move in and stop him. Perhaps set up an alternate command to take over NSA if needed, without his knowledge."

"Give him enough rope?"

"Yes, sir. If I'm wrong, then no harm done. If I'm right, sooner or later he'll do something that proves it. Then we'd get a chance to find out who else is involved. I'm working on that now."

"I want you to get to the bottom of this. Carter will be our direct liaison. After today, no one will think it unusual if he is seen with me on occasion. I take it you have a secure location to work from?"

"Yes, Mr. President. Sir, please don't misunderstand me. Dysart is bound to be observing everything. You must be very careful about the people you choose to confide in. I recommend no contact with Langley regarding our suspicions."

Nick kept his face neutral. Not many people tell the President of the United States to be careful about what he does or who he should talk to, much less tell him to stay away from the CIA. Harker had balls.

"You believe CIA is involved?"

"I don't know, sir. But Langley has leaks. Any involvement with them about Dysart will give everything away."

"I'll take that under advisement, Director. I appreciate your candor. Keep me informed of any progress, any new information."

"Yes, sir. Thank you for your trust, Mr. President."

"You've earned it. One more thing."

"Yes, sir?"

"Whoever did this must be revealed for who they are and shown to the world. It is the only thing that can stop what has begun. Work quickly, Director."

Rice ended the call.

CHAPTER THIRTY-FIVE

Elizabeth, Stephanie and Selena returned to the Project building and cleaned out everything relating to Dysart and Nick's mission. They found the bug on Selena's car and moved it to another vehicle parked nearby, then both cars headed toward Virginia. In Harker's rear view mirror, the gray building housing the Project receded behind them.

Elizabeth kept checking the mirrors, looking for tails. Nothing stood out. That didn't mean there wasn't someone there. She knew how easy it was to switch cars behind you, follow from in front or from the air, change the look of surveillance in an eye blink, track from the sky, but her intuition was calm.

They turned onto the rural state highway that led toward the safe house. There was still no sign of a tail. Traffic was light. Elizabeth allowed herself a small measure of relaxation.

"Dysart might make a mistake," Stephanie said.

"This has to go way beyond Dysart." Elizabeth swerved to avoid a pothole in the road. "War between the Muslims and Israel could go nuclear. Who would want to see that happen?"

Stephanie mused out loud. "*Qui Bene?* Who benefits? Not Israel. Not the Muslims either."

"No one in the Middle East benefits, except the ones who don't want peace," Elizabeth said. "The Islamic fundamentalists would never destroy al-Aqsa. It can't be them."

"Profit? War is going to disrupt the financial markets. There could be big profit in that."

"That's an idea. We could look at the markets in the last six months and see if someone is about to get rich if a war starts up. We can ignore little trades, just look at the big ones. If we see a pattern, perhaps we can track it back to whoever it is that 'commands' Dysart."

"Yes. 'At your command'. Dysart doesn't strike me as the kind of man who'd take orders from just anyone."

"Israel could be destroyed, and half of the Middle East with it. That's bigger than money. The Iranians, perhaps? The Syrians? But they're Muslim, too. No way they'd blow up the Mosque."

They turned into the drive leading up to the house. A minute later they were inside the garage, the door closing behind them.

Safe.

CHAPTER THIRTY-SIX

In one of the windowless detention cells below Shin Bet Headquarters, Khalid recited his prayers. Even here, imprisoned by the Jewish occupiers, he could still face Mecca and find the strength that had deserted him earlier. He shuddered, remembering the look in the eyes of the Jew as he whispered the things he would do to Khalid's family. Surely the Jew was a demon, a jinn sent to test him. Allah, the All Compassionate and All Merciful, would forgive Khalid for his cowardice. He rose from his prayers. A metal view slot opened in the steel door of his cell.

Someone peered in. The slot shut. Khalid heard bolts being drawn, a murmured conversation. He sat down on the bare metal ledge bolted to the wall that served as table, chair and bunk and waited. Khalid was passive. He knew it was futile to think of physical resistance. He swallowed and thought of his family, and prepared to be interrogated.

İn'sh'allah. As God wills.

The man who entered the cell wore an army uniform. He closed the door behind him. His face was bland, almost featureless, almost kind. He held a covered box in his left hand.

"You are hungry?" the man said.

Khalid shrugged, ready for a blow, a lie, a trick. There was no trusting these Israeli dogs. The man's Arabic was fluent, with a hint of an accent.

"You have been helpful," the man said. "I've brought something to show our appreciation." He reached into the box with his right hand.

The silenced pistol spat once and a small, dark hole appeared in Khalid's forehead. He never felt the second shot that entered his ear.

The Visitor replaced the pistol in the box. He lifted Khalid's body onto the narrow bunk and turned his face to the wall. Anyone looking in would see a sleeping prisoner. The Visitor left the cell and closed the door, bolting it after him. Five minutes later he had disappeared into the crowds on the street outside. Another soldier, hurrying to his appointment with the god of war.

Back in his apartment, the Visitor made a call.

"It's done."

"Good. Your time there is finished." A brief silence. "You failed with the agent."

"It was unavoidable. I lost three people. He is a worthy adversary."

"It doesn't matter. Return to Washington. Call when you are settled."

The Visitor could hear an opera playing in the background, something by Wagner.

"Yes."

The Visitor broke the connection, smashed the phone with his heel. He began packing. When he was done, he sat on the edge of the bed. He closed his eyes, his mind soaring to a summer meadow high in the Bavarian Alps.

CHAPTER THIRTY-SEVEN

At Andrews, Rice ordered the Secret Service to provide Nick with transportation. They gave him a shiny black Suburban with armor reinforced doors and wheels, tinted bullet proof glass and a Remington pump twelve gauge set upright between the front seats. The vehicle was fast, too. He watched for anyone following and took a circuitous route around the city. When he was sure no one was behind, he headed for the safe house.

He pulled into the garage and went inside. Ronnie and Selena were at the kitchen table. Ronnie was flashing cards filled with diagrams and data at Selena, teaching her to store essential information in her mind with only a brief look.

"Hey, Mr. TV personality himself. Welcome home, Nick." Ronnie put the cards on the table.

"TV Personality?"

Selena said, "You've been on the news all day. The networks can't get enough of you jumping into that hole and protecting the President. Over here, you're a hero. In the Mid East, you're a murderer. You've even been hung in effigy. They've made a martyr out of the man who tried to shoot you and Rice."

Nick felt a headache starting. Harker and Stephanie came into the room. Director Harker wore casual sweats. The outfit was black and white, if not up to her usual standard of elegance. She looked tired, more frayed around the edges than he'd ever seen before.

"Nick, I know you just got here, but we need to go over what we've found out."

"You mean Dysart?"

"That and more. Let's sit down."

The silver pen came out and Harker began tapping. The sound echoed in his head like a ball ratcheting around a pinball machine.

"Dysart mentioned Antarctica in his emails. A German research station in Antarctica burned to the ground two nights ago. The fire was set with phosphorous grenades and all personnel were shot and killed. A plane landed and took off around the time of the raid. The German government has sealed the whole thing off and clamped the lid down on inquiries."

"If they aren't talking, how come we know about it?"

"Stephanie hacked into Berlin's intelligence network looking for reaction to the Jerusalem bombing. She found the Antarctica reports."

Steph made a mock curtsey.

Nick rubbed his forehead, then the back of his neck. The headache was kicking in big time. "What's got them going?"

"Nazis."

"Nazis? As in Hitler, swastikas, all that stuff? How do Nazis come into it?"

"Two scientists found an old bunker complex in the mountains the day before the station was attacked. No one knew it was there. They discovered a radio station, barracks, generators and crates marked with swastikas. They opened one of the crates and found rare paintings missing since the war. The radio had swastikas on it and one of those Enigma coding machines next to it. There was also a vault they couldn't open.

"They called it in to Berlin. That was on Wednesday afternoon. Early Thursday morning someone showed up, blew the door off the vault and cleaned the place out. It looks like a military op. They didn't leave anyone behind to talk about it. Berlin thinks this was a secret Nazi base rumored to exist since the war, built to research experimental weapons. Everyone thought it was a myth, until now."

"What was in the vault?"

"No one knows. The only things left behind were files. Inventories of jewelry, gold teeth, wedding rings and other property stolen from Holocaust victims. All neatly cataloged."

Carter thought about that. Gold teeth and wedding rings. Who could fathom the pathological cruelty of the Nazi mind?

Harker continued. "Inside the vault were two mummified bodies in World War II German naval uniforms. They'd been shot at close range with a pistol. One of them had ID that showed they came off a submarine, U-886."

"You think this is what Dysart was referring to in his email?"

"It must be. There's not much happening in Antarctica. The email said the 'key' to Parsifal had been found there, whatever that is."

"How do we use the Antarctica connection?" Nick tugged at his ear.

"We need more data."

Harker's pen tapped. Nick wanted to snatch it from her and break it in half. His head was throbbing. The room vibrated with a faint light.

"What about the sub those mummies came from?" Ronnie said. "Why was it there? If we knew that, we might know why someone came back years later and took out that research station. That's pretty cold, killing a bunch of civilian eggheads studying penguins and snow."

"We have the number of the sub." Harker tapped her pen. "There should be records, maybe an action report. Almost all the U-Boats have been accounted for. We could start by tracking it down."

"That's easy. We can Google it." Stephanie got her laptop and plugged it in. It booted up and routed through the mainframe sitting in the other room. Steph tapped keys and entered a search. In a few seconds the display screen showed a numerical list of all Nazi submarines. She clicked on U-886.

U-886 was listed as a type IX D2, built in July 1944 by AG Weser at the Bremen yards. She'd been sunk with depth charges by a British destroyer on 22 February, 1945. Stephanie pulled up the Admiralty report. The co-ordinates of the action placed the sub's grave at fifteen miles east and south of Mar del Plata on the Argentine coast, on the continental shelf in 35 fathoms of water.

Elizabeth coughed. "It looks like they were running for Argentina. Type IX D2's were converted to carry cargo. They must have had something on board."

"Or they left something behind," Nick said. "If the sub was carrying something away, wouldn't they have taken the crates with the paintings?"

"Why leave anything in Antarctica? The war was almost over and they were heading for safety." Selena looked at the screen. "They couldn't have planned on coming back anytime soon."

Nick thought. "They killed two of their own. Why would they do that?"

"Only one reason makes sense," Ronnie said. "Whoever shot those guys didn't want them talking about what was in the vault."

"And the paintings were outside, not in the vault." Stephanie picked it up. "So whatever was in there was more important to the Nazis than a bunch of Old Masters. That's got to be something pretty special."

"Whatever it was, they never came back for it," Ronnie said.

"Until a few days ago." Harker tapped her pen, set it aside. "Why not before?"

"Maybe they didn't know where it was." Ronnie cracked his knuckles. "Maybe the location went down with the sub. When the scientists found it someone jumped on it before the German government could step in."

Harker frowned. "That means someone would have to monitor transmissions from the Antarctic or have deep contacts in Germany. Then they would have to mount an armed expedition and get it on site in less than a day. That's pretty sophisticated."

The pen came out again, tapping.

"Steph hasn't been able to track the other end of those emails yet. It might be worth it to see if there's anything left on that sub. Something that could tell us what Dysart was referring to."

"If we can find it," Nick said. "Even if we could, there's not going to be much left. It's a waste of time."

He didn't usually argue with Harker, but he was tired. The headache was stabbing him in back of his left eye. He felt nauseous.

She looked at him. "Do you have a better idea?"

"No, but it sounds like a wild goose chase to me."

"We've got the coordinates in the action report. It's a long shot, but if we can find the wreck, I think it's worth a try. It's the only direct connection to Antarctica and whatever happened there. The only connection to Dysart."

"How are we going to get to it?"

"We'd have to dive on it. You must know someone, Nick."

"As a matter of fact, I do know someone. Ronnie knows him, too. His name is Lamont Cameron. He just got out of the Seals."

Ronnie nodded. "Shadow? He'd be perfect."

"Shadow?" Harker's pen stopped moving.

"His mom named him after Lamont Cranston," Nick said, "the Shadow on the radio show. That's how he got the nickname."

"Can you get hold of him?"

"Probably. His mom lives in D.C. She would know where he is. I can track him down, but I still think it's a waste of time."

Harker looked annoyed. "Do that. If he's interested, brief him and bring him here."

"What did Arslanian's flash drive have on it?"

"It's encoded. Steph hasn't cracked it yet."

Later, after he'd gone upstairs, Nick sat on the edge of the bed. His head was splitting. The stitches on his leg were inflamed and sore, he ached from being blown down twice in almost as many days, and he was jet lagging from the air journeys. His left hand was painful and stiff. He didn't know if he should lie down or throw up.

I'm getting too old for this, he thought. Not for the first time.

Selena sat down on the bed. The movement made his stomach turn over. He reached the bathroom just in time. When he came out, Selena helped him undress.

The last thing he remembered was the feel of her slipping into bed beside him and the warm curling of her naked body against his.

CHAPTER THIRTY-EIGHT

Ronnie and Nick met Lamont Cameron at a bar popular with past and present members of the various SOCOM units. It was crowded. It smelled of stale beer and overcooked frankfurters. No one ever came there for dinner.

Lamont looked good for pushing forty. His head was shaved and smooth. His skin was dark reddish brown, the color of fresh ground coffee. His eyes were an odd pale blue, a genetic trait inherited from his Ethiopian ancestors. He had even features, square cheekbones, and an aquiline nose.

A thin, jagged ridge of pink scar tissue cut through one black eyebrow and across his nose, a souvenir from Iraq. He'd left the Seals as a Master Chief. In the Seals that was a real accolade. Lamont was one of the smartest and toughest men Nick had ever met.

He was at a table in the back. He stood up as they approached. The three men high-fived.

"Hey Nick, you look a little rough around the edges."

"Yeah, good to see you too." Lamont signaled the waitress.

"Double Jameson's for me," Nick said, "soda back."

"Coke, with a lime if you've got it," Ronnie told her. Ronnie didn't drink. On the Reservation he'd seen what it could do.

Lamont held up his half empty bottle.

"Another Bud." When the waitress had gone he said, "Saw you on the tube saving the President's ass. What were you doing there, anyway? You Secret Service now?"

"Nope. That's part of what we want to talk with you about. How've you been, Shadow?"

"Can't complain. Nobody would listen anyway." He grinned, lifted the beer in mock salute.

"How's civilian life?"

"Not what it's cracked up to be. I'm staying at my Mom's for now, keeping her company. Lots of changes since the last time I came home and none of them good. I'm trying to get her to move to a better part of town, but she's stubborn. Her church is there, her friends. She'll never move."

Carter had been to the house. It was in part of the city where the landscape looked like a war zone. Decent people like Lamont's mother lived with drive-by shootings, gang bangers and iron bars on the windows as part of life. It was one of those places most of America didn't want to know about. Right in the heart of the American dream, the nation's capitol. Even the cops didn't go there unless they had plenty of backup.

The waitress brought the drinks. Nick downed the Irish and ordered another before she left.

"You have any plans?" he said. "What you're going to do?"

"I know a guy who's a commercial diver. I was thinking maybe I'd hook up with him. He wants to open a dive school."

"Pretty tame." Ronnie lifted his coke, sipped.

"Yeah." Lamont looked a little depressed. Nick figured it was time to cheer him up.

"What would you say if I told you there's another option? Not so tame?"

"Not so tame, like whatever you were doing in Jerusalem?"

"Yes."

"Tell me all about it, amigo."

During the next hour they filled him in on Harker and the Project. Nick kept the Irish coming. After the fourth one something let go. He began to relax for the first time since he'd left for Israel.

"What do you think, Shadow? You want to meet Harker?"

"You talked with her?"

"She pulled your jacket and cleared you earlier today. It's up to you. Travel, pay, exotic places, meet new people—what more could you ask?"

He smiled. "Damn." He held his hands out and spoke in a whispery Marlon Brando voice. "Just when I thought I was out, they pull me back in."

"Your Brando sucks, and besides it was Pacino said that."

Cameron shrugged. "Hey. As long as we don't leave the gun. When do I meet her?"

"Tomorrow. We'll pick you up."

They clinked glasses.

The team was getting stronger.

CHAPTER THIRTY-NINE

Morning light filtered through the windows of the safe house. Lamont looked spiffy in a light blue suit and lavender tie. Ronnie had on his usual Hawaiian riot. Nick's black turtleneck and gray jacket suited the throbbing hangover he had. The aspirin hadn't kicked in. His .45 felt like it weighed fifty pounds. Something kept squeezing his back. Selena looked fresh and ready to go.

Harker gave Lamont the pitch, an ID, a Glock and had him sign his life away. He cracked the slide, checked the magazine and clipped the holstered pistol onto his belt with the ease of practice. She briefed him on Dysart and the week's events. She told him about the sunken submarine.

"Yeah, Nick told me about it."

"If we found that sub, could you dive on it?"

"Thirty-five fathoms? That's two hundred and ten feet down. Sure. Straightforward, unless there are bad currents and poor visibility."

"That deep you should have a partner, but you're going to have to go it alone."

"He doesn't have to go alone." It was Selena. "I've got enough experience. I've been deep before."

Something made Nick say, "Is there anything you can't do?" His headache stabbed him.

There was a brief silence. Selena's face closed down. Lamont's expression was unreadable.

Harker's pen stopped moving. "You're an experienced diver, Selena?"

"I've done over a hundred recreational dives and two dozen deep, technical dives."

She looked at Lamont. "I know it's not the same as what you've done. But you need someone with you, in case there's trouble."

"We're talking seventy meters," Lamont said. "That's not recreational diving. Something goes wrong, it's pretty far to the surface."

"If something goes wrong and you're by yourself, you won't make the surface."

Strong words. Lamont raised his eyebrows. She went on. "We're not just talking about diving an old wreck. We're talking about getting inside it, looking for something. We don't even know what it is we're looking for. That's dangerous. You need backup."

"I could maybe get some ex-Navy guys I know to help out."

"There's no time for that," Harker said. "Besides, they'd have to be vetted, cleared. It's not an option."

Lamont asked Selena, "You checked out with rebreathers?"

"Yes. I've been to three hundred and fifty feet with one."

Steph said, "What's a rebreather?"

"It's diving apparatus. It cycles breath and breathing gas within a closed circuit system. We used them all the time in the Seals." Lamont rubbed his palm on his leg. "The advantage is no bubbles going to the surface if you're in a combat situation. You don't need big tanks and you can stay down longer and deeper than with the open circuit stuff. With the right mix the decompression stops aren't as long."

The pen started up, then stopped. Harker made up her mind. "Selena's right. If you can find the sub, she goes down with you. Nick, you and Ronnie will back them up on the surface. I'll requisition a plane to take you to Mar del Plata. Take weapons. I'll clear you for entry, you shouldn't have trouble. We have an arrangement with the Argentine military and it's friendly at the moment. They have an air base near there."

Lamont said, "We'll need gear."

"Tell Ronnie what you need. Mar del Plata is a big fishing port, right on the Atlantic. It shouldn't be a problem to rent a boat down there. I'll arrange for accommodations and a vehicle. Selena, you speak Spanish, don't you?"

"Fluently."

Harker put her pen down. "Any other questions?"

"When do we leave?"

"Tomorrow."

"Hey, I always wanted to see Argentina," Lamont said.

CHAPTER FORTY

It was a warm October morning in the nation's capitol, the sky blue and cloudless. Senator Gordon Greenwood was in his office on the Hill, thinking about an upcoming meeting with a group of deep pocket constituents. His secretary interrupted his thoughts.

"Senator, Acting Director CIA is on line two."

"Thank you, Addie."

Greenwood chaired the Senate Intelligence Oversight Committee. He picked up his phone and activated the scrambler.

"Wendell, how are you?"

"Fine, Gordon. A beautiful day out there, isn't it? Have you got a minute?"

Senator Greenwood knew Wendell Lodge well. The two men often played together at the elite Bull Run Country Club, overlooking the Civil War battleground. From the club it was possible to see the spot where General Jackson had stood immovable as a stone wall, the air around him filled with minie balls and grape shot. At Bull Run the minie balls had been replaced by golf balls arcing toward the blue sky.

CIA was political. Hearings were coming up to move someone into the Director's slot and Wendell Lodge wanted the job. No one would get to the Director's office at Langley if the senator decided to oppose him. It didn't hurt Lodge's chances that he and Greenwood were Yale classmates and members of Skull and Bones.

All the same, a little shared information of the right sort went a long way. There were lots of ways to get information in Washington. It came down to who you knew. In the Capitol, power was the name of the game and information was the currency of power. You needed money, a lot of it, but information was the more valuable commodity.

Lodge said, "There's something that needs your attention as Chairman of the committee."

"Oh?"

"Are you briefed on the Project?"

Greenwood allowed a small laugh. There wasn't much he didn't know about the intelligence community. "You mean the President's attempt to circumvent your agency?"

"That's the one." Lodge considered his next words. "I know the Director of the unit, Elizabeth Harker. One of her people was in Jerusalem. You probably saw him on TV, shooting the man who went after Rice."

"Yes, I know about Harker."

"I've just learned she's sent her team to Argentina on some covert mission. She's acting under Rice's authority. I thought in your capacity as Chairman you might be interested in knowing about it. I'm getting a bit tired of her antics. She's stepped into my bailiwick before, and when she does she makes a lot of trouble."

"Where in Argentina, Wendell?"

"Their flight plan ends at an Argentine air base near Mar del Plata, on the Atlantic coast. They took diving gear, weapons and underwater communications equipment. I don't think they're down there for a vacation."

Greenwood sipped from a glass of water on his desk. "If Rice and Harker are in collusion about something and hiding it, a look by the Committee into what's going on might be in order."

"My thought exactly, Gordon. Right now Rice is riding the popularity generated by that bomb in Jerusalem, but that won't last. If public hearings turned up Presidential involvement with questionable covert operations, it wouldn't hurt your potential candidacy any. It might even help us get you nominated and into the Oval Office. There's strong sentiment you would make a good candidate. You know you can count on me."

"I appreciate your call, Wendell. Let's get together at the Club next weekend."

"I look forward to it."

Greenwood set the phone down and looked out his window. After a moment, he picked up the phone again and dialed.

On the seventh floor at Langley, Wendell Lodge placed another call, this time to South America.

CHAPTER FORTY-ONE

Carter looked out the window at the endless canopy of jungle greenery passing below. They were somewhere over South America.

He didn't like this mission. He didn't like deep water. He always imagined something with teeth waiting for him under the surface. Lamont, on the other hand, had probably been born with flippers and a mask and if something with teeth tried to bother him, Nick was pretty sure he knew who'd win. He wasn't worried about Lamont. Selena was a different story.

He didn't want to worry about Selena. He told himself it would be different if she'd come out of an intelligence or military background. It would be different if he'd never slept with her. It would be different if he'd never met her. It pissed him off, having to worry.

He had to hand it to her. Not many people would jump at the chance to dive on a Nazi wreck two hundred feet down. He glanced over at her. She was reading an article on gender specific phrases in proto Indo-European languages. Nick had been reading a mystery about a wise-cracking detective couple in Boston that hung out with a psychopathic sidekick. Sometimes he saw a little too much of himself in the author's fictional hero, but it passed the time.

He felt a headache starting. He went to the mini-bar for another whiskey. The view from the window hadn't changed. After awhile he fell asleep.

Darkness. It was cold, very cold, a chill that ate into his bones. He was in a small room, pitch black except for a dull, reddish glow coming from somewhere. In the glow, something was lying on the ground. He wanted to see what it was, but he didn't want to see, either.

He went over to it. It was a corpse dressed in a naval uniform, a seaman. He turned it over. The face was dried and sunken in on itself, eyes open and glazed. The pupils were a splotched milky white. The skin was brown and dry and shrunken like old leather. The lips were pulled back in a horrible smile. Stained teeth grinned at him in the eerie light.

He stepped back, afraid. The light came from a box glowing dark red in the darkness. He knew he had to see what was inside. He forced himself to walk to it and place a hand on the lid.

Then the lid was open and he was looking at his own severed head. He screamed.

"Nick!" Selena was shaking him. "Nick. Wake up."

He opened his eyes. The sound of the engines droned outside the window. The endless jungle canopy passed below. She sat down next to him. "You were having another nightmare."

Nick rubbed his face. "God, I hate these."

"I know Israel was rough." She rested her hand on his arm. "I've been thinking about you. About these nightmares and headaches you're having."

He looked out the window. "I don't know what to do about these dreams. It's getting so I don't want to go to sleep."

"You haven't been getting much sleep. Maybe that's part of the problem."

"Catch 22, huh?"

"Maybe you ought to think about seeing somebody."

"Like a shrink?"

"No, not a shrink. A counselor. Someone who could help you deal with the stress."

"You think I'm stressed?"

She laughed. "Are you kidding? Your week wasn't exactly relaxing."

"Wasn't boring, though."

"You know about PTSD. You know you've got it. If you talked with someone it could help."

"You want me to see someone."

"Yes."

"I'll think about it."

"There's something else. You're drinking a lot."

He'd been about ready to get another drink when she said that. "You think I'm drinking too much?"

He started to get angry. It came out in his voice.

"Let me see if I've got this right. You think I need a shrink and that I'm drinking too much. Anything else you want to say?"

"Not a shrink. And yes, you're drinking too damn much. And no, there's nothing else."

She got up and went back to her seat.

Nick got his drink and looked out the window.

He looked at the whiskey in his hand and set it down. His head hurt.

CHAPTER FORTY-TWO

Tourist brochures called Mar del Plata the "Pearl of the Atlantic". From the air it didn't look much like a pearl. The city was gray and bleak under overcast skies. The plane banked out over the water on final approach. Below them a scimitar of smooth sand sliced into the cold, white capped waters of the Atlantic. A long, unbroken crescent curve of beach ended in a rocky cape jutting out into the ocean. Miles of hotels, houses, beach cabanas and high rises lined the shore. In the summer tourist season thousands of people would come here and pack together like sardines on the beach. Now it was mostly deserted.

Selena's Spanish charmed the suspicious Argentine Major who met them at the air base outside of the city. His eyes kept going to her breasts. He gave her his phone number.

The diving gear weighed several hundred pounds. It was packed into four bulky aluminum cases. A fifth case held weapons. Personal things were stuffed into four black bags. The team loaded everything into a dented white van and headed into town, trailing blue exhaust smoke behind.

The house Harker had secured was eight blocks from the beach. They took the gear inside. Heavy, dark furniture covered in brown fabric and cracked leather weighed down the rooms. The house smelled stale, of shut in dust and old cooking. Dark brocade drapes covered the windows.

It was like stepping back into the nineteenth century.

The team gravitated to the kitchen and gathered around a large table. Lamont spread out a chart of the waters off the coast.

He gestured at the chart. "This whole area is called the Argentine Sea," he said. He'd marked a small "X" where the British Admiralty report stated the sub had gone down.

"The coastal shelf goes out a ways and then falls off big time, thousands of feet deep. Doesn't look like we're going to run into anything unusual, but we're dealing with the Falkland Current. It's strong. At that depth and fifteen miles offshore, it will be a factor."

Lamont spread a large blueprint of a Nazi submarine over the chart. The U-Boat was huge, almost the length of a football field. The drawings showed one large deck gun forward and two twin

20MM antiaircraft guns mounted on the deck aft of the conning tower.

"These plans are for a Type IX D. They were used as command vessels for the Wolf Packs in the early days of the war. After the Nazis took France, they built radio transmitters on the coast to take over command functions and most of the Type IX's were converted to carry cargo."

He ran his hand over the plans. "The one we're looking for is a D2. It's the same as this, except the engines were better and the Germans took out the torpedo tubes to make space. There could be something in the aft or forward storage areas. Even if we find the sub, there may be no way to get inside. If we can, the best place to look for anything is the storage areas and the control room and captain's quarters."

He tapped his finger on the drawing. The captain's quarters were a tiny space little bigger than a bunk, set off with a curtain for privacy. It was located next to the control room and aft of the conning tower on the port side.

Ronnie frowned. "The Captain didn't rate a separate cabin?"

"Nope. No privacy on a Nazi sub. It wasn't fun. The crew wore the same clothes the whole time they were out. Regulations allowed one change of underwear and one extra pair of socks. No one bathed for three months at a stretch. Their Navy issued cologne to cut the stink."

"What are we looking for?" Selena brushed hair back from her forehead.

Carter looked at the plans. "Anything that could tell us why the sub was in Antarctica. A log book or record of the voyage, or any cargo she carried. Someplace they'd keep important records, like a locker or a safe."

He still thought this was a waste of time. Nothing on paper could have survived after all those years under water.

"No way we'll get into a safe," Lamont said. "We don't even know if we can find the wreck, let alone get into it."

"Maybe it's a little late to ask," Nick said, "but you sure you've got the gear you need for this?"

"Yeah, we're set. Full face masks with transceivers good to five hundred meters and voice activated mikes. The electronics on the rebreathers adjust the mix according to pressure and demand. We won't have to sweat oxygen toxicity."

Ronnie said, "Oxygen is toxic? I thought you needed it to breathe."

"You do, but at 50 meters, the pressure drives oxygen in the blood stream to toxic levels. The deeper you go, the less oxygen you need. Too much and you get oxygen narcosis. First thing you know, you're in trouble. That's one reason the full masks are good. You can't spit out the mouthpiece and drown if you have a convulsion. The gear will feed us the right amount of breathing gas as we need it."

"Sounds easy."

"Nothing's easy two hundred feet down." Lamont scratched his nose.

"How long do we stay on the bottom?" Selena asked.

"Deep is always dangerous. I think we ought to limit it. Say ten or fifteen minutes max. That will speed up the decompression stops also."

Nick looked at them. "Anything else?"

No one spoke. He looked at his watch. "Let's hit the rack. Long day tomorrow."

They went to their separate rooms.

CHAPTER FORTY-THREE

The harbor at Mar del Plata was big and crowded with bright yellow fishing boats. The waterfront was busy. Hundreds of screeching gulls circled and dived above the docks. The sea air smelled of fish and diesel and food cooking in stands and restaurants along the waterfront. The sun cast little warmth and the spring weather was clear and cold. Nick pulled up the collar of his jacket against the breeze sweeping in off the ocean.

He didn't want a local captain along asking questions. He could handle a moderate sized boat and read the charts and had the certifications with him to prove it. Some fancy talking and extra hard cash got them an older wooden boat with a high, glass enclosed wheelhouse. The engine might have been new when Peron was in power. The boat was painted red and white. It was equipped with radio, a fish finder, gasoline generator, a small galley and a bilge pump that clanked with an ominous sound.

The team headed east and south, past Cape Corrientes and out onto the Argentine Sea. Ronnie and Selena laid the gear out on deck. Lamont set up the underwater communications station in the wheelhouse, an Aquacom STX transceiver designed for military use. Once in the water, Selena and Lamont would have continuous contact with the surface.

Two hours later, Nick throttled down at the coordinates posted in the Admiralty report. Whatever was left of U-886 waited somewhere below. Lamont fired up a deep scan sonar unit he'd brought from the States. Nick set up a grid pattern. They started a slow search of the area.

Two and a half hours later they hadn't found anything.

"I hate this part." Lamont watched the sonar screen.

"Waiting?" Nick rubbed his ear. It was tingling.

A cold chill swept over him. A flat humming started in his ears.

"We're close," he said. He shook off the chill. He could almost hear his grandmother muttering.

"What? Hey, wait a sec." Lamont peered at the screen. "There's something coming up."

The depth indicator read two hundred and thirty feet to the ocean floor. A scattering of small black blips appeared on screen. Then a long, cigar shape. Nick throttled down.

Lamont gave Nick a strange look. "That's got to be it! How did you know? That's a debris field. She opened up when she went down. Keep us over the wreck."

He stopped as if he were about to say something, shook his head and went aft. He dropped a mooring line with markers and an ascension ladder over the side. The line was a crucial safety factor for Selena and Lamont underwater. If it wasn't on target they'd have to come back up and start over again.

Lamont and Selena got their gear on. Nick listened to them talking.

"Down there, you follow my lead. We clear?"

"Got it."

"If you have to bail out, don't mess around, you won't have a lot of time. Head for the surface, remember your stops, don't panic. I'll be right behind you."

She nodded and donned her face mask. She made a minor adjustment and gave a thumbs up. Her voice came over the speaker.

"It's good."

Lamont buttoned up, adjusted his mask. "Comm okay?"

Nick spoke into his headset. "Loud and clear."

Lamont and Selena entered the water. They surfaced for a moment. Seconds later they were gone from sight beneath the waves.

"How's the signal?" Nick said into the microphone.

"Five by five." Lamont's voice came back.

"Five by five," Selena said.

He tugged on his ear. Now there was nothing to do but wait.

CHAPTER FORTY-FOUR

The water was cold and clean. Selena matched Lamont's steady, rippling movement as they followed the mooring line down. There was plenty of light. It was a stroke of luck to get a bright, sunny day. Even at 70 meters, there would still be light to see by. Selena felt the tug of the Falkland current, but it was only an annoyance. Something to be aware of and compensate for.

The sub was somewhere out of sight below. The blue of the water deepened as they passed 30 meters. She breathed easily with the full mask. She felt a little lightheaded. She checked the mix, but it was only the thrill of it, the love of the unexplored.

And the danger.

Selena loved diving. This was the dive of a lifetime.

She didn't know the names of the fish swimming around her, but there were a lot of them. So far she hadn't seen any sharks. Sharks didn't bother her; she'd seen plenty in the past. There were supposed to be sea lions in the area. She felt for the razor sharp knife at her side. She wasn't sure she wanted to see a sea lion. They were aggressive and territorial, nothing to fool with. This was their world, not hers.

"Selena." Lamont's voice sounded in her headset. "Coming up on fifty meters. Check your oxygen level."

"Roger."

Selena looked at the meter that measured oxygen partial pressure level. It was well away from the 1.4 bar that meant narcosis and possible death. Everything was working. Closed circuit rebreathers were the only way to go for deep dives. At least they were the way to go if everything kept working.

The water was getting darker. Bits of floating sediment drifted all around. The sea floor came into view. Selena began to see objects scattered about. A layer of greenish-brown silt covered everything, softening the outlines of debris spewed from the submarine when she'd plunged to her death. She saw a cook stove lying on its back. A large and ugly fat lipped fish peered out at her from the open oven. Selena thought of pans of eggs and sausage and soups and cakes being cooked on that stove.

They swam over a scattered string of phallic shapes, artillery shells for the guns. There were box like outlines, unidentifiable mounds. Then a pair of boots, the toes splayed outward. She wondered what his thoughts had been, this German seaman, in those last seconds when the water rushed in.

The hulking ruin of the sunken submarine emerged from the blue-green gloom of the deep. Ghost-like and silent on the ocean floor, U-886 still looked like the menacing predator she had once been.

The sub had struck end on and settled upright. The stern section was crushed and buckled. The bow pointed straight down a steep slope covered with thick mud and silt. The slope ended at an undersea cliff that dropped off into fathomless depths.

Sea growth encrusted the wreck. Bizarre clumps and shapes hung from the railings and guns. Pale yellow fronds and long green streamers trailed in the current. The sea floor around the submarine was stained reddish brown from rust, as if U-886 had bled to death in her final agony.

The visibility was good, but Selena reminded herself to be cautious. It wouldn't take much to stir up a cloud of particles and turn everything murky.

The British depth charges had ripped a long, ragged gash on the starboard side, exposing the central corridor to the sea. A painted white shield with a black sword and swastika was still visible on the conning tower.

Nick's voice sounded in Selena's earpiece.

"Lamont. What's your status?"

"It's the right sub. We're looking at her. She's almost upright. She's ripped open and the stern is collapsed. We're not going to find anything aft. The center section looks accessible. I'm going to take a look now."

"Roger that. Selena, you okay?"

"I'm good. You should see this. There's a painted badge on the tower, sword and swastika on a white shield."

"Most of the U-Boats had badges. They identified the boat and her crew."

Lamont and Selena reached the breach in the hull and turned on their lights. The bright white beams lit up the dark interior of the wreck. Cables and wires hung down and swayed in the current, their crisp outlines blurred by sea growth. Fallen pipes lay rusting on the deck.

Selena's light cast strange shadows inside the sub. If this were a recreational dive, she'd never have thought of going in. The opening into the hull was jagged and sharp. It reminded Selena of the maw of a primeval beast, waiting for unsuspecting prey to swim through.

Waiting for her and Lamont.

The transceiver crackled. "Nick, I'm ready to go in. Selena, you hang back behind me, give me some light."

"Roger."

Lamont eased through the gap and hung suspended. He shone his light down the passageway.

"I can see the control room. The hatch is open, that's a break. They must not have had time to get it closed. Some pipes down, cables, not too bad."

He moved into the blackness of the sub's interior. Selena followed him in and shone her light through the dark water after him. Through the open hatchway she could see the periscope column and a bank of gauges in the control room. Clusters of valve wheels, rusted pipes and sagging conduit lined the ceiling and walls. Debris lay everywhere, covered in yellowish silt. Lamont's passage sent small clouds of sediment drifting in her beam.

Her light caught something white. A half buried skull looked up at her from the floor.

Lamont paused in the control room. "Bones on the deck," he said. "The depth gauge glass is cracked and the needle is stuck right on 76 meters. 228 feet. That's about right. There's a box by what's left of the radio. I'm going to open it."

Selena watched Lamont fumble with something out of view.

"It's junk. Looks like some kind of typewriter."

Lamont moved about in the wreckage of the control room. He tugged on a cabinet door above his head. The door came open in a cloud of rust particles. He reached in and withdrew a flat, black object. It turned to a soggy mass in his hands.

"Found what was probably the log book. It's no good, turned to slime." He dropped it on the floor. He turned away from the periscope column.

"Now I'm looking at the captain's corner. There's still a piece of the curtain left."

Selena felt a vibration. She glanced outside. Sediment swirled around the sub.

"Lamont, the current is picking up."

"Roger. Hold your station." She saw him grasp a bulkhead and disappear from view as he moved into the captain's alcove.

Lamont shone his light around the confined space. A disjointed skeleton lay on the floor. Fragments of dark cloth clung to the bones. The empty sockets of a narrow skull gaped up at him, the lower jaw fallen away. The legs still wore high leather jack boots, turned a soggy, brownish green. Something poked through the white bones. Lamont reached down and pulled it out, brushed silt aside. It was a brown oilskin pouch. He placed it in the bag hooked on his belt.

The sub moved. The delicate balance keeping U-886 in place for so many years had been disturbed.

"Lamont, the sub's moving. Get out!" Selena tried to keep the fear out of her voice.

"Roger."

The submarine groaned and tilted. Selena braced against the movement. Pipes broke away from the ceiling and Selena saw one strike Lamont on the head. A sudden, thick cloud of particles blocked her view.

"Lamont. Lamont, talk to me."

There was no response.

"Selena, what's going on?" Nick's voice came over her headset.

"The sub moved. Lamont's hurt. He's not answering. I'm going in after him."

"For Christ's sake, be careful. Talk to me, Selena. Let me know what you're doing." Fear flooded her body and her heart began thumping in her chest. She forced herself to slow her breathing. With more than two hundred feet of water above her, too much breath could be fatal.

"I'm going in. I can't see much, too much stuff in the water. I can't see Lamont yet. There are pipes and cables down, but I can get past them." She pushed a tangle of wires aside, death traps moving about in the murk like slime covered spiders reaching for her.

"Talk to me." Nick's voice was calm, soothing. "Take your time. Lamont's gear will keep him alive. Don't rush."

"A couple of pipes came down in the corridor, but I think I can get through them. Wait one."

Selena pushed one of the pipes aside and swam past. She swam through the hatchway. In the swirling silt she saw Lamont pinned against the deck, a pipe across his chest. His eyes were closed behind the mask, his mouth open.

"Lamont's unconscious. There's a pipe across him, not too big." She reached down with both hands and lifted the pipe away. She heard a strange groaning, an eerie, low, metallic moan. She felt the sub moving. She wanted to get out of there. She fought her panic, concentrated on Lamont.

Selena started back through the passage, pulling Lamont behind her. The sub groaned again and began to vibrate. The water inside was filled with clouds of silt. She could see nothing at all in the murk. She worked by touch and instinct through the fallen pipes, dangling wires and cables, praying she wouldn't get snagged. She reached the opening in the hull and pulled Lamont out. The wreck was beginning to move away under her feet. Grasping him under one arm, she backpedaled toward the mooring line.

The sub picked up speed as it slid down the steep slope. Roiling clouds of silt churned out from under the stern, as if the huge engines had come back to life. The black swastika and white shield gleamed like a demon's eye in the ocean light as the long, narrow shape moved away. Streams of seaweed trailed from the conning tower. They look like flags, she thought. Flags, on a ship of the dead.

The submarine went over the edge of the cliff.

For a brief moment she held her course, as if a ghostly hand was at the helm. Then the bow nosed down and the wreck disappeared into the black depths. A thick cloud of particles billowed up from the sea floor.

"Nick, I've got him, I'm coming up. The sub's gone." She looked at Lamont's oxygen meter. Still safe.

"Roger. Remember your stops."

Selena began the ascent. She watched her depth meter. She felt the cold weight of what seemed like miles of water above her.

Lamont's eyes fluttered, opened. He looked at Selena, her mask next to his as she swam upward. She saw him open his eyes.

"I've got you. You're okay. Your meters are good."

"What happened?" His voice was hoarse.

"You got knocked out. We're going up. At one hundred fifty feet now. Decompression stop."

"I can swim."

"You sure?"

"Yeah, hook on to me, but let me go."

Selena tethered him to her belt and let him go, ready to grab him if she had to.

"Shadow. Can you hear me?"

"Yeah, Nick. It's all right. We'll be up soon. I found something."

When at last they reached the surface, Selena had never been so glad to see the blue sky above her.

CHAPTER FORTY-FIVE

"You might have a concussion." Nick held up three fingers. "How many?"

"Three."

"Good answer." Nick peered into his eyes. Both pupils were the same size.

"I think you're good. But pay attention, will you?"

"I'm fine Nick. It's just a bump on the head."

Selena had changed into sweats and jacket and was sitting near the stern, watching the wake trail out behind.

Lamont walked to the stern and sat down next to her. He looked out over the water, then down at the deck.

"When I was a kid, I almost drowned."

Selena waited.

"It was a hot summer day. I was eight years old. My mom took me to the city park, to the pool. It was mobbed. Everyone was running around, rough housing, splashing each other. You know how kids are."

"Sure."

"There was this long line for the diving board. The water was twelve feet at the deep end and kids were piling off the board, one right after another. I got on the board, ran to the end and jumped. A big kid jumped in right behind and kicked me in the head. It knocked me out and I went right to the bottom. When I came to I was breathing water. Then everything got kind of peaceful and I started drifting down there, on the bottom of the pool."

Lamont looked out over the South Atlantic.

"I remember the paint on the bottom was blue and it was all chipped and cracked and there was this Baby Ruth candy wrapper stuck on the drain. It felt easy. I wasn't struggling or choking, just drifting in the water. Then someone grabbed me and pulled me out and dumped me on the cement by the pool. I never saw who it was, only a pair of feet walking away. Then my mom was yelling and pounding me on the back and I coughed up water and got sick."

Lamont paused.

"That pipe hitting me down there, it was like when that kid kicked me. I gotta tell you the truth, I wasn't sure about this when we went over the side, about having you down there. You know, Seals—we have our own way of doing things." He looked embarrassed. "Thanks for getting me out."

"You'd have done the same."

"Yeah, but thanks anyway."

In the wheelhouse, Ronnie turned the pouch Lamont had found over in his hands.

"Let's wait until we're back on shore to open it." Nick made a course adjustment.

Ronnie set the pouch down. "Boats heading toward us." He pointed out over the water. The line of cliffs and beaches along the coast was still three or four miles away. Dark, low shapes were coming hard over the waves, throwing water behind them in a wide wake.

Carter scanned them through his binoculars.

"Three speed boats. Big engines. They're in some kind of hurry. Two men in each."

The boats were headed straight for them.

"You call for pizza, Ronnie?"

"Don't think so."

"Break out the weapons." Nick lowered the binoculars.

Selena had come back to the wheelhouse. "How would anyone know what we were doing?" she asked.

"We seem to be asking that question a lot these days. I don't know. But whoever they are, they're coming this way. They're not here for the fishing."

Ronnie lifted MP-5s out of the weapons case. Lamont took one and inserted a 30 round magazine. He tapped the magazine with his hand to make sure it was seated. He racked the bolt and grabbed an ammo belt with five extra magazines.

"Reminds me of the old days," he said. "I carried one of these for years."

Nick moved the throttle forward and turned west. The speedboats altered course.

"No doubt about it. They want to intercept us. They're a lot faster, they'll get here in a few minutes. Ronnie, you and Lamont cover the stern."

Ronnie pulled an Airtronics RPG-7 launcher out of the case. It looked like a ray gun from a pulp science fiction novel. It had an elongated trumpet on one end, a large bulbous section in the middle and a black pistol grip and trigger in the front. He opened a knapsack with five rockets sticking out of it.

"Latest stuff," he said. "Your basic Russian design but made in America with improvements. We're ready to rock and roll. The guys in those boats are in for a little surprise."

"Selena," Nick said. "You position yourself here in the wheelhouse. Don't get behind that launcher. I may have to do some fancy turns and I need you to watch my back. We'll play it by ear until we know for sure they're hostile."

She nodded and loaded her weapon. Cocked and locked and ready to go. She put on her sunglasses and stood calmly in the wind and sun looking out at the approaching boats, legs slightly apart and holding the MP-5 across her chest.

Nick watched her. The sun gleamed off her weapon and framed her hair in a halo of light. She looked like an avenging Amazon from a new, modern myth of war. He felt something clench in his gut. He put it out of his mind.

For the next few minutes nothing happened. The three boats fanned out in a widening arc, angling to come at them from the stern and sides. Nick looked through the binoculars again.

"Armed. Looks like AKs. I guess they're not friendly."

The sides of the boat offered some protection where they rose above the deck. It wasn't much. Ronnie and Lamont crouched behind a large metal fish locker near the stern. The lead boat closed and the passenger lifted his assault rifle and fired. Splinters flew from the fantail.

Ronnie and Lamont opened up. Two of the boats thundered by on each side of the wheelhouse. The roar of their engines blotted out the sound of AK's firing from the cockpits. Nick and Selena ducked.

The wooden frames of the wheelhouse turned to splinters. The windows shattered into a thousand bits of glass.

Selena stood up when the boats had passed and fired after them. Nick gripped the wheel and pushed the throttles to the firewall. Two of the attackers veered off into another turn. The third boat crossed in front and raked the wheelhouse. What little glass that was left disappeared.

Selena waited until it was past, then emptied her magazine. The bullets made a trail of spouts up to the stern of the speeding boat and into the rear. The gas tank exploded. The boat skewed left and stopped. Black smoke roiled skyward as the burning craft sank by the stern. The two men in the boat were screaming, engulfed in flame.

Nick tried to ram one of the pursuers. The boat roared past. Aft, Lamont let off short, steady bursts. Ronnie picked up the launcher.

The two remaining speedboats came in for another run. Bits of wood flew all around. Bullets smacked into the metal locker and whined away. Ronnie knelt with the launcher and fired.

The rocket shot from the tube in a trailing curl of white smoke. It passed over the lead boat and was swallowed in the water beyond.

"Damn," Ronnie said. He loaded another. Selena slammed in another magazine. Lamont was firing. Nick spun the wheel to port and the boat heeled over. Ronnie lost his balance and slid across the deck. He recovered, stood up and zeroed in on one of the boats. This time the rocket went straight in. The boat disintegrated in a billowing black and orange fireball.

The third boat turned and raced for shore.

Ronnie took careful aim and fired another rocket. It streaked toward the last attacker and blew the craft out of the water. A body flew into the air and splashed into the waves. What was left of the boat sank in seconds. As they passed over the spot there was nothing to see but fragments of fiberglass and a slick of burning oil floating on the surface.

Carter throttled down and headed for Mar del Plata. He kept one hand on the helm and looked around. Everything seemed lit with bright light.

The railings of the boat were splintered and broken. The metal fish locker was holed and pocked from multiple hits. The deck was torn up in gouges where rounds had struck or ricocheted. All the glass was shot away from the wheelhouse and it was in bad shape. Only the corner posts still held the roof on.

No one was wounded. That qualified as a minor miracle.

"I don't think the guy that owns this boat is going to be happy," Lamont said. "What do we tell him?"

"Pirates. We tell him pirates." Selena brushed hair away from her forehead. She looked angry.

"Pirates off Argentina?"

"Why not? They seem to be everywhere else. Why not here?"

"We'll compensate him," Nick said. "We'll buy him a new boat. I've got ten grand right here." He patted a money belt strapped around his waist. "Hell, its government money."

"We were lucky." Lamont cleared his MP-5 and placed it back in the case.

"Yeah, Lamont, it's been your lucky day."

They entered the harbor by the southern breakwater, past a tall statue of Christ waiting with open arms to welcome sailors home. It was a comforting sight. They headed for the dock.

***

A non-descript man in a tan straw hat stood fishing on the end of the pier. He watched the battered red and white boat ease into the dock and a black man jump off and tie her down against the fenders hanging alongside. The fisherman noted the destroyed wheelhouse and bullet-scarred sides. He watched the four people on board begin unloading their gear. The owner of the boat appeared and started shouting and waving his hands in the air.

The fisherman picked up his rod and sauntered past the curious onlookers beginning to gather. When he reached the street he stopped and turned back to look at the scene, then took out a phone and placed a call to Washington.

CHAPTER FORTY-SIX

The boat owner was hysterical.

"Selena, talk to him," Nick said. A crowd was forming. It didn't look friendly. There was a lot of muttering.

She began speaking to him.

"Sir, calm down. It's not our fault. Pirates came after us. They must have thought they could take your boat from us. We had to fight them off. But we will pay to fix her. Please, be calm. We'll pay. There's no need to be upset."

Nick took cash from his money belt and held it in front of the man. His eyes bugged as he saw the wad of hundred dollar bills. Maybe more American dollars than his boat was worth.

Lamont and Ronnie watched the crowd. It was a lot of money, out in the open. A siren announced the approach of the local *policia*.

"Give him five thousand dollars," Selena said. "He may want more. I'm going to call for help." She took out her cell phone and punched in the number for the Argentine Major.

An hour later and eight thousand dollars lighter, plus five hundred for the Chief of Police and five hundred more for the Major, they were allowed to leave the pier. Maybe it was because of Selena's fluent Spanish, or maybe the fact that the Major couldn't stop ogling her breasts.

Breasts or not, he made it clear they had overstayed their welcome.

Back in the house the team was ready to move out. They sat around the table with cups of strong Argentine coffee, looking at the pouch Lamont had salvaged from the U-Boat. Carter unsealed the oilskin packet, expecting seawater to pour out. Inside was a slim, brown book. The pouch had held up. The book was dry. He opened the hard bound cover. A name was written across the flyleaf in black ink.

Obergruppenfuehrer Dieter Reinhardt.

Nick turned the page. The writing was in German.

"It's a journal." Selena pointed at the first entry. It was dated in the European style, 30-4-41. April 30, 1941.

"Can you read it?" Nick thought about how she'd looked standing on the deck of the boat just before they were attacked, the sun shining off her hair and the metal of her MP-5.

"Yes." She scanned the entry. "It's the diary of an SS General."

"What was an SS General doing on that sub?" Lamont sipped his coffee.

"Probably escaping to Argentina," Carter said. "A lot of the SS made it out of Germany at the end and came down here. What does the first entry say, Selena?"

"It's a description of his initiation into a secret SS order headed by Heinrich Himmler."

"The chief of the SS?"

"Yes. Listen to this. This is in the spring of 1941. Walpurgis Night, May Eve."

"The witches' night."

"Yes."

30-4-41

Tonight I was initiated into the Council, the greatest honor of my life. I knelt before the Reichsfuehrer in the holy circle. The Knights of the Grand Council looked on. Heydrich was there, and Eicke, Frank, Dietrich, Muller, Nebe, Lorenz.

The blood offering was exchanged. I swore my oath, kneeling before Grand Master Himmler and my peers. While I knelt, Heydrich invoked the power of the Spear, chanting in the old language. Heydrich spoke the words, but it was the Reichsfuehrer himself who touched my shoulders with the most sacred talisman, the Holy Lance of Vienna, to seal the oath.

"The Vienna Lance? Wasn't that captured by Patton in 1945?"

"Yes. It's back in Vienna now. I wonder why Himmler had it? Hitler grabbed it when he entered Austria. He took it to Nuremberg." Selena pointed at the page. "That list of names is a who's who of the SS. Eicke commanded Dachau. Heydrich was number two after Himmler. The Czechs called him the 'Butcher of Prague'."

"What's this Council he's talking about?" Ronnie added sugar to his coffee.

"Himmler created a Nazi round table modeled on the legends of King Arthur, called the Grand Council of Knights. There were twelve plus Himmler, all senior SS Generals. They met in Himmler's castle."

"How do you know this stuff? Nazi Knights?" Nick tugged on his ear.

"Just something else I know."

He remembered his wise ass comment about her knowing everything.

Selena looked at him and took pity. She decided to explain.

"I was researching Indo-European languages. Studying the evolution of archaic languages into modern ones. Himmler and the Nazis used language as one of the tests in all that pseudo-scientific nonsense about the 'Master Race'. I came across a discussion of Himmler and his so-called Council. He advocated a return to the old German religion. He was supposed to have conducted secret ceremonies in archaic German, but nobody knows what those were."

She turned a page.

20-1-42

We met today in the Wannsee district to discuss the Jewish question. The conference was led by Heydrich. He was inspiring, pointing out that the conference would resolve fundamental questions of organization, transportation and coordination of efforts between all of us to achieve the final solution.

Our aim must be to cleanse the Fatherland and all the territories the German people will occupy in the future of the corrupting stain of the Jews.

It was decided to accelerate the transportation of the Jews to the East, where facilities for work and reeducation are available and they can receive special treatment.

"He's talking about the death camps!" Lamont set his cup down. "Special treatment was Nazi speak for the gas chambers."

"There's a list of the people who were there," Selena said. "SS big shots and Nazi Party officials. He says the notes were taken by Adolph Eichmann."

"Skip ahead, Selena. See if anything jumps out at you." She turned a page.

4-6-42

A great Knight has fallen! Heydrich was brutally attacked in Czechoslovakia. He struggled bravely with his wounds, but succumbed to poisoning of the blood. They will pay.

"The guy who wrote this was a real piece of work." Ronnie gestured at the book. "Heydrich was a psychopath. The Nazis burned a whole town of people alive in retaliation for Heydrich's death."

4-2-43
Bad news from the Eastern Front. Stalingrad has fallen. Paulus and Schrenk, both surrendered. The Fuehrer refused to recall the armies, and now 600,000 men are gone. Many rings have been sent back from the front. The Russians now have the advantage.

"Rings? What's he talking about?"
Selena said, "SS officers wore silver skull rings. Himmler ordered the rings sent back to him when an officer was killed. After the war they found a box with thousands of them in his castle."
She turned another page.

21-6-43
Trudi and I were married today in the Chancellery. Reichsfuehrer Himmler presided over the ceremony. The Fuehrer himself was there, and Goering.

"He got married on the Summer Solstice," Ronnie said. "This guy seems to have a thing for dates of ancient celebrations."
"That fits with the movement toward the old German gods and pagan religion among the Nazis," Selena said. "Reinhardt was probably a believer. The SS had their own pagan versions of Christian ceremonies like baptism and marriage."

17-4-44
I have a son! Trudi gave birth today. I have named him Eric. Our pure Aryan heritage will carry on. We shall raise a warrior for the Cause.
I leave for an inspection tour of the camps tomorrow. I have completed my arrangements in Switzerland. If I should fall, Trudi and Eric will be well protected.

"I wonder if they survived the war, his wife and boy." Selena said.

"At least here's one good Nazi who didn't. Skip to the end, Selena. See if there's anything about the sub or Antarctica." Nick emptied his cup. She turned pages.

"Here's something."

8-12-44

I met with the Grand Master. He has tasked me with a sacred mission. The Holy Lance is in my care. I leave tonight for Antarctica.

She turned a page. "This is the last entry. Three days before the sub went down."

19-2-45

We arrived in New Schwabia today. At last. The trip from Spain was difficult. We spent most of the time submerged. The new snorkel unit kept us out of sight of the enemy.

I took the Lance to Station 211 and placed it in the vault, as instructed. When I left, I concealed the entrance. No one will find it.

Now we are underway for Argentina. Parsifal has begun and we will continue. In time, victory will be ours.

The journal ended there.

"Well." Selena put the book down on the table. "Now we know what the submarine was doing in Antarctica. Hiding the Vienna Lance."

"There wasn't much future for the Nazis in 1945," Ronnie said. "Why go all the way to Antarctica to hide a Christian relic? Who's Parsifal?"

Selena said, "Parsifal was a knight who sought the Holy Grail. Wagner wrote a whole opera about it. Parsifal had to retrieve the Holy Spear from an evil magician named Klingsor. That must be what Dysart's email was about. The Spear. The Lance. That's the Antarctica reference, and Parsifal is some kind of code name for whatever is going on."

"I don't get it." Lamont rubbed the bump on his head. "What's the big deal about this spear?"

Selena brushed her hair back. "It's supposed to be the spear that pierced Christ's side on the cross. Sometimes it's called the Spear of Longinus, after the Roman legionnaire who wielded it. It's said to have mystical powers because it was bathed in the blood of Christ. There's a legend that whoever has it will rule the world. All the great conquerors of Europe carried it, starting with Charlemagne. The Holy Roman Emperors, Barbarossa, Frederick the Great. People like that. That's why Hitler wanted it."

"Napoleon?"

"No, it was hidden from him. Then it ended up with the Hapsburg Emperor."

"But Patton's army found it, didn't they? So how could it be in Antarctica?" Lamont picked up his empty cup, set it down.

"They found something that looked like the one Hitler stole in Vienna," Selena said, "but there have been tests on it since then. It's no older than the sixth or seventh century CE. It couldn't have been the actual spear at the crucifixion. It does have a first century piece of iron attached to it that's supposed to be a nail from the True Cross."

"Then what's this one, the one he's talking about in the journal?" Lamont asked.

"According to that diary Himmler used the Lance for his Council of Knights," Carter said. "I don't think Hitler would have let him do that. Himmler could have made a copy to fool Hitler and taken the real one."

Selena picked up the diary, put it back in the pouch. "There have been rumors for years saying the lance Patton found is a copy and that the Nazis hid the real one. Maybe it's true."

Ronnie peered into his cup. "So when Himmler sees that time's up for the Third Reich, he sends one of his generals down to the South Pole to hide the lance in a secret base nobody knows about."

Selena stood up and went to the stove, poured herself some more coffee. "The journal says they will continue. He's talking about his Nazi Council. Do you think they could still exist? Could they be behind the attack in Antarctica?" She set the pot back on the stove.

"There are plenty of Nazi groups," Nick said. "None so organized they could intercept information sent to Berlin and mount an armed expedition within hours."

"None that we know about," said Lamont.

"Someone knew the Vienna Lance was in that vault. They must not have known *where* it was until the research station notified Berlin. When they found out they went and got it. It's like they were waiting."

"Waiting for almost seventy years? That's too weird."

He stood up. "We need to get back and get this to Harker."

As they walked out to the van, Nick touched Selena on the arm. He had to say it.

"You were good out there today. I'm sorry for that crack I made about everything you know how to do. I don't know why I said that. If you hadn't been down there Lamont would have died."

"Is that an apology?"

"Maybe you're right about talking with someone."

"Maybe we both should. You're not the only one on the edge."

Two hours later they were in the air.

CHAPTER FORTY-SEVEN

It was a pleasant evening. The windows of the safe house were cracked open. A cool night breeze brought the pungent scent of burning leaves from somewhere. Nick tried to relax on the couch. A ceiling fan turned above. Selena sat across from him in a wingback chair.

"We have a lot to talk about," Harker said. "Stephanie broke the encryption on Arslanian's drive."

"I figured out most of it," Stephanie said. "Arslanian was researching the Holocaust. He visited Germany two weeks before he was killed and found documents written by Himmler. They were stashed away in one of the old Stasi archives in what used to be East Germany. He scanned them and that's what's on his drive."

"Stasi?" Lamont said.

"The East German Secret Police," Harker tapped her pen. "Kind of like the Nazi Gestapo."

Stephanie said, "Himmler knew Germany would lose the war. Sometime in 1943 he prepared a plan for afterwards. He wanted to establish the Fourth Reich right here in the US. The plan is code named 'Parsifal'. It details money transfers, land purchases, deep cover agents in the US and South America and political action plans for subverting our electoral process and taking over the government."

"What's the part you haven't figured out?" asked Lamont.

"It's a separate piece in itself, written in runes. It's several pages."

"Runes?" Selena came alive. "Nordic runes, the old Norse language?"

Stephanie nodded.

"Can you bring them up on screen?" Selena asked.

"Sure." Stephanie tapped on her keyboard. "Here's the first page."

Selena got up and went over to the monitor.

"This is Elder Futhark," Selena said.

"Excuse me?"

"Elder Futhark. That's what you call this variant. Although it might be using the Nazi variation. They made up their own meanings for some of the symbols, like the SS lightning bolts. That's a double Sig rune. The SS used runes everywhere, on birth certificates, graves, military markings—everywhere." She squinted at the screen.

"You can read it?" Harker tapped her pen.

"Yes. Elder Futhark is an Indo-European language, Germanic. I had to study it during my Master's program."

"What does it say?"

"It says, 'Aufruf vom Alten'. It's a direct translation from modern German."

"What does that mean?"

"Invocation of the Old One. What's the next page. Steph?"

Selena studied the writing, let out a breath. "Whoa. This says, 'By the blood of the Spear, call the Old One. With the Sacred Blade, prepare the circle with the blood of the sacrifice'."

Ronnie and Nick looked at each other. "Okay, who's the 'Old One'," Ronnie said.

"Someone you don't want to meet," said Selena. "A demon, or even Satan himself. I think we've got some kind of magical ritual here, something Himmler and Heydrich cooked up."

"You think they wrote a ritual to evoke a *demon*? Are you serious?"

"I have to read the rest of it. How many more pages, Steph?"

"Another twenty-five. There are twenty-seven altogether."

Selena nodded her head. "That fits. Twenty-seven is three times nine. Nine and three are magical numbers in the old Germanic culture, used in rituals and spells. Give me an hour and I think I can translate it all."

It took her an hour and a half.

"I knew the Nazis and Himmler were into the occult, but this is something else." She seemed uneasy and stopped. Everyone waited for her to go on.

"There was a strong occultist movement in Germany. These pages are a black magic rite. Himmler created a special SS Bureau to study the occult. He sent teams all over the world looking for secrets of magical power. The Nazis even used mystical power symbols to call on supernatural forces."

"Power symbols?" Nick finished his whiskey.

"The swastika is a good example. It's thousands of years old. The Nazi swastika turns counter-clockwise. As a symbol it can represent the dark side, the left hand path, the path of darkness away from the sun."

"The dark side? Like Darth Vader?" Ronnie shook his head. "When you look at what the Nazis did, it must have worked."

"The ritual on these pages is about using the Vienna Lance as a magical power object to ensure victory. According to this, it requires a blood sacrifice. Human sacrifice."

"A magical object requiring human sacrifice?" Lamont looked at Selena in astonishment. "I thought the Lance was supposed to be something good, something associated with Christ."

"That seems to depend on who possesses it and what they intend to do with it. That Lance was carried by the commanders of armies that slaughtered hundreds of thousands of people. People like Charlemagne and Barbarossa and Frederick the Great. There's been a lot of blood spilled under the shadow of that spear. That's a lot of psychic energy. Blood sacrifice, if you like."

"You believe in that stuff?" Lamont asked.

"It doesn't matter if I believe in it. It's clear Himmler and Heydrich thought the Lance was magical."

"If people think something is imbued with mystical power, they'll act like it is," Nick said. "It doesn't mean anything more than that."

"Are you sure about that?" Selena said. "What about all those stories of miraculous events associated with the relics of Saints or the like? Or the healing miracles that happen at places like Lourdes? Or that man down in Brazil who does operations with a rusty penknife while spirits help him out? And what about those dreams you have, the ones that foreshadow the future?"

"That's different."

"How is it different?"

"Well, you can't pick up a dream. It's not an object."

"Yes, but it's still mystical somehow. How can you know things that haven't happened yet?"

"I don't know that. I just get images of things that later turn out to be connected to something in my life."

Harker tapped her pen on a glass.

"This is all very interesting, but it doesn't get us any closer to finding out who's behind the Jerusalem bombing, or why Arslanian was killed."

"We should be able to figure it out," Nick said. "At least some of it. The documents and the diary say there's a Nazi plan for after the war, 'Parsifal'. Arslanian found out about it and they killed him. The plan must be active and someone is following it. Dysart mentioned Parsifal, so we know he's involved."

Harker set her pen down. "Yes, but he's taking orders from someone else."

"Dysart and whoever 'commands' him knew about the Lance." Nick looked at the others. "The Lance was hidden in 1945. The only people who could have known that were the Nazis in Himmler's secret Council. Maybe the Council kept going after the war and Dysart is one of them. If he is, someone in the Council could command him."

"You think a secret SS Order is still in business?" Harker picked up her pen.

"It would explain a lot. If they are, we'd better find out what the hell they're planning."

CHAPTER FORTY-EIGHT

The thirteen members of the Council sat at a large round table made of dark oak. The Grand Master sat in a wooden armchair like the others, the only distinction being that his chair was upholstered in black. The others were brown. The wooden box recovered from Antarctica rested on the table before him. The lid bore a golden wreath and a large swastika of solid gold set with hundreds of diamonds. The diamonds glittered in the light of the overhead chandelier.

General Dysart sat on the right of the Grand Master. Next to him was Eric Reinhardt. He was the son of SS General Dieter Reinhardt, the man who had hidden the Lance in the last months of the war.

Reinhardt had come to America with his mother in 1948. The money concealed by his father in Switzerland had provided the capital needed to start his business ventures. Now almost seventy years old, Reinhardt had built an industrial empire. He was one of America's largest defense contractors. His company had developed the new explosive that had brought down the Mosque in Jerusalem. His device had led to the hidden base in Antarctica.

Two of the members of the Council, like Reinhardt, had been born into families of SS officers who had made their way into the United States in the years after the war. The others were from families of deep cover agents known only to Himmler and a few of the original Council, placed in America before the war had begun.

All were dedicated to the SS philosophy; annihilation of the Jews, purification of the race and loyalty to the cause of Aryan supremacy and it's leader. All had attended the best American universities and colleges. All had risen to the top of their respective professions. They represented the success of Himmler's plan, if not yet the culmination.

PARSIFAL.

No one would have thought there was anything unusual about this gathering, if they had bothered to pay attention. It was common for these powerful men to meet for a social evening of cards and drinks. Everyone knew that. It was even dubbed "The Movers' Club" by the media.

The Council had been gathered for over an hour. The Grand Master addressed the group.

"Everything is now in place." He placed his hand on the box containing the Lance. "The Holy Spear is in our possession. Our success is assured. Events are going well in the Middle East. The Muslims are convinced the Jews destroyed al-Aqsa. They are preparing to attack. The Jews argue among themselves. They are likely to launch a preemptive strike, provoking an even greater response."

The Grand Master turned to Dysart.

"It's time to begin the next phase. Is everything ready?"

"Yes. The warhead will detonate on the Jew Sabbath. Our analysis indicates full-scale escalation within 24 hours. This isn't 1967. The Jews will be defeated. This time, the Angel of Death won't be passing over."

There were smiles and chuckles all around the table.

Dysart went on. "Intelligence after the blast will point to Iran. The Jews are certain to retaliate but it will be too late."

"What about the oil fields?"

"None of our scenarios indicate more than moderate damage to the fields. If the Jews use nukes they'll aim for the cities, not the oil. Mecca, Tehran, Damascus, perhaps Cairo, perhaps Islamabad. Most of their nuclear arsenal is tactical, but their missiles are capable of long range accuracy. They will simply aid us in ridding the world of more non-Aryans."

The Grand Master turned to a man on his left.

"What is the status of our naval operation?"

The man cleared his throat. "Everything is ready. Elements of the Fifth Fleet will be attacked in the Gulf of Hormuz by what appear to be Iranian gunships. There will be American casualties."

"And Rice?"

"Rice will be in Chicago addressing a convention when he receives the news. When he leaves the building, he will be assassinated."

The speaker nodded at another man sitting at the table.

"Our new President will engage the Iranians. After the air and missile strikes, the follow up invasion will leave our military overextended. It will take time to bring back the draft and increase war production, but it is so easy to manipulate public opinion.

Within two years we will have the armies we need, with weapons and resources our forefathers only dreamed of."

Dysart spoke. "We have an ongoing problem, minor, but it needs to be handled. The woman, Harker. She knows too much. She needs to be eliminated, along with her unit."

"Why hasn't it been done?" The Grand Master gave Dysart a cold stare.

"They've been lucky. They escaped us in Argentina and until today I didn't know where they were. That location has been determined. I intend to take care of it personally."

"See that you do." The Grand Master looked around the circle. "Are there any other issues we need to address?"

No one spoke. Almost as one, the men stood. They raised their arms high in the Nazi salute. "Sieg, Heil!"

Hail, Victory!

CHAPTER FORTY-NINE

Elizabeth pulled into the garage at the safe house. She'd made a run with Steph and Selena for supplies while Ronnie kept watch on the security monitors. They began unloading the car. Lamont's mother had needed emergency surgery and he'd gone to the hospital in the Capitol. Nick was meeting with Rice's principal aide at a discreet restaurant in Washington.

Elizabeth, Selena and Stephanie walked into the kitchen, their arms full of groceries. Ronnie sat with his hands on the table before him. His expression was rigid.

"Hey, Ronnie, we're back." Stephanie looked at him. "What's wrong?"

General Dysart stepped into the kitchen from the living room. With him were six men holding Ingram Mac-10s with noise suppressors. Nicknamed "whispering death" in Vietnam, the Macs put out over a thousand 9mm rounds a minute. Obsolete technology. Very, very lethal. Elizabeth froze in place.

"You've caused me a lot of trouble, Harker." Dysart clenched and unclenched his hands. "Put those sacks down. Slowly."

They set the bags on the floor.

"Take your weapons out and lay them on the floor. Put your hands in back of you. One mistake, my men fire. Don't tempt me."

Elizabeth saw Stephanie think about going for her pistol.

"Don't, Steph. Do as he says." They laid the guns down on the floor. One of Dysart's men kicked them aside.

"Get down on your knees, all of you. You, too." Dysart pulled Ronnie's chair out from under him.

One of the men handed his weapon to Dysart and took plastic ties from his pocket. It took only a minute to truss everyone's hands together behind their backs.

"You can't get away with this," said Elizabeth.

Dysart laughed. There was no mirth in it. "Of course I can."

"How did you find us?"

"Your computer hacking. Difficult to trace, but here we are. You're not as clever as you thought. You shouldn't go looking at other people's emails." He sat down by the table. "Why don't you tell me what you've learned?"

"I've learned you're a traitor." Elizabeth said. "But you already know that."

Dysart stood up, walked over and punched Elizabeth hard in the face. She fell to her side, dazed. Blood poured from her nose. Ronnie made a movement toward Dysart. One of the men hit him in the back of his head with a gun, knocking him to the floor. Dysart turned to Selena and Stephanie where they knelt on the kitchen tiles.

"You won't make any trouble, will you? No, I didn't think so."

Dysart smiled at Selena, an unpleasant, frightening smile. "We have something special planned for you."

He reached down and grabbed Elizabeth's hair, jerked her to her knees. "I enjoyed that." His eyes glittered. "Tie their ankles."

They were trussed up with more ties. "Take them into the cellar and make sure they can't go anywhere. We'll wait for the others to get back and question everyone at the same time. It's instructive when you show someone what happens when they don't want to talk."

Dysart's men dragged them down a narrow flight of stairs into the cavernous cellar. Elizabeth's head bumped on the cellar steps. Their captors bound them sitting against two columns supporting the floor above.

One of the men crouched down in front of Selena. She could smell his stink, a rank, sour smell of unwashed body odor and cheap cigarettes. He reached out and squeezed her breast, twisting her nipple with his fingers, watching her reaction. He grinned as she winced.

He pursed his lips in a mock kiss. "You're mine, sweetheart."

"In your dreams, asshole." Selena's feet were tied but her legs were free. She brought her knees to her chest in one fluid motion and kicked her tormentor hard below the belt. He grunted and flew halfway across the room. His companion laughed.

The man rose to his feet, face black with anger, clutching his groin. He started toward Selena.

"That's enough, Carl," the other said. "There's time for that later. Come on, the General wants us upstairs."

"You'll pay for that, bitch," Carl said.

"That's original. You get that line from a movie?"

"Come *on* Carl."

The men went back upstairs and closed the door to the kitchen behind them. A single, dim bulb cast scarce light into the basement gloom.

In another time, long ago, wounded soldiers from the Army of Northern Virginia had lain in rows in this same basement. The damp stone walls had seen more than their share of pain and misery.

Elizabeth was frightened. She blew a bubble of blood from her lips. She took a labored breath and thought of her father.

The Judge had been sitting in his favorite green wingback chair by the fire in his study, a fresh glass of bourbon in his hand. Elizabeth had been fourteen years old. Outside, the sub-zero cold of a bitter Colorado winter had covered the Western Slope in ice and snow, but in the Judge's study it was warm and comfortable. They'd been talking about Stephen Crane's book, The Red Badge of Courage. Elizabeth had wondered aloud how men could overcome their fear, be so brave that they would march into the mouths of cannons and almost certain death.

"Everyone gets afraid, but sometimes you just have to go ahead."

"What do you do when you're afraid, Daddy?"

"Well, the first thing I do is admit it to myself. It doesn't do any good to pretend I'm not scared, or that I don't feel the way I really feel. That's where courage comes in."

"Courage?"

"Courage is accepting your fear and doing whatever needs to be done anyway. Cowards are people who can't face up to their fear and let it get the better of them. There's always a place for courage. There's always something that can be done. You might not see it right away. Sooner or later something comes to mind that can help you through it. You make up your mind that it's okay to be afraid and you are going to be all right. Then you do what has to be done. That's courage."

Courage. She needed that now.

Elizabeth heard Ronnie groan.

"Ronnie, are you okay?"

"Unnh. Yeah. Head hurts. I'm all right. I'm going to kill that bastard."

"How did they get in?" Elizabeth took a deep breath through her mouth.

"I was watching the monitors. Next thing I knew there was a muzzle at the back of my neck. I never saw them or heard them coming. They beat the alarms somehow. NSA bullshit."

Elizabeth took another breath through her mouth. "Dysart has to kill us. We've got to figure this out, and fast. I wonder if he knows about the tunnel?"

"Doesn't help unless we can get free."

Stone fireplaces took up each end of the basement, big enough to stand in and wide enough for eight foot logs. In the days before central heating they had warmed the house above. The concealed escape tunnel began behind the back wall of the fireplace at the far end. On the other side of that wall were weapons and a straight route out of the safe house. It might as well have been in China for all the good it did them.

"How long you think we've got before they come down and start asking questions?"

"I don't know, Ronnie." Elizabeth spit blood. The flow from her nose had slowed to a trickle. She coughed, gasped for air.

"Your nose looks broken." Selena looked over at Elizabeth. "The bleeding's almost stopped."

"When is Nick due back?" Elizabeth breathed through her mouth.

"He didn't say." Ronnie twisted in his restraints, but it was no use. "I hope it's soon."

They waited for their executioners.

CHAPTER FIFTY

Nick tried raising Harker and the others. Lamont didn't answer. He was still at the hospital with his mother and probably in a place where a cell phone would set off fifty heart attacks. Nick's ear felt like bees were crawling on it. Under Alpha Red, no response to communications within two minutes meant trouble. Something was wrong.

He was still driving the armored Suburban. It was already deep twilight. He parked well away from the safe house and moved on foot until he could see the front of the building. There were no cars out front. Everything looked normal. He stayed low outside the stone fencing and followed it around the property. In the back, a light burned in the kitchen window. Two black Jeeps were parked under the trees.

He crouched behind the wall and thought about his options.

Two vehicles meant at least two men, probably four, maybe more. He'd never make it to the house undetected, past the alarms and cameras. But there was another way in. He went back to the Suburban and drove with his lights off, past the house to where the highway came to a wide stream. He pulled as far as he could off the road and parked. He took the shotgun and a flashlight and followed the bank of the stream until he came to the grill sealing off the escape tunnel.

The tunnel looked like a large, rectangular storm drain. Carter disabled the alarm, pulled the grill away and set it aside.

The tunnel was dry and high enough to walk in. The light from his torch shone on cement walls stained with damp. Bugs and spiders scuttled out of his way. He reached the end of the tunnel. He looked through a spy hole behind the fireplace and saw the others bound to columns, feet stretched out before them on the floor. Harker's face and blouse were bloody.

Nick stepped through the back of the fireplace. He set the shotgun against the wall, pulled his knife and started cutting them free. First Ronnie, then the others.

"Nick!" Ronnie whispered. "Dysart and six others. Heavy firepower."

Ronnie picked up the shotgun and ran to the bottom of the stairs. He eased the slide back, checking to see if a round was chambered. Selena rubbed her wrists. She touched Nick on the arm, as if making sure he was real.

Stephanie ran to the tunnel, opened a steel locker and took out weapons. She handed an M4A1 to Selena, one to Harker and quietly racked the bolt on her own. They loaded up.

"They've got Mac-10s," Ronnie said in a low voice.

Nick took out his pistol. "What do you think? Should we go up, or bring them down here?"

"Up. There's no way to get them all down here at once. We have to go after them."

"Is the door locked?"

"I don't know. Probably not. They think we're helpless." He smiled. Nick knew the look. Ronnie was mad. It wasn't a good idea to get Ronnie mad at you.

"Black flag, Ronnie."

He nodded. "I'll go first." He patted the stock of the Remington. "More spread, close quarters, lots of noise. Should take them by surprise."

Nick felt the adrenaline rush. He took a few breaths to calm himself.

"Stephanie, Director," he said in a low voice. "You wait down here. Take them out if someone gets by us. Selena, you follow Ronnie and me up. Cover us. Lay down fire when you can. You get a clear shot at one of the bad guys, take it. Don't get yourself killed."

The three moved silently up the stairs. Light and the murmur of voices slipped through the crack under the door. Ronnie put his left hand on the knob and turned it in a slow, even movement. He nodded.

Nick held up three fingers, mouthed the count. One. Two. Three.

The door flew open. The man who had mauled Selena sat with one of the others drinking beer. Their guns were on the table in front of them. They went for their weapons.

The Remington blew the first man out of his chair and painted the wall in back of him with blood. Nick fired twice as the second lifted his gun. The big hollow point bullets drove him into the stove and to the floor. Two down.

Nick caught movement in the living room and dove to the side. He heard Selena's weapon behind him. The arch around the entrance to the living room disintegrated in a shower of plaster.

A long burst from a Mac-10 sprayed the kitchen with rounds. He could hear the bolt snicking back and forth over the soft stuttering of the suppressor. Ronnie fired twice, the twelve gauge loud as thunder inside the house. The double ought buckshot lifted the shooter off his feet and threw him backward.

Nick got to his feet and reached the living room. Another burst from a MAC-10 chopped the kitchen cabinets into bits. China and glass shattered behind him. Ronnie fired and a shape behind the sofa collapsed. Someone stood and Selena shot him. He went down firing, the bullets stitching a pattern into the ceiling and blowing out the chandelier. In the next room a man reached around the doorway and fired. Selena fired a short burst and he crumpled.

A man in uniform ran for the front door. Nick let off three rounds into his back. He slammed face first into the door and slid to the floor, arms spread wide, leaving broad smears of blood behind on the smooth, white enameled surface.

Loud silence.

The rooms filled with the smell of cordite, blood and the stink of emptying bowels.

"I count seven," Ronnie said. "That's all of them." He racked the slide on the shotgun, ejected an empty casing. It bounced with a hollow clatter onto the wooden floor.

They checked the bodies. Dysart lay by the door, his green uniform dark with blood. That was the good news. The bad news was that he wasn't going to answer any questions.

Selena stood frozen in the kitchen, her rifle still held close to her cheek. Nick walked over and laid his hand on her shoulder.

"You're all right."

Something changed in her eyes. She lowered her weapon.

Harker and Stephanie came into the room. Harker looked at the carnage and shook her head.

"I'd better call the President," she said. "He needs a new spymaster."

CHAPTER FIFTY-ONE

They moved the bodies into the garage. Harker called Rice. They sat around the table in the ruins of the kitchen.

"I've got to set your nose," said Ronnie. "This is going to hurt, Director."

"Go for it."

He placed both hands on the side of her nose and moved the cartilage back into place with a quick movement. She gasped. Tears came to her eyes. Ronnie taped it in place.

Nick called Lamont and filled him in. Stephanie made coffee and threw brandy in it. The team sat for a few minutes with the cups, thinking their own thoughts. Harker broke the silence.

"I didn't think Dysart could find us. I was wrong. Whoever's behind this just upped the ante. The question is why? Why would Dysart himself come after us like that?"

"We know too much," Nick said. "They can't know what it is that we know, but it doesn't seem to matter. We know why they tried to stop us in Jerusalem. They wanted to blow up the Mosque and kill Rice."

"And keep us from finding out what Arslanian knew. About Himmler's plan." Harker took a deep breath through her mouth. "That must be why they're still after us. There must be more to it than the bombing."

Nick sipped the brandy and coffee. "Himmler's plan was to try and take over the US. There are plenty of would-be Nazis around. It's hard to believe they could be powerful enough to pull it off."

"They have first rate intelligence. How did they know we were in Argentina? Maybe Dysart figured it out, but I don't see how." Ronnie yawned and stretched.

Harker looked at her watch. "Let's get some sleep. I can't think straight anymore. Set the alarms, but I don't think we're going to get any more visitors tonight."

They went to their rooms.

The adrenaline had worn off and Nick was bone tired. Selena came out of the bathroom and sat on the edge of the bed. Things were good between them again. She looked at him, shuddered.

"Jesus, Nick."

He put his arm around her. "Yeah."

"I don't know if I can keep doing this. The team, I mean. I thought I knew what I was getting into. When we were tied up in the cellar, I thought they were going to kill us."

"They were. But they didn't. That's what counts."

"But what about next time?"

"You can't think about that. If you start thinking like that you'll lose your confidence."

She looked into his eyes.

"We're so different, you and I," she said.

"How so?"

"You always seem so, I don't know…detached. It's like you turn on a switch and after that everything is action until the shooting stops. You don't seem to worry about it. It's instinct with you. With me, I have to think about it. Don't you think about it, at all?"

"Not much when things are happening. After, I do. It's probably because of my training. To know what I'm supposed to do."

"I think it's more than that. I do things I'm trained to do that people think is crazy, like jump out of airplanes for the fun of it. But I've thought about it first. It's a choice, something I've reasoned out."

She looked down at her hands. "Today wasn't something I chose to do. Nick, I was scared. Reason has nothing to do with people like Dysart."

"People like Dysart give reason a bad name." Nick paused. "I don't think we're so different. In the end, you did what had to be done, scared or not."

"You don't understand what I'm saying. It seems natural for you. It's not, for me."

Nick could feel a headache starting. Selena had just called him a natural born killer. It wasn't what he wanted to hear.

CHAPTER FIFTY-TWO

The President sent a clean up team. They said nothing and asked no questions. They took the bodies away. Pretty soon the media would announce that the Director of the NSA had suffered a heart attack or a fatal car accident. The need for secrecy and stability meant what really happened would never be made public.

Rice appointed an obscure General to fill in at the agency until things could be sorted out. With the safe house compromised and Dysart dead, there seemed no point in keeping away from Project headquarters. The team moved back into town.

They met in Harker's office. The Director had two black eyes and a broad white bandage across her nose. About all you could say for it was that it complimented her black and white outfit. Nick waited for her to start and thought about what Selena had said the night before. It bothered him.

He'd never known a woman like her. To say they were different was a hell of an understatement. That was all right. It was the thought that killing was natural for him and not for her that got under his skin.

Out came Harker's pen. She began tapping. "There are new developments, bad ones. First let's talk about Dysart. He's gone, but there are others. They've made a determined effort to take us out of the picture. I'm wondering if we need to keep out of sight?"

"You think they'll keep trying?" Nick asked.

"They might not. I've been subpoenaed to appear before the Senate Intelligence Oversight Committee, to answer questions about 'questionable and unauthorized covert operations in Argentina'. It can't be a coincidence."

"That's Senator Greenwood. How did he find out about Argentina? What's he up to?" Carter scratched his ear.

"There's a lot of media mileage in an investigation. Greenwood has a shot at the Presidency and an investigation could embarrass the President. That might be reason enough but I think there's more to it. I think Greenwood wants to stop what we're doing."

"Like Dysart," said Ronnie.

"Steph and I had an idea that whoever was behind this might be looking to profit from war in the Middle East. We've done some checking. Senator Greenwood made large trades in the last six months, moving funds into domestic gas and oil and military contractors. If there's a war he'll make a killing.

"If Greenwood is one of the conspirators, this could be a change of tactics on their part. Knock us out with legal moves and expose the Project. He could discredit us and Rice at the same time."

Nick said, "Greenwood is one of the powerhouses in the Senate. How high does this go, anyway?"

"It goes damned high, almost to the top. That's the other development, bigger than Dysart. We've gained access to all of Dysart's files. You aren't going to like what we found. Steph, would you run it down, please."

Stephanie cleared her throat. "Dysart's encrypted emails show communication with several key correspondents. There are repeated references to 'Parsifal'. We know that's Himmler's plan to subvert our government. It took a while, but I was able to back trace most of the recipients. It's a scary list. By definition, all these men are traitors."

Lamont said, "Who's on the list, Steph?"

"You can start with the Vice-President."

"Earlston? You're saying the VP is part of a Nazi conspiracy?"

She nodded. "That's what it looks like. Justice Smothers is another."

Selena looked shocked. "Smothers? The Supreme Court?"

"Yes. Also Admiral Lang and Senator Blackfriar."

Ronnie sat up straight. "Lang runs Naval Intelligence."

"Blackfriar makes or breaks the money for defense appropriations," Nick said.

Harker said, "We still don't know who told Dysart what to do. But these others—I think we've stepped right into a snake pit. Without proof, no one will believe these men are anything but dedicated public servants. There are other emails that appear to be in the nature of Dysart's job, but some of those people might be involved also. Acting DCI Wendell Lodge is one of them."

"CIA. Shit." Ronnie shook his head.

"What do you think they're trying to do?" Lamont said.

"I think they want to destroy Israel and get control of the oil fields." Harker tapped her pen. "The bombing of the mosque sets up war. The Middle East will explode and we'll be sucked right into it. If Rice were out of the picture, Earlston would take over. They could pretty much do what they please."

Harker set the pen down. "If there's a war, people like Admiral Lang could create chaos. It would get covered up in the general madness of the fighting. There's a pattern of co-opting our intelligence resources. NSA, Naval Intelligence and perhaps CIA. And now I'm called to appear before Greenwood's committee."

"They're playing hardball. Two can play that game."

"What do you mean, Nick?"

"Why don't we pay a visit to Greenwood's office? Maybe there's something that ties him to the conspiracy."

"You want to raid the office of the Chairman of the Senate Intelligence Oversight Committee?"

"Why not?"

"If you're caught, it will make Watergate look like a little white lie. It will blow us out of the water."

"If Greenwood succeeds in busting you it will blow us out of the water. Rice as well. We can't stop them by ourselves. Even if we get proof, it's going to take some fancy footwork by the President to break open this rat's nest. These people are powerful."

"I'm open to ideas."

"I don't think his office is a good bet," said Lamont. "Besides, he has two official offices. We'd have to hit both of them. If you were part of a conspiracy, would you keep incriminating stuff lying around where some intern might discover it?"

"You have a point." Harker picked up her pen.

Ronnie shifted in the chair. "If I wanted to keep something private, I'd keep it at home. Less chance of someone stumbling over something. Why don't we creep his house? He can't be there all the time."

"Daylight penetration while he's at work?" Nick said.

"Maybe the old exterminator trick, or gas and electric. Telephone repair. We go in the open and the neighbors see what they want to see. We could bug his home while we're at it."

"If he's got anything to hide, he probably sweeps the place."

"Yeah, but until he finds one we might get lucky. Hell, they bugged us, didn't they? Turn about is fair play, right?"

"If he's involved."

"Any bets he's clean? I'll give you ten to one he's dirty as Dysart."

Nick tugged on his ear. "Can we get plans for his place?"

"Plans are public record." Stephanie went over to the computer console. A few keystrokes and the plans for Greenwood's home appeared on screen. Records showed he had completed a major expansion and renovation of his basement, five years before.

Greenwood lived on ten acres of privacy in an upscale suburban development in Montgomery County, just over the District line in Maryland. The house was five thousand square feet of pseudo English Manor, complete with tall windows and Mansard roof.

Stephanie clicked again and a live satellite view of the area appeared. She zoomed in on Greenwood's address. Behind the house was a large, formal garden. A gardener trimmed a row of hedges as they watched. A high fence and mature landscaping concealed the house from neighbors.

"Who goes in?" Nick asked.

"I think Selena and Lamont." Harker paused. "We'll use the telephone repair ploy. Ronnie, you put together what they need—a van, uniforms, you know the drill."

"Is this legal?" Selena asked. "We can go in and bug a US Senator because we think he's involved in something?"

"We have to know if Greenwood is part of this. No, it's not legal. But we don't always play by the rules. Look what's at stake."

She took out a tissue and coughed into it. "All right. We'll see if Greenwood is involved. In the meantime, we still need to think about our own security. Any ideas? Nick?"

"I don't think we can keep out of sight. The safe house is blown. If we couldn't stay hidden there, how can we expect to pull another vanishing act and have it come off? If we duck and cover, we take ourselves right out of the game. I don't want to do that."

Selena said, "Nick's right. Time's running out. A war's going to start any moment."

"That's what I think." Ronnie brushed a fleck of something away from his shirt, where palm trees waved on a red and yellow background in the ocean breeze. Lamont and Stephanie nodded agreement.

Harker said, "We'll proceed as usual, then, with extra caution."

CHAPTER FIFTY-THREE

Nick opened his door. Selena had dressed in heels and a sleek designer creation of blue silk cut low over her breasts. The fabric rippled when she moved. A chain and earrings of Black Hills gold picked up the highlights in her hair. A soft black jacket completed her outfit. Her smile was enough to make Nick forget all about Nazis and plots.

They were going out for dinner, the date she'd talked about when he was in Jerusalem. The first date he'd had since Megan died. He'd dressed in his best suit, a gray weave over a light blue shirt and dark blue tie. The look was only slightly marred by the bulge of the .45 under his jacket.

"You look wonderful," Selena said. "I thought we'd go over to DuPont Circle. I know a place with a good wine list and great little things to eat."

"Sounds good. You look terrific. Really terrific." Nick took her arm. They rode the elevator down to the first floor of his building. They nodded at the security guard and walked out into the chill of an October evening on the East Coast. The street was deserted, unusual for this time of night.

They strolled toward the corner to look for a taxi. The evening bore a hint of coming winter in the air. A garbage truck rumbled by and stopped up the block ahead of them. Two men in overalls and baseball caps climbed from the cab. They began emptying cans lined in the alley.

Nick and Selena came abreast of the truck. One of the garbage men pivoted and drove the metal lid from a can into Nick and knocked him to the pavement. The second grabbed Selena. Nick felt a hard boot in his ribs and rolled to get away. Out of the corner of his eye he saw Selena struggling.

A second kick came at his head. He caught the foot and twisted in and down with all his strength. The man screamed and fell to the sidewalk. He reached inside his overalls and pulled out a dark, blue automatic. Nick fired, the roar of the .45 harsh in the night air. The phony trash man sprawled on the sidewalk.

Selena grasped her attacker and hurled him into the side of the garbage truck. He bounced against the metal and pulled out a pistol.

Before he could fire, she leapt into the air and planted a flying kick in the center of his chest. He slid down the side of the truck and collapsed, his head slumped over his chest. Blood poured from his nose and mouth. He coughed twice and died.

It had taken no more than half a minute.

"Are you all right?" Nick got to his feet.

"Yes." She looked down at her dress.

The sleek blue was ripped down the front, exposing her breast. She pulled the jacket tight around her and cast an eye over him.

"You look pretty good, yourself."

His suit was trashed, the soft, gray weave torn and dirty. Nick went over to the man slumped next to the truck, felt for a pulse.

"He's dead."

"He should be. I've practiced that strike for years. It's supposed to kill. I never thought I'd have to use it for real."

"He had a gun."

"I know," she said, "but it doesn't help."

Sirens sounded down the block.

CHAPTER FIFTY-FOUR

"Some date," Selena said.

She tossed her purse on the couch. Harker had called off the cops. They were back in Nick's place.

"I'll never complain again about how you can do everything," he said. "You walk on water, too?"

"Only on a jet ski." She sat down next to him on the couch. "Why did they come after us?"

"They wanted us alive or we'd be dead. Maybe to find out what we know. Maybe some other reason. It has to be the same people."

"The Nazis."

"Yeah. But dumb ones. That was really bad planning, to try and grab us on the street like that. They're making mistakes and that's a good sign. Somebody sure as hell doesn't want us getting in their way."

"Greenwood?"

"I don't know. We might find out tomorrow when you go over there."

Selena got up, went to the liquor cabinet and took out a bottle of Jameson's. She came back with the bottle and two glasses. She handed him a glass, poured, then poured one for herself.

"I'm beginning to see why you like this stuff."

"It's all right if you don't overdo it. When Megan died, I hit it pretty hard."

Selena looked at him. He'd never told her about Megan. All Selena knew was that he'd loved her and she was dead.

"It's a lousy fix, the bottle. My father was a drunk, and I know better. But for awhile, it seemed to help, after she died."

Selena waited. Then she said, "How did she die?"

He remembered. The worst day in his life.

"I was on leave," he said. "We'd had a good week." Acid churned in his stomach. "We went to the airport."

He emptied his glass. He got up and went to the bar and poured another drink. he sat down next to Selena.

"I was rotating back to Iraq. Megan was going to San Diego. She had a new job..." He stopped, remembering.

"Anyway, her plane left before mine. I went over by the windows to watch her take off. You know those big windows they have at the San Francisco airport?"

"Yes."

"Her plane lifted off and then it did something strange. It kind of joggled. In the air. Then the nose went down, then one wing tipped down and the plane went straight into the ground. It blew up. There wasn't anything I could do to stop it. Anything. I had to stand there and watch her die."

He put his hand over his eyes. "There was nothing I could do. Nothing I could do."

Something broke inside him.

Then he was sobbing and Selena had her arms wrapped around him.

CHAPTER FIFTY-FIVE

The Visitor watched his target walk to the front door of her Georgetown Brownstone. The woman paused in the mullioned yellow light from the antique coach lamps set on either side of the door. She fumbled with her keys and went inside. It was after eleven. The night was cold, the warmth of the day a memory. On the deserted, tree-lined street, all the post-dinner strollers had gone home to the safety of their beds.

The Visitor drove his car down the block. He turned off his lights and pulled into the service alley behind the buildings. He parked. He got out of his car and slipped to the rear of the target's home. He opened a gate in the fence and became another shadow blending into the tall bushes in back of the house.

The scent of wet leaves and the coming of winter filled the night air.

Lights came on in the second story, where the Visitor knew the bedroom was located. He pictured the interior of the house in his mind's eye, the location of the alarm box. He went through how things would happen and repeated the mental exercise. When he felt ready, he moved to the back door, opened it in seconds and slipped inside. He had only a minute to disable the alarms.

A red light blinked steadily on the alarm box. On. Off. On. Off. He took out a small electric tool and unscrewed the cover on the box. He took a device from his pocket and clipped leads onto the terminals. The blinking red light turned green. The Visitor started for the stairs.

Upstairs, Elizabeth had changed into her robe. She was sitting at her dressing table brushing her hair. Her holstered Glock was on the table in front of her, in the midst of an assortment of bottles and containers. After the events of the last days it was always in reach. She looked in the mirror, at the purple bruises around her eyes, her damaged face. She sighed and set the brush down.

Elizabeth tried to take a deep breath and coughed. She picked up the latest lab reports from Johns Hopkins.

Lymphangioleiomyomatosis. She couldn't even pronounce the damn thing. The doctors called it LAM for short. It was rare, so rare she was one of only five hundred some cases diagnosed in the US. It affected only women. It was going to kill her.

For a long time she and her doctor had thought it was a case of nasty chronic bronchitis. Finally, her doctor ordered an MRI and they had discovered the truth. There wasn't any real treatment. She'd already been through heavy antibiotics, but they hadn't done anything except destroy her digestion. Then hormonal therapy, but that hadn't worked either. Then an experimental regimen of something called Rapamycin. Now she was on another experimental drug. Something new, they said. It might work, they said. It might not. It left her with a dry mouth and occasional dizziness. It was too soon to know if it would do the job.

Her lungs were filling up with tissue that shouldn't be there. She was tired all the time, now, although she didn't think the others had noticed yet. She had a powerful inhaler, a bronco-dilator for when she couldn't catch her breath, but she didn't like to use it. Acupuncture brought temporary relief, but it was difficult to find time for visits to the cheerful Chinese doctor. In any event, it wasn't a cure.

At this rate she'd be dead in two years. If the new regimen didn't work, the only possible alternative was a full lung transplant. Elizabeth wasn't holding her breath on that one.

That bizarre thought made her laugh. She bent over the table in a fit of coughing, her hand resting on the Glock.

A movement in the mirror that shouldn't have been there. She half turned and stared into the barrel of a silenced automatic, held by a tall figure standing in the doorway. The man was dressed in dark clothing, his face bland and unremarkable, the face of an assassin. The hand with the pistol was unwavering.

"Please do not move." His voice was soft, neutral, a hint of an accent.

She stopped turning. "What do you want?"

She knew what he wanted—to kill her. The hard black grip of her holstered pistol was cold under her hand. The assassin had come in while she was in front of the mirror. He couldn't have seen the Glock lying in the midst of the bottles and jars on the makeup table surface.

Elizabeth knew there was little time. She would have only one chance. She closed her finger around the trigger. Had she chambered a round?

"To help you," the man said. He moved closer.

Elizabeth spun the Glock around with a swift, fluid motion and pulled the trigger as the intruder fired. She heard the soft sound of the silencer and felt the bullet strike her skull, a sharp, hammering pain that knocked her backwards off the low stool where she'd been sitting.

The Glock bucked in her hand as she tumbled to the floor and she smelled the leather of the holster burning. The assassin staggered backwards as she fired again, then again. His pistol clattered onto the floor and he fell back into the hall. She could see his feet sticking through the doorway. As she slipped into unconsciousness Elizabeth saw that one of the soles of his black, shiny shoes was almost worn through.

CHAPTER FIFTY-SIX

Nick tossed and turned in his sleep.

They come in out of the sun, low over the village, the beat of the rotors echoing in his helmet and hammering inside his head. It's Afghanistan again, back where he will kill a child, back where he'll feel the grenade try to tear him apart.

The dream is different this time. This time, he knows he's dreaming. He tries to wake up but he can't and his Marines jump out into the dusty market street, as they always do in the dream.

Megan is standing in the middle of the street.

"Nick."

He begins weeping. The dream changes, and now he and Megan are standing in front of a building on a street in a strange city, a place he doesn't recognize. Blocks of gray apartment buildings recede into the distance. People hurry past, their faces averted. Something is burning. A man walks by in a round, fur hat, dressed in black, with a beard and long ringlets of hair. He gives Nick a frightened stare as he passes.

Israel. He's in Israel.

"You have to stop it." Megan looks sad.

"Stop what? I don't understand."

Megan points at the building. There's a sign, but the letters keep changing and it's hard to read. He can see words. 'Jaff' then 'Arms', 'toilet', then a phone number in blue. It looks familiar, but he can't place it.

"Call him. Look, Nick, here's a phone."

She hands him a large, old fashioned black phone. It's ringing. He picks up the receiver. "Hello?" he says. "Hello?"

His phone was ringing on the bedside table. He picked it up.

"Yes." The clock on the dresser read 3:04 A.M.

It was Stephanie. "Nick, someone tried to kill the Director."

He came wide awake. "Is she all right?"

"She's in Bethesda. The assassin is dead, she put three rounds in him but she was shot in the head. The bullet was a .22. They're operating as we speak."

He watched the numerals tick over on the clock.

"There's more. Elizabeth is ill. She's got some kind of rare disease. It's fatal. Nobody knew about it, but when they got her to the hospital they figured it out from the meds in her purse. They called her doctor and he confirmed it."

He'd think about that later. "Have you called the others? Selena's not here, she's at her hotel."

"You're the first. How shall we handle this?"

"You're in charge, Steph. What do you want to do?"

"I think we need to notify Rice and meet right away. Something bad is happening and we need to stop it."

You have to stop it.

"I'll be there as soon as I can."

While he dressed he thought about the dream. There was something about that phone number. He'd seen it somewhere. The dream had seemed to be set in Israel. An Israeli number? Then Nick remembered where he'd seen it.

On Ari Herzog's card.

It was already past ten in the morning in Israel. Herzog was probably in his office. Nick looked in his wallet, extracted the card. What was he going to say? That he'd had a dream where his dead lover said he should call?

He decided to begin by bringing Herzog up to speed on Harker and what they'd found out about Himmler's plans. He punched in the number.

"Herzog."

"Ari, this is Nick Carter. Are you on a secure line?"

"I'll call you back."

Nick disconnected. Thirty seconds later his phone signaled the call.

"We can talk now. What's up, Nick?"

"I'm not sure, Ari, but a lot has happened here. Someone tried to kill my boss tonight. You need to know what we've discovered."

He ran it down. The raid in the Antarctic, the Nazi sub. Arslanian, Himmler's Nazi Council of Knights and the Vienna Lance. He told Ari about PARSIFAL. He told him about the raid on the safe house and Dysart's death. He told him it went high and that key figures in the government and military were involved. He didn't tell him who they were or that one of them was the VP of the United States. That was Rice's call.

Herzog only interrupted twice as he spoke, to clarify a detail. Nick told him about the attack outside his building and the attempt on Harker's life.

Then he told him about the dream.

There was a long silence at the other end. Nick looked at the phone to make sure they were still connected.

"You are saying that there is a Nazi conspiracy of powerful men in your country and that they wish to destroy Israel."

"Yes."

"Then you tell me about this dream. Do you realize what this sounds like?"

"Like I'm some kind of raving lunatic, yeah, I know. But PARSIFAL is no dream. Something's going down in Israel soon and has to be stopped before it happens. The dream is trying to warn me about it. Warn you. Why else would I see your phone number? Maybe it's only my subconscious putting things together, but whatever it is I think we've got to pay attention to it."

"Tell me again about this dream."

Nick described the street, the man, the building, as best as he could remember.

"I am looking at my computer as we speak," Ari said. "There is an apartment complex in Tel Aviv called the 'Jaffa Road Royal Arms'. It's in one of the older sections of the city. Have you visited Tel Aviv?"

"Never. Only the airport."

"So you would have no way of knowing about this building. Mmm."

"Ari, I know it sounds off the wall. I don't know why I get these dreams. My Grandmother had them, too. I only know they're important. Maybe you could check that building out."

He needed to make Ari understand.

"Are you aware of what has been happening here, Nick?"

"Only that things are heating up."

"We are hours away from all out war. I am dealing with a continuous flood of intelligence. It is necessary to prioritize."

"Ari. We don't know each other well. Please trust me. I have a really bad feeling about what will happen if you don't follow up on this."

Another silence.

"All right, Nick. Keep me informed. I will do the same."

"Thanks, Ari. Good luck, over there." He remembered words he'd seen carved over a Roman tomb. "Don't let the bastards wear you down."

Nick thought he could hear Herzog smile on the other end.

CHAPTER FIFTY-SEVEN

It was breaking dawn outside. Streaks of vermillion and gold and yellow illuminated a shotgun sky filled with rows of puffy gray clouds. Stephanie sat in the Director's chair. It was strange to see anyone else sitting there. Harker's silver pen lay silent on the desk. Nick half expected Stephanie to pick it up.

"Elizabeth is out of surgery," Stephanie said. "The bullet bounced off the orbital ridge above her left eye and lodged alongside the skull. She was lucky it was only a .22. If the shooter had used something bigger it would have blown the top of her head off. They got the bullet out and she's in an induced coma while they wait and see if there's going to be any further insult to the brain—hemorrhaging, fluid build up. It's too soon to evaluate her neural functioning, if she's lost any capacity. The doctors are hopeful."

"What about the son of a bitch who shot her?" Ronnie kneaded his knuckles.

"No information yet. No ID. He was dressed in clothes of European manufacture. We're running his picture and prints through Interpol and everyone else. If he's ever been picked up, we'll find out who he was."

"She got off three shots after taking a bullet in her head?" It was Lamont.

Stephanie nodded. Lamont let out a sigh.

"I want to tell you about a dream I had," Nick said, "and a conversation with Herzog in Israel."

When he was done, everyone was silent.

"It feels like everything is coming to a head," he said, "but I'm damned if I know what it is. The thing outside my building—they must have wanted Selena and me alive, at least until I started shooting. Then, going after the Director like that. They're trying to stop us and they've turned up the pressure. It must be something set to happen soon."

Stephanie shifted in Harker's chair.

"We'll continue as planned. Get into Greenwood's house and see if we can find anything linking him to this conspiracy." She turned to Ronnie. "Are we set with the logistics?"

"We are. I got us a phone truck, uniforms, tools, all that stuff, plus some nifty little bugs we can scatter around. We'll be able to hear everything that happens in there after that."

"I pulled up Greenwood's schedule. He's in meetings all day. His wife is back in his home state. The maids don't come today and it's the gardener's day off. If you go in this morning it should be fine."

Stephanie picked up the pen, quickly set it down. She was showing the stress. "What I can't figure out is how these people know so much. We stopped Dysart. That should have been enough. It's like they know everything we're thinking about."

She turned to Nick. "I notified the President about the attack. He wants you at the White House this morning. It looks like a photo op to give you a medal for your actions in Jerusalem. It's a cover for a private meeting."

"What time?"

"At ten. You go in the front way, where the press can see you. The ceremony is in the Rose Garden. After the award, he'll invite you inside for a private chat. No one will think anything of it." She looked around. "Any other thoughts? No? Then we'll meet after Selena and Lamont get back from Greenwood's."

Stephanie stood up and Harker's wheeled executive chair slipped out from under her. She grabbed for the desk and her hand sent the picture of the Twin Towers skittering lengthwise along the polished surface. It flew off the desk and landed at Nick's feet. He reached down and picked it up.

A tiny, black rectangle was stuck on the bottom of the picture frame. Carter swore to himself. He held up his hand at the others, touched his lips and held the picture high where they could see it, pointed at the bug.

He said, "We've got a long day ahead of us. Anyone up for breakfast? I'm buying."

"I'll go with you," said Selena. "Come on guys. Let's all go."

Nick set the picture back on the desk. They left the room. No one said anything in the elevator or out in the parking lot. They drove to a restaurant down the road. The place was slow. They took a corner table where they could see the entrance.

The waitress brought the order. Nick mashed toast into his eggs and thought about the listening device on that picture.

"No wonder they know what we're thinking. They've heard every word, all along."

"The sweeps didn't pick it up," said Stephanie. "It's got to be something new. High tech. How did they get it past all the security?"

"We'll find out." He put more sugar in his coffee.

"Whoever is listening knows we're going after Greenwood." Ronnie talked between bites. "If he's part of this, he's going to try and stop us. What if we found something in his house that could pin him down? He couldn't risk that."

Everyone nodded. The team was on the same page. Nick looked at Selena and she smiled at him, just a little.

"If Greenwood is dirty," Lamont said, "he'll be waiting for us. He's got no reason to think we'd be looking for an ambush. If I were him, I'd have people waiting outside and inside. We should be able to spot them outside. Then we'd know he's part of this for sure."

Ronnie munched on a piece of bacon. "That would tell us he's one of the bad guys, It wouldn't get us inside his house."

"How about this," Nick said. "If he wants to play rough, he's got to do it out of sight, inside the house. You go out there like we planned. You check things out. You spot someone, plant a bug in his phone box outside, but don't go inside. Then drive away. He thinks you did what you came to do. Then we come back when he's not expecting us."

"That could work." Stephanie pushed her half eaten eggs aside. She made up her mind. "Lamont and Selena, you go as planned. We'll leave the bug in place in Elizabeth's office. We've got an advantage, now. They don't know that we know they're listening"

Carter looked at his watch. "I have to get ready to meet Rice. Steph, as soon as I'm out of there I'll call you."

"Elizabeth briefed the President on those emails we found on Dysart's computer. What I don't know is how he thinks it should be handled. Find out, Nick."

CHAPTER FIFTY-EIGHT

Nick stood next to the President in the Rose Garden. Rice made the requisite remarks about service and duty and presented him with a boxed medal. The cameras flashed. It was a relief when they went inside to the Oval Office.

Rice took a seat behind his desk and motioned Nick to a chair. They were alone except for a Secret Service agent standing by one of the curved doors set into the wall.

"How do you like the limelight, Nick? You don't mind if I call you Nick, do you?"

"Of course not, sir. I don't like cameras much, to tell the truth. Don't you get tired of it?"

"It goes with the territory. Don't be surprised if someone wants you to run for Congress. You've got name recognition, now."

"I'd make a lousy politician, Mr. President."

He laughed. "Yes, you would. You're too willing to say what's on your mind. Even when you don't, your face gives you away. Don't get into any poker games, Nick."

Rice turned serious. "I was sorry to hear about Director Harker. How would you feel about taking over for her?"

It took a moment to absorb that. "Sir, I'm no administrator. And as you pointed out, I wouldn't make a very good politician. A lot of what she does is political. I'd screw it up."

Rice picked up a letter opener, set it down. "What is your evaluation of Harker's deputy?"

"She's very competent. She's fully capable of running things and she knows everything that's going on. She and the Director have been an excellent team. We're all comfortable with her in charge."

"Hmmm. Then for now we'll leave things as they are."

Nick briefed him on Greenwood. He relayed Steph's question about how to handle the implications of Dysart's emails to the conspirators. He could see Rice thinking about what he was going to say next.

"This situation will tear the country apart if it becomes public. It was bad enough about Dysart, but the rest of it..." His voice trailed off. His eyes had a glint in them. Nick had seen it before, in the eyes of men getting ready to go into combat, an inward look of calculation, determination and something else.

"When I think of what this country has given these men," Rice said, "the honor and position—to have them throw it in our faces because of some rabid Nazi philosophy of hatred makes me want to puke. You have to get me proof, Carter. Proof. I can't move against them without it."

"Yes, sir."

Rice stood up and Nick rose. The President walked over to the windows and looked out into the Rose Garden. He had his hands clasped behind his back. The knuckles were white and his voice was tight, controlled.

"I thought I'd have an eight year run here. Time enough to do some good, get the country back on track, wind down the war. If this becomes public, I'm finished. My VP is a Nazi. No one can spin that away."

Rice was speaking to the window. Nick couldn't see his face.

As if it were an afterthought, he said, "If General Dysart had been taken alive and tried, it would have been a bad day for our country."

"Yes, sir, it would have been." The message was clear. The President didn't want these men to come to trial. But he hadn't said the words out loud.

"Meanwhile, I still don't have what I need to show it wasn't a Jewish group that bombed the Mosque."

Rice turned back to face him. "I must have something, or I will not be able to stop what is happening over there. It may be too late, anyway, but I've got to try. I've spoken with the Presidents of China and Russia. They're willing to work with me to try and broker a solution, but without a clear trail of evidence showing the Israelis weren't behind it, there's not much any of us can do that will make a difference. This bomb has ignited hatreds that have festered for a thousand years."

"I understand, sir. I'll do my best."

Rice reached across the desk and shook his hand. "I know you will. I'm counting on it."

CHAPTER FIFTY-NINE

The dreary façade of the Jaffa Road Royal Arms in Tel Aviv would never find its way into the tourist brochures. A large, faded sign in Hebrew and English on the front of the building advertised "Furnished Rooms/Apartments To Let".

Ari wondered how he'd let himself be persuaded by Nick's phone call to mount this operation. He was beginning to think it was a good thing he had. Earlier his agents had checked out the building. A conversation with the manager and a look at the tenant list and Ari called in his teams.

The entire block was due to be leveled as part of a comprehensive program of urban renewal. Rents were cheap. All of the units except one in the Jaffa Arms were occupied by pensioners and older people down on their luck. Most had lived here for years. The one exception was a one bedroom unit rented only two months before by a middle-aged tourist couple from America. In this building, that rental stood out like a neon sign. The manager hadn't seen the tenants for a week. He did remember that several packages had arrived by private courier ten days before.

The street was sealed off. Anyone looking would see only the road barriers and work crews common when the utility company was digging something up.

Ari followed his six man team up the stairs. Outside the building, men watched the fire exits and escapes. The elevator was out of commission. The only way out from the upper floors was down these stairs he was now climbing.

The hall corridor on the fourth floor smelled of stale cabbage and cigarette smoke. Flickering fluorescent lights did nothing for the scuffed linoleum on the floor. Cracked and peeling yellow paint covered the ceiling and walls. The door to 416 was painted dull green. Ari put his ear against the wood. There was no sound from inside the apartment.

The lead man inserted a key the manager had given them. The key would not turn. The lock was shiny and looked new. Perhaps the tenants replaced it, Ari thought. Perhaps there was something in there they didn't want anyone to see.

One of the men held a ram ready. Ari nodded and the ram slammed into the door, splintering the lock and frame. The men boiled into the apartment, guns ready, and spread into the rooms, calling out.

"Clear."

"Clear."

The apartment was empty. The curtains were drawn. Ari pulled them back in a cloud of dust to let in some light.

A large, shiny metal case with reinforced corners and a black plastic carrying handle sat on a chipped brown table in the kitchen. Ari bent close and listened. He could hear nothing. He was tempted to open the case but he knew better. Maybe it was a travel case. Maybe not.

"Call the bomb squad. Clear the building and get out of here."

Three hours later, he gave Nick a call.

"Shalom, Nick."

"Shalom, Ari. What did you find?"

"Your line is secure?"

"Yeah, go ahead."

"My friend, please do not hesitate to call me again if you have one of your dreams."

"Come on, Ari, what did you find?"

"A nuclear warhead rigged to an electronic timer and set to detonate on the coming Sabbath."

Nick couldn't think of what to say. Ari continued.

"The warhead is of Russian manufacture. The container and detonator materials are Iranian. There's quite a debate going on right now about that. There's a lot of pressure on the acting prime minister. You can imagine what the hardliners want to do about this."

Nick found his voice. "Nuke Iran back into the stone age?"

"Exactly. There is going to be real trouble no matter what. If that warhead had gone off, a large part of Israel would have been gone in a mushroom cloud. We are a small country, Nick. With the fallout and aftermath one nuclear explosion could wipe us out."

"What if it's not Iran? What if it's these Nazis we're after? They want Israel destroyed. This could be misdirection, like the Mosque explosion. Hell, the whole world would get involved if nukes go off in the Middle East. Pakistan has the bomb. We'd never get the genie back in the bottle."

"It's not my call, Nick. All I can do is keep feeding information to the powers that be. What is happening on your end?"

"We have a suspicion about who's at the head of this organization but we don't have proof yet. We've mounted an operation to find out. Rice is behind us, all the way. I have to tell him what you've found."

"Mmm. What do you think your President will do?"

"I don't know, but I trust him. He doesn't want this to escalate. He's got Russia and China backing him up."

"You didn't get this information from me."

"Of course not. But this isn't a time to keep secrets, is it?"

"No. There's too much at stake. Too many mistakes get made because governments keep secrets. Soldiers know that, I've never understood why politicians don't. Let's not give them the option."

"You're a good friend, Ari."

"I do this for Israel, Nick. But I would be pleased to see you again when this is over. In friendship."

Ari ended the call and thought about the conversation. Some might condemn him for passing information to the Americans. It might ruin him if it came out, but Ari knew he had not betrayed his country. Politics and country were not the same thing.

CHAPTER SIXTY

Lamont and Selena parked down the street from Greenwood's house. The street was wide, pleasant and shady. The houses in the development were in the two million dollar plus range. Landscaped lots of ten acres, with mature trees and plenty of privacy. The American Dream. Or maybe a nightmare.

A long blacktop drive led to Greenwood's house. It circled under a covered entryway in front of the house and around a large Italianesque fountain before it rejoined itself. The fountain featured four smiling cherubim relieving themselves. They sat in the van, watching. A bird sang somewhere. The engine made a ticking noise.

Selena said, "In the blue BMW, reading the paper. He hasn't turned a page since we got here."

"Yeah, I see him. There's another pretending to walk his dog, over there." Lamont lowered his binoculars. He pointed at a man some distance away leading a muzzled German shepherd on a tight leash.

"I guess we've got our proof."

"Proof enough for us. Not enough to bring him down. Plan B, we don't go in. Ready?"

Selena nodded. Lamont started the van and drove to Greenwood's driveway and up to the front of the house. He parked and they got out. Lamont walked up to the front door and rang the bell, just as any telephone repairman might do. They waited. No one came to the door. Selena kept her hand on the Glock concealed under her shirt.

Lamont opened the back of the truck. He buckled on a tool belt. He went around to the side of the house where the phone box was located. Selena followed a few steps behind. There was no one in sight.

Lamont opened the box. He took his time pretending to check the connections. He installed the bug, tightened everything up and closed the box. He didn't think the bug was going to be there for long. They got back in the van and drove away. Now they'd wait to see what would happen.

Across town, Senator Greenwood set his phone down. He looked out the window of his office on the Hill. Things were not going according to plan. He was annoyed. More than annoyed, he was angry. Why hadn't those meddlers gone inside? If they had, they would not have come out again.

The Visitor had failed. Always, his assignments had ceased to exist, ceased to create problems. Now he was dead. At least that damned woman was out of the picture. Greenwood hoped she suffered. He hoped she died.

He took a deep breath and calmed himself. There was no point in over-reacting. The meeting was still set for tonight. The last element would soon be in place. It had been botched yesterday, but that final detail would be taken care of today.

Tomorrow would bring the dawn of the Fourth Reich. Of course, it wouldn't be called that. This wasn't 1933. There wouldn't be parades of jackbooted soldiers or gigantic squares filled with troops. Modern times demanded modern techniques. The appearance of democracy was everything. By the time America realized what had happened, it would be too late.

The bomb would detonate in Israel. Rice's assassination would create panic. In the confusion, no one would see what was happening. Earlston would step into the Presidency and let Israel and the Muslim states destroy one another. He would intervene only to protect the oil in the region. The war drums would beat against Iran. When the dust settled, the Jewish state would be only a bad memory. Control of the resources of the Middle East would rest in the hands of the Council. His hands. The New Leader.

It was all coming together, just as he'd planned.

CHAPTER SIXTY-ONE

Selena stepped out of the elevator and walked down the hotel corridor toward her rooms. The team was meeting at seven. She wanted to shower and change clothes. It was going to be a long evening.

A uniformed waiter rolling a large food cart draped with white linen came down the corridor. Selena noticed that the sleeves of his uniform jacket seemed too short for him. Trays of food under glass domed covers filled the top of the cart.

Selena was hungry. She decided she had time to order room service before meeting the others. Breakfast hadn't been much more than coffee and a few bites of toast. She'd had nothing to eat since, except a power bar in the van.

She paused in front of her door and took her key from her purse.

"Good afternoon, Ma'am," the waiter said.

Selena inserted her key. Something stung her neck and everything went black.

Then she was awake.

The first thing she felt was pain. Pain in her arms and hands and shoulders. Something cut into her wrists and ankles. She opened her eyes. She could see nothing. Wherever she was, it was pitch black. A hard, rough surface scraped against her skin.

She was naked.

She hung from something. Her arms stretched above her, her legs buckled under. She straightened her legs and the strain eased in her arms.

She remembered the waiter in the hotel corridor. She remembered inserting the key in her door. Then a brief pain, like a bee sting. Then nothing.

A wave of primal fear rocked her. Her mind cleared, as if someone had thrown a bucket of ice water in her face. She waited for her heart to stop pounding. She closed her eyes and drew upon her training in martial arts, remembered her teacher's words.

Fear does not exist, except in the mind. There is only being, only chi. All else is illusion. Meditate on this. Believe. Then you will be invincible.

She began the meditation to gain control of emotion. To focus the mind and gather power, the warrior's way. Her breathing settled to a steady, slow rhythm.

Selena opened her eyes. She could see nothing, but the meditation had created a heightened state of awareness. She could feel the space around her. It was large, she could tell that. The wall behind was of stone. The floor under her bare feet was cold and smooth. Polished granite or marble, or tile.

She was cool, but not cold. It was very quiet, with a sense of weight all around. There was a whisper of ventilation, a mere breath of air moving against her body. She thought the room must be underground. That would explain the complete silence, the feeling of containment. Her eyes were adjusted to the darkness but there was still nothing to see, except the suggestion of a faint, reddish glow across the way. It could be her imagination.

She was clamped by metal cuffs to the wall. Tight enough to prevent any slippage, any Houdini-like escape.

What time was it? She had no way of knowing. She was due to meet the others. When she failed to show up they would know something was wrong. Was it seven yet? How long had she been out? Was it the same day? Did they know she was missing? How would they find her?

She thought it was the same day. Probably no more than a few hours since she'd been taken.

Light erupted in the room, blinding her. When the flare subsided behind her eyes and she could see, she felt the fear trying to return.

The light came from gas torches set in brackets of black iron. She was in a large, windowless chamber of stone. Shadows from the flames danced around the room. A pattern was inlaid in green marble on the polished granite floor. Selena recognized it.

The Black Sun.

Die Schwarze Sonne. The dark opposite of light. She'd seen a floor just like this one in Germany, in the Generals' Hall of Himmler's Westphalia castle.

In the center of the circle was a vertical wooden pole. Two iron rings were set into the pole, one high and one low. The top of the pole was crowned with a replica of the Black Sun fashioned of gold. Near the pole was a low table. A silver cup studded with emeralds rested upon it. There was a polished wooden box next to the cup, carved with the lightning bolt runes of the SS.

There was a picture of her tacked to the pole.

The circle of the Black Sun was ringed by twelve chairs of wood and flat leather. A thirteenth chair was made of polished wood, larger and more ornate than the others. The chair was carved with runes and swastikas in a design of leaves and branches. Runes were branded into the leather of the other chairs.

Power. Victory. Life. Death.

Repeated, again and again. On one side of the carved chair stood a large Nazi flag. On the other, a flag in black and silver. Words were inlaid in black marble on the wall behind the chair, outlined with gold.

Meine Ehre heist Treue

My Loyalty is True. The SS motto.

Off to the side was a heavy, arch-topped wooden door. The door opened, and Gordon Greenwood entered the room. He was dressed in black under a monk-like robe of white, the cowl thrown back onto his shoulders. The robe was tied across the front with a black cord. The black sun was embroidered over his left breast. A wide black band embroidered with silver runes circled his left sleeve. Beyond the door a flight of stone steps led upward.

Greenwood came over to her.

"Awake? Good, we want you alert."

Selena was angry. "You've made a big mistake, you Nazi cretin."

Greenwood laughed. "Oh, no, I don't think so, *Doctor* Connor. You're the one who made the mistake. You should never have meddled in things that didn't concern you. But it all works out well in the end."

She heard steps on the stairs. Others began filing into the room. They were dressed like Greenwood in white robes with the black sun on the left breast. Only Greenwood bore the band around his sleeve. Selena recognized Smothers and Earlston. She was shocked to see a man she'd watched countless times anchoring the evening news.

The last one to enter the room was a blond man in his mid twenties. He examined her as if she were an interesting but loathsome bug.

"A beautiful specimen, Father."

"Yes. She even has good Aryan bloodlines, but she is a traitor to her race. She is perfect for our needs. For *His* need."

Selena didn't like the way Greenwood said that.

"This is my son, Frederick, Doctor Connor. Frederick did a wonderful job in Jerusalem, don't you think? Frederick is here because you succeeded in removing General Dysart. The number of the Council must be preserved. He's a bit young for such responsibility, but I'm sure he'll grow into the task."

"Robes are out of style, Greenwood. I read that Hitler used to dress up when he was little. Are you carrying on the tradition? Didn't you get enough play time in mommy's clothes?"

Greenwood's face reddened. He stepped forward and slapped her, hard. Selena's head slammed back against the wall.

"Go to your place, Frederick. We begin."

Blood trickled from Selena's mouth. Greenwood stood in front of the carved chair. The others took their seats. From his robe, Greenwood withdrew a book. The cover was black, emblazoned with the SS insignia in silver. He began reading aloud in a slow and measured cadence. It took Selena a moment to realize he was speaking in the old Germanic tongue, the language of the runes. A ripple of fear moved through her as she recognized the ritual Arslanian had encoded on his flash drive. The torches flickered.

Nick, she thought, *where the hell are you?*

CHAPTER SIXTY-TWO

Nick's ear felt like it was on fire. Selena would never be late like this. He couldn't raise her.

Lamont, Ronnie, Stephanie and Nick were in a McDonald's in downtown DC. It was a safe bet no one would look for them there. Even so, Ronnie had his black box out. It sat in the middle of the cardboard containers of hamburgers and fries. It was going on 8:40. Selena was over an hour and a half late.

Stephanie said, "I got the trace on the email to Dysart. About commanding him. It's Greenwood. We were right about him. He's the one running the show."

It was Halloween, the last night of October. A scattering of teens in bizarre costumes sat at tables nearby. Across the room, four sullen bikers in leather jackets and dirty jeans eyed Stephanie. Lamont gave them a cold look. They went back to whatever they'd been talking about.

Nick dipped a fry in ketchup, set it down. The slick surface of the table felt cold under his fingers.

"Selena's in trouble." It was a physical feeling, a bad feeling.

Stephanie's phone rang. She answered, listened, disconnected.

"That was someone I sent to her hotel. They found a waiter stuffed in a maintenance closet on Selena's floor, unconscious. His uniform was missing. Her key was still in the door slot of the room. Someone's grabbed her."

Nick felt like someone had punched him in the stomach.

"Where would they take her?" Ronnie ate the last bite of his Big Mac.

"I can think of one way to find out," Nick said. "We grab Greenwood. He'll know." He thought about how he would question him. "I can persuade him to tell us."

"Back to his house?"

"Yes."

Stephanie glanced over at a teen dressed as a vampire.

Her face paled. "Nick! That rite Heydrich wrote down. It's Halloween. In the old religions, it was the most powerful night for magic. A night of sacrifice."

It registered on everyone at the same time.

"Selena. They're going to sacrifice her, perform that ritual."
Nick crushed the plastic cup of soda he held in his hand.

"There can't be much time," Ronnie said. "I've got my stash in
the Hummer."

Ronnie's black Hummer had a concealed compartment in the
back. He had weapons, ammunition and a variety of useful things for
an emergency.

Nick nodded. "You, me and Lamont. Someone has to work the
political and legal angles if this goes bad." He turned to Stephanie.
"That's you, Steph."

She set her coffee down. "Gee, I love being Director." She
looked at them. "Well, what are you waiting for?"

An hour later they were down the street from Greenwood's
home. A tall hedge ran all along the front of the property. There
were lights on in the house. One upstairs behind drawn blinds. One
on the ground floor.

They'd changed into black clothing and body armor. They had
pistols and silenced MP-5s.

Ronnie had brought a tranquilizer gun. Silent, auto loading three
rounds, designed for use on humans, it featured a fast acting nerve
agent that took the target down on the spot. The target got violently
sick when he woke up but that was better than being dead.

A half dozen cars lined the circular drive in front of
Greenwood's house. There was a meeting going on inside.

Carter scanned the drive with night vision binoculars. "There are
two guards in suits by the entrance," he said. "What do you think,
Ronnie?"

"If Earlston is inside, the suits could be Secret Service. Maybe
we need to go easy."

"Okay, we'll trank 'em."

The moon was hidden, blanked out by thick, dark clouds. The
night was black as Hades. They got out of the car, shadows in the
darkness. They worked their way along Greenwood's hedge. They
listened for signs of alarm. Dogs, a neighbor's voice, anything. There
was only the whisper of a chill night breeze in the leaves of the
hedge.

They came to the driveway entrance. One of the guards yawned
and looked at his watch. Ronnie aimed and there was a soft hiss. The
guard grunted and dropped to the ground. His partner turned toward

the sound. Ronnie fired again and the second man crumpled to the grass. The team ran to the house.

Nick laid his hand on one of the cars. The hood was warm. There was cigarette smoke on the night air. Nick went to the end of the house and risked a glance around the corner. Halfway down, a figure leaned against the wall, smoking. No suit. He was dressed in black and had a MAC-10 slung under his arm. The man dropped his cigarette and ground it out under his foot. He began walking toward the front of the house.

Nick signaled. One coming this way. They faded into the bushes. The guard turned the corner and passed in front of Ronnie. The tranquilizer gun spat and he went down. Lamont turned him over.

Black paramilitary uniform, military haircut. Silenced MAC, fully loaded. A scar on his face. No ID. Definitely not Secret Service.

A silent, dark shape launched itself from the night and knocked Lamont down. Lamont jammed his arm between jaws trying to tear out his throat. They rolled on the ground and Lamont struggled to draw his knife. There was a strangled yelp and the dog convulsed and died. It was a large German Shepherd.

Lamont wiped the blade and sheathed the knife. His sleeve was torn and blood stained the ripped fabric.

"Waste of a good dog," he said under his breath. "They must have cut his vocal cords. I hate it when someone trains a dog like that."

They ran to the back door. A few seconds and they were in. An alarm box mounted on the wall blinked green. Another stupid mistake. Someone had failed to set the alarms.

They were in a laundry room. A night light burned over the washer/dryer. The door from the room opened into a dark kitchen. The crash of ice dropping into the bin of an icemaker sent Nick into a crouch, gun high by his cheek. A hallway led to the front of the house, where light spilled over from the living room.

He signaled with his hand. First him, then Ronnie, then Lamont. They nodded. They crept down the hall, the rubber soles on their shoes silent on the wooden floor.

Nick didn't like houses where someone might start shooting at you. Corners you couldn't see around. Stairs leading to God knew what. Closets and crannies and rooms and doors, and every one of them could hide someone waiting to kill you.

The house was quiet. Too quiet. There was no sound of conversation, nothing to indicate where the people from those cars were meeting.

It wasn't in the living room. Two men waited there, crouched behind furniture on different sides of the room.

Nick saw their reflection in a glass picture frame on the wall. He signaled Lamont and Ronnie. Two hostiles, right and left. Wait.

He slipped back to the kitchen and picked up a cushion from a stool next to the counter. The men in the living room had to be on an adrenaline trip wire. Back in the hall, he signaled the others and threw the cushion up and out and into the room. The Macs opened up, shredding the cushion to confetti. Nick and Ronnie reached around the walls and fired to both sides, then came through the opening low and firing.

The silenced weapons stuttered and jumped, spraying the room with bullets. The MACs weren't silenced, and their barking shattered the night.

The nine millimeter rounds tore into Greenwood's expensive walnut paneling. The shooters went down, tumbling backwards. The MP-5s chopped up the walls and furniture around them.

"Upstairs," Nick shouted. No need for hand signals now. "Lamont, cover us." Another shooter appeared on the second floor. Ronnie fired and he tumbled down the stairs. An ugly man, dressed in black like the others. Ronnie followed Nick at a run up the stairs. Lamont took up position at the bottom in case someone came up from below or from another part of the house.

Upstairs were five large bedrooms and three baths, all empty. Greenwood wasn't there and neither was Selena. They retreated back to the ground floor. Less than five minutes had passed since they'd entered the house.

"The library." Nick pointed with his MP-5.

The adrenaline rush was in full swing. Where was everyone? They must have heard the shooting. Another hallway led from the living room to the library, where a single desk lamp burned in the darkness. The light reflected from a crystal pen and inkwell on the desktop and the silver surface of a closed laptop computer. There was no one there. There was no one in the garden, or the downstairs bathrooms, or the closets, or the maid's room, or the garage.

"Has to be the basement," Ronnie said. "That's all that's left. They're here somewhere."

They found the door to the basement and pulled it open. A light was on. They descended a flight of wooden steps into a room with a cement floor. The walls held shelves and a workbench. Boxes were stacked in one corner. Aside from storage, it was empty.

"What now?" Lamont said.

"Something's not right." Ronnie scanned the room. It looked like an ordinary basement, the kind you'd find almost anywhere. "This room is too small. Remember the plans? Greenwood did a major make over here a while back. It was a lot bigger than this. There's got to be a hidden door."

They walked around the room. There was a faint mark on the floor, like part of a crescent moon, at one end of a high bank of shelves. Nick tugged on the shelves but they didn't move. He felt around the side.

Nothing.

He traced his fingers along the upper edge and felt something plastic. A switch. He pressed it and the shelves swung away from the wall. They started down a flight of stone steps.

CHAPTER SIXTY-THREE

Greenwood's voice made the hairs on the back of Selena's neck stand on end. She'd always heard about that. There was something primal in the harsh rhythm of the old language. Barbaric. Threatening. Frightening.

Still chanting, Greenwood went to the table in the center of the room. The chanting stopped. He opened the box. Selena saw a flash of diamonds and gold in the torchlight as he lifted the lid away. Greenwood took something from the box.

Greenwood said, "Bring her."

Four men moved away from the circle and came over to where she hung helpless. Each man took a key and unlocked one of the iron cuffs that bound her, grasping an arm or a leg. Selena struggled. The men lifted her naked body and brought her to the pole in the center of the room. Two men kept her arms and legs imprisoned while the other two bound her with leather thongs to the rings embedded in the pole. Then they returned to their places in the circle.

Greenwood stepped forward and held up a long, tapered blade in front of her face. It was brown and rusted with age, notched and pierced and wrapped in gold.

The Vienna Lance.

Greenwood spoke to her in German. Something moved in his eyes, as if more than one person were looking out at her.

"My name is Gruenwald," he said, his voice guttural and wet. "My father was Master of the Council before me, as Himmler was before him, as my son shall be after me. Tonight, the Reich is reborn. Your blood will open the passage."

Greenwood took the Lance and made a deep cut in Selena's forearm, opening a vein. The ancient blade dug into her flesh. She clenched her teeth against the pain. Greenwood picked up the emerald cup and caught the blood running down. The point of the Lance gleamed red in the flickering light of the torches. Selena twisted in her bonds and hot blood ran down her arm, down her side, draining into the cup.

When the cup was almost full, Greenwood stepped away. Blood continued to flow down her arm and over her breast. It ran down her side, down her leg, dripping on the floor. She was getting dizzy. She fought it.

"Bind her wound," Greenwood said. "We don't want her to die yet."

Smothers taped a compress over the bleeding vein. He wasn't gentle. Greenwood went to the edge of the circle of the black sun. He dipped the Vienna Lance into the chalice of blood and began to draw the blood along the circle. He moved counter-clockwise, chanting in the grating rhythm of the Old Germanic tongue as he moved.

The air turned freezing cold. Selena blinked, blinked again. A darkness was forming in the room, a thin, black cloud near the ceiling. It had to be an illusion, brought on by the wavering light of the torches, the loss of blood. She fought to stay conscious.

She wasn't going to give up, no matter what. But she hoped the others had figured it out and were on the way. She didn't think she had much time left.

CHAPTER SIXTY-FOUR

There were thirteen steps. At the bottom, a short corridor paved with stone led to an arched door of thick, heavy oak. The hinges were of hammered iron, the black iron handle shaped like a snarling wolf's head. The door looked medieval. There was a faint sound beyond the thick door, a rhythmic chanting, harsh and guttural, rising in pitch.

Nick shifted the selector switch on his MP-5 to semi-auto.

"Lamont, you pull the door open, we go in. On three." He signaled with his fingers. The door opened and they stepped into the room.

The first thing Nick saw was a group of men dressed in white robes, standing in a circle in a stone room lit by flaming torches. The room was freezing. The next thing he saw was Selena, naked and slick with blood, bound to a pole set in the middle of the room. A man stood in front of her. He was chanting. His back was toward the entrance. There was a strange darkness hovering around him. He raised both his hands high over his head. Between them he held a long, dark blade, pointed down toward Selena.

Nick's bullet took him somewhere between his shoulder and spine, spinning him away from Selena. The blade flew from his hands and clattered against the polished floor.

An older man in the circle reached for something inside his robe. Lamont shot him in the chest. He staggered and crumpled over, the front of his robe bright with blood. The rest of the circle froze in place.

Nick slung his MP-5 and ran to Selena. He reached up and cut her bonds. She slumped into his arms. He caught her and laid her down. Ronnie and Lamont kept their weapons trained on the others.

Blood oozed from under a crude bandage on her arm, dark red against her pale skin. He felt her pulse. Strong, but erratic. Lying on the floor not far away, the man he'd shot groaned. Nick recognized Greenwood.

"Ronnie, get me one of those robes."

Ronnie walked over to the Vice-President. "Take it off."

Earlston drew himself up to his full five foot nine. "Do you know who I am?"

Ronnie put the muzzle of his gun on Earlston's forehead and pressed.

"I don't give a shit if you're the Queen of England. Take it off."

Earlston stripped off the robe. Ronnie tossed the robe over and Nick wrapped it around Selena. Her face was white. She opened her eyes.

"Nick."

"You're okay now. It's all right."

"It took you long enough." She closed her eyes.

He picked her up and carried her across the room, sat her down in a fancy carved chair. That was when he noticed the Nazi flags. He looked around the room, at the swastikas, the torches, the words on the wall. He looked at Selena, pale in the light of the torches. He wanted to hurt someone. He wanted to hurt someone badly.

One of the robed men started toward the figure groaning on the floor.

"Don't move," Lamont said.

"That's my father, he's hurt."

"Tough shit. Don't move."

"You wouldn't dare shoot us."

Lamont looked at the speaker. Admiral Lang, Chief of Naval Intelligence.

"Do you know who we are? Do you understand what is going to happen to you if you harm us? I am your superior officer. I order you to drop those weapons, now."

Ronnie and Lamont looked at each other and began laughing. Lang looked confused.

Selena opened her eyes. "Take care of this, Nick. I'm fine." Her eyes were clear.

He walked over to Lamont. They stood with their backs to the open door.

"Nick, what are we going to do with these shitbirds?"

"Damned if I know."

"You will do nothing. Drop your weapons. You and the schwarze."

The voice came from behind them, from the passage beyond the door. Whoever was there couldn't see Ronnie, standing to the left of the doorway.

People who point guns expect the target to freeze. There's only a fraction of a second to react. Training took over. Nick and Lamont rolled in opposite directions away from the door and the line of fire. Nick came up kneeling with his pistol in his hand.

Ronnie opened up toward the hall, bouncing rounds off the walls of the passage at the unseen speaker. Shots came through the open door.

Selena dived for the floor. Lang pulled a pistol from under his robe and shot Ronnie. The bullet knocked him off his feet and back against the wall. He fell to the floor. Carter shot Lang twice, the .45 bucking in his hand. The circle of robed men scattered and more pistols came out. The room echoed with gunfire.

Ronnie's armor had stopped the round. He raised his weapon from where he lay and began firing. Lamont fired. Carter fired at anything moving in a white robe. Bits of stone flew and the air filled with rounds whining and ricocheting off the walls. The slide locked back on Nick's pistol.

Sudden silence. The flames from the torches flickered and danced, casting strange shadows on the walls.

The room stank of gunfire and blood. Empty shell casings littered the marble floor. Ronnie climbed to his feet, holding his side where the round had punched his armor. Lamont took a quick look around the door frame, ducked back, and looked again. He moved into the doorway, his MP-5 held up by his cheek.

"Clear," he said.

The floor of the room was carpeted with white-robed bodies. The stone walls were chipped and pockmarked. Nick ejected the empty magazine from his .45. He fed in a new one, racked the slide and walked over to where Greenwood lay on the floor. He felt sudden goose bumps all over. There was something nearby. Something to be feared. He looked around but saw nothing.

Greenwood lay in a spreading pool of blood. He looked up, his face contorted in rage. Nick thought about killing him, but Greenwood was already dead. He just didn't know it yet.

"It is not over," Greenwood said. He coughed and blood bubbled from his lips as he spoke. "We are everywhere. You will never defeat us." Suddenly he was watching something over Nick's shoulder. All the color drained from his face.

"No," he said. "Oh, no."

Something colder than ice brushed Nick. Something dark. Something foul. Greenwood shuddered.

"NO!" he screamed.

He died. Suddenly the room was warm. Whatever it was Nick had felt was gone. He took a deep breath.

He reached down and picked up the Vienna Lance, damp with Selena's blood. It twisted in his hand and cut his palm. He swore and hurled it against the wall. The brittle iron broke with a sharp, snapping sound and the Lance fell in pieces to the ground.

Ronnie and Lamont walked among the bodies. Smothers lay on his side, clutching his abdomen and moaning. Senator Blackfriar had a sucking chest wound and lay on his back laboring for breath, staring at the ceiling. Greenwood's son crawled across the floor in a trail of blood, clutching his stomach. A strange, mewling whine came from him. The rest were dead.

Lamont had a deep gash across his cheek. He touched it, blotted it with his sleeve.

"Let's go." Carter holstered his pistol.

Selena stood up. "What about that?" She gestured at the bodies.

"Leave it. We'll let Rice handle it. We've got to get out of here."

Then he remembered Rice's comment about Dysart never coming to trial. What would happen if this got out? He looked at Ronnie and Lamont.

"This can't go public," he said.

They nodded.

"Take Selena upstairs and go get the car. I'll finish up here."

"You sure?" Lamont said.

"You go ahead. I'll be right behind."

Lamont and Ronnie helped Selena to her feet. They went up the stairs.

Nick moved around the walls and snuffed all the torches except one. The hiss of escaping gas grew loud. He found an adjustment, turned the remaining torch down to a tiny flame and left it burning.

He went into the hall. A man in black uniform lay on the stones, his weapon beside him. His lifeless eyes were open, cold and blue. On his collar he wore a silver oak leaf insignia.

Nick closed the door to the Nazi chamber and the soft whisper of gas. He hurried up the stairs, past the basement and up to the first floor. He ran into the library and took the laptop from Greenwood's desk. He ran to the front of the house and out the door, past the silent cars and the Italian fountain. As he reached the street Lamont pulled up in the car.

In the back seat, Nick held Selena close. She shivered, waves that rippled across her.

They were blocks away when the explosion lit up the night.

CHAPTER SIXTY-FIVE

On the way in, Nick called Stephanie and briefed her. She was waiting for them in front of Nick's building. He gave her Greenwood's computer. Maybe it had the proof the President needed. Rice had to get things under control, fast. Before anyone figured out what had really happened.

It wasn't the first time Nick had showed up at his building looking like anything but a normal tenant. The security guard eyed Selena in her bloody robe and Nick in his black gear. He shook his head without saying a word as they made for the elevator.

The apartment was furnished European style. Simple wood and glass and clean Scandinavian accents. Nick sat Selena down on a wide couch of brown leather and cleaned the wound on her arm. It was a brutal gash, deep and red. He put antibiotic ointment on it and bandaged the cut. It would do for now. He got up and poured her a whiskey. She was pale, still wrapped in the robe with the black sun embroidered on the breast.

"Here, this will help." He poured one for himself. It was two in the morning. The night was quiet, cold and dark. No traffic on the street ten stories below. No garbage trucks. No Nazis.

She drank, coughed, drank more.

Nick sat down next to her. She clutched the glass in both hands. She had the thousand yard stare. Watching something a long way off.

He watched her and thought about Megan. He'd wanted to keep Megan safe and had thought he could. That illusion had vanished in flame at the end of the airport runway. After Megan, he'd never wanted to feel pain like that again. Hadn't wanted to risk letting anyone in. Looking at Selena, he knew what he had done.

"It's okay," Nick said. "It's over. You're safe."

"What was that in the room?" she said.

"I don't know."

"It was evil," she said. "And the look in Greenwood's eyes. He was going to plunge that spear into my heart." She shuddered.

Nick put his hand on her arm. "I saw you hanging there—I didn't know if you were dead. All that blood. I wanted to kill him. All of them."

"You did," she said. "Give me another." She held out her glass. He got up and poured two more. He set his down and went into the bedroom and came back with a Turkish robe of blue cotton.

"Put this on." She slipped into it, the sleeves too long for her arms. Nick stuffed the Nazi robe in the trash.

She pulled the robe tight. Her color was coming back as the whiskey worked into her system. She was going to be all right, but she'd live with tonight for the rest of her life.

He cleared his throat, said, "I've been kind of stuck the last few months."

"What do you mean?"

"Words come hard for me. About you. About Megan. What I'm trying to say...if you had died tonight I couldn't have handled it. I had to see that. I've pushed you away because I didn't want to admit I cared that much. But I do. I'm sorry."

She reached up and touched him on his face. "It's as much my fault as yours. You scare me sometimes. Your dreams, all of it."

"Selena..."

"It's all right, Nick. It doesn't matter now."

She was right. It didn't.

CHAPTER SIXTY-SIX

Morning. The team gathered at the apartment. The smell of fresh coffee drifted across the room. The TV was on. Every station carried stories about the freak gas explosion at Greenwood's home that had killed the Vice President. After a few minutes Nick turned it off.

"Greenwood had everything on his computer," Stephanie said. She held up a disc. "It's all here. The Jerusalem bomb came out of Syria. Greenwood's son planted it at the Mosque. One of the council was Eric Reinhardt, the industrial magnate. His father wrote the diary you found on the sub. Reinhardt provided the explosives and the nuke in Tel Aviv."

"Where did he get it?" Lamont said.

"On the East European black market, one of those warheads that went missing after the Soviet Union collapsed."

"What else was on the computer?" Nick asked.

"They were plotting a coup. Rice was going to be assassinated. There was going to be an 'incident' in the Gulf of Hormuz, a *casus belli* pointing at the Iranians. Like the Tonkin Gulf in '64."

A North Vietnamese gunboat raid in the Tonkin Gulf provided the excuse President Lyndon Johnson needed to escalate the war in Vietnam. Nick thought it had been a set up. That war had bled the country for ten years and cost 58,000 American lives and more than a million dead Vietnamese. Greenwood and his Nazi Council had wanted to do it all over again, on a bigger scale.

Greenwood was dead, but the war he'd started was alive and well.

Nick tugged on his ear. "It's the proof Rice wanted. I don't know if anyone will believe it."

"Speaking of Rice, you're going to the White House again. He's sending a car. You can take this to him."

"I keep going over there, maybe he'll give me a spare key."

Stephanie gave him the disc.

"Does he know what's on it?"

"Yes."

"I wonder how he handled it? Freak gas explosion looks a lot better than what happened."

"If you find out, let me know."

The black Lincoln Rice sent took Nick to a rear entrance of the White House. A grim faced Secret Service escort took him to a workout room on the third floor. Rice was riding a stationary bike. He was dressed in sweat pants and a green tee shirt that said USMC across the front.

Rice got off the bike. He mopped sweat from his forehead with a towel and beckoned Nick over to a bench. His Secret Service detail stood a discreet distance away. Carter gave him the disc. There was tension in the room Nick hadn't felt on his previous visits.

"Tell me about it," Rice said.

Carter told him. Rice drank from a bottle of water. He sat for a moment, thinking.

"Do you know how the situation was sanitized, Carter?" It wasn't "Nick" today.

"No, sir."

"Wendell Lodge will become the next Director of the CIA."

He didn't need to say more. Nick thought it was a devil's bargain, like clasping a snake to your breast.

"I'm sorry to hear that, sir."

"Yes. However, it's done and my VP is an honored victim. I may get my second term, after all." He drank from the water bottle.

"Carter, you and your team have done a great service. You understand, I cannot acknowledge it."

"Of course, sir. We never considered that. I'll tell them what you said."

Rice set the bottle down. He looked frustrated. "Israel and Iran are at war. The Israelis took out the Iranian nuclear facilities at Natanz and Arak last night. They hit Qom as well. We're at DEFCON2."

Natanz was where the Iranians had most of their centrifuges for uranium enrichment. Arak was a heavy water plant. Aside from sheltering another enrichment plant, Qom was a holy city with a famous mosque. Because of that it was another Muslim flash point.

Nick kept quiet.

Rice continued. "The Iranians retaliated with missiles. No nukes, though, thank God. They still don't have them. There are heavy civilian casualties on both sides."

He mopped sweat from his face. "Two hours ago Israel fought an aerial battle over Lebanon and the Sinai against a combined strike of hundreds of planes sent by Syria, Iran, and Egypt. It was the biggest air battle since World War Two. The Israelis drove them off.

"The Saudis and the Turks have held back so far, which means we can still preserve an illusion of cooperation with them. They're our last hope for any kind of diplomatic solution in the Islamic world."

Rice paused.

"The Saudis stand to lose a lot if the war spreads. They cannot appear to compromise with us, but they're panicked. They're worried about Israeli nukes. They should be. I know Litzvak, the acting Prime Minister of Israel. He's a rabid Zionist, brought in by Ascher to placate the extremists. He'll use nukes if Israel is pressed too hard. Mecca and Riyadh are probably on top of his target list. He hates the Arabs."

Rice sipped from his water.

"Iran, Iraq and Syria have announced a pact of 'mutual military cooperation' and Iran is beginning to move troops and supplies across southern Iraq. They're setting up an invasion and using Iraqi airspace. Litzvak will never allow it to happen. He'll throw everything he's got at them."

"What are you going to do, Mr. President?"

Rice gave him a calculating look. "What would you do, Carter, if you were me?"

"Well, sir." He stopped. "Sir, it seems to me that you have two problems that combine to give you a third."

"Go on."

"There's the trigger event, the bombing at the Mosque. Then there's the underlying situation in the region. The hatred, the fanaticism, the religious beliefs. That's what's driving things now. Nothing you do can change that."

"You don't think reason will prevail." Rice's voice was flat.

"No, sir. I don't."

"You said three problems. You've defined two. What is the third?"

"The third is the war itself. If it can't be stopped by reason, it has to be stopped by emotion. The only emotion I can think of that's strong enough is fear. There's plenty of that already. I think you have to use that, find a way to, ah, encourage these governments to see it's in their own best interest to back off. Then sweeten it with something that lets everyone save face and claim they won something valuable for themselves and their people."

Rice smiled. "Encourage?"

"I always liked Teddy Roosevelt's philosophy."

"Speak softly and carry a big stick?"

"Yes, sir. If you can get some other big sticks to go along, maybe the combatants will listen."

"I can't reveal what really happened. You brought me the proof I asked for, but it can't be used. Someone must be held responsible for the bombing."

"Then I guess you'll have to make something up, Mr. President."

Rice looked at Nick as if he had just realized he was there.

"Perhaps you should consider a career in politics after all. You're suggesting I manufacture a bomber and a plot and sell it to the world."

Nick said nothing.

"I'll think about what you've said, Carter."

"I'm sure you'll find a way, Mr. President."

"That's what I like about you, Carter. Confidence." He stood up and Nick rose with him.

"I'm told that Director Harker will be unable to return to work for some time. In your opinion, is her deputy competent to take over?"

"Yes, sir. She's been with Harker since the beginning, she knows all the players. She's a good choice."

"You're sure you wouldn't like the job?"

"Stephanie will make a great Director, Mister President."

No way did he want the job. No way. He'd last about ten minutes in the political snake pit of the Capitol.

Rice nodded. "Then here's what I want you to do. I want both of you to assume leadership of the Project. Will you do that for me?"

"Sir..."

Rice held up his hand. "Don't say anything right now, Carter. Take some time off. Think about it."

"Yes, sir." What else was he supposed to say?

Rice stopped at the door. "I was supposed to be assassinated in Chicago today. It's a strange feeling." He looked at Nick. "Well done," he said. Then he was gone.

Nick left the White House. He wondered what the rest of the day would bring. He wished he was sitting on his cabin porch or maybe lying on the beach in Maui. Maybe he should resign. Maybe he would.

Years ago, he'd talk with Megan when he had a tough decision to make. She'd had a way of looking at things that helped him get his head straight. But Megan was gone. He'd talk it over with Selena.

CHAPTER SIXTY-SEVEN

Ronnie sat on Nick's couch munching cashews and watching television. The networks were covering the conclusion of an extraordinary meeting in Casablanca.

"It looks like Rice pulled it off," Ronnie said.

"He had some help." Nick stood by the kitchen counter. "No one wants World War III. At least the shooting's stopped."

Rice had spent eight days in Morocco meeting with the leaders of the Islamic world and of Israel, Russia, China, France and Great Britain. On the third day of the conference Israel and Iran had walked out. On the fifth day they declared a temporary cease fire. Nick wondered what kind of heavy arm twisting and deal making had gone on behind the scenes.

Rice had decided partial truth was the best strategy. In a speech televised around the globe, he revealed that Eric Reinhardt was behind the destruction of al-Aqsa, in a neo-Nazi plot to start a war and destroy the Jews. He presented proof. It got Israel off the hook. It shocked the world.

Rice emphasized that Reinhardt was not a native-born American. Everything about him had been uncovered. Rice pointed out that Reinhardt's father had been an SS General. He made no mention of the existence of the Council or its membership and influence.

No one knew Reinhardt had been at Greenwood's house. Rice said he'd been killed in a fiery car crash while trying to escape Federal Agents sent to arrest him. Dental records confirmed his identity. The remains of his incinerated body were shown to the world. He then announced a coalition of nations would rebuild the Mosque. He condemned hate groups and called for a new era of understanding and compassion.

Two days after the speech, Elizabeth was out of her induced coma. The team gathered in her hospital room. Her head was swathed in bandages. Her left eye was covered. It was too soon to calculate the full extent of damage to her brain, but she was weeks ahead of schedule in her recovery. She could speak, with a slight blurring of some of her words. She could think clearly.

Nick told her what had happened.

"They were going to sacrifice Selena? Really?" Her voice was a whisper.

"Yes. But no one will ever find out. The house went up in a firestorm. The fire trucks couldn't get near it. Everything turned to slag and ashes. Lodge shut the locals down before they could get going. It's amazing what the phrase 'National Security' will do. There's nothing left, nothing to point a finger at a Nazi conspiracy."

"The Lance?"

"Gone. Melted into nothing, and good riddance. They still have the copy in Vienna. As far as the world knows it's the real deal."

"Rice owes Lodge. I wonder how that will work out?" She coughed, reached carefully for a tissue. "I need a long rest." She looked out the window. "I'm tired, Nick." The words came out slurred.

Nick kept his face neutral. "You'll be back soon, Director."

She looked at him. "We both know it won't be soon. Maybe never. Rice spoke with me about you taking over the team with Stephanie. What's your decision?"

"I don't know. He said take some time to think about it."

"Rice needs you. With Stephanie, you'll be fine. She can handle the political and administrative side, but you're the best choice to deal with the tactical and strategic decisions. The two of you can make it work." She coughed. "Rice needs you," she said again.

A headache began. He needed time to think about it. He'd go to the cabin.

Stephanie said, "We've talked about it. We've got you covered, Nick. Take some time off. I'll call you if anything important happens."

Nick looked at the others. The team. His team. His friends.

"Thanks," he said.

EPILOGUE

Selena and Nick headed up into the Sierra Foothills. They turned off the paved road, bounced over a stretch of dirt and gravel and pulled up in front of Nick's cabin.

The cabin was at the end of the road on top of a good sized hill. Built of old, dark wood, it had a steep, hunter green metal roof sloping down over a covered front porch. The foothills rose up behind. East were the High Sierras. West was a wide vista to the coastal range. It looked like the Pacific might not be too far away, but it was a hundred and fifty miles or so to the beach.

The cabin was home. He always seemed to think better here. The place in D.C. was only where he stayed.

They stepped from the car under clouds of black, gold and deep red.

He unlocked the door, dropped his bag on the couch and opened a window. He opened the grate on the woodstove and set a match to the kindling and wood laid there.

He opened a bottle of wine. They went outside and sat on the porch, watching the sun go down in splashes and streaks of vivid color behind the Coastal Range. Shadows lengthened under the trees. The air smelled of wood smoke from the stove.

After a few minutes Selena said, "Do you think we got them all?"

"I think we wrote the last page of Himmler's medieval fantasy. But Nazis are like the Hydra in that Greek myth. You cut off the head, two more spring back. You can't ever get them all. But Greenwood's bunch, yeah. We stopped them."

Selena looked out at the afterglow of the sunset. "I was thinking about what I said a while back. About us being so different. How it was natural for you to jump into action and start shooting, but not for me."

He tensed. Natural born killer.

"Maybe we're not so different. It does seem to me that you...that you're more reckless than I am. But there's something that's the same."

"What's that?" he set his glass down.

"Instinct. You can't get where I am in martial arts without that. It's a zone, a place where I just *do*. Or it does me. I don't think about it. You do it too. Our training and experience are different but we both act out of instinct without thinking. So, it's the same."

She drank some wine. She frowned.

"I always thought my martial arts would protect me."

He waited.

"I couldn't get out of those bonds in Greenwood's room. I can't stop a bullet with a side kick. I can't use my skills to deflect it. It scares the hell out of me."

"Bullets scare the hell out of me, too."

"I guess it goes with the territory."

"You could quit."

"No. I don't want to. It would let everyone down. The team means a lot to me. It's the first time in my life I've felt like I was part of something important. I've got a real purpose in life, now. Bullets or not."

Selena pulled up the collar of her jacket. The night was coming on and it was getting cold.

"Are you going to take Rice up on his offer?"

"I don't know."

"Do you trust him?"

"As much as any politician. But he's the President. He's always got to think of protecting the office of the Presidency. He could disown us if something goes wrong."

"I've known him since I was fifteen. He and my uncle were good friends. I don't think he'd hang us out to dry. But you're right, he has to do what the office demands. Why do you think he set up the Project in the first place?"

"He knows people like Lodge don't tell him the truth. He needs someone outside the agencies. We're a counterweight so he can find out what's what. It puts us at odds with everyone. CIA and DIA and the others are always jockeying for position. There's a lot of stonewalling and competition. They protect their turf and argue about the meaning of intelligence and what should be done about it. They hide things from him."

"You make it sound like they're the enemy."

"I don't mean it that way. But things get lost in the bureaucracy and there are a lot of personal agendas. Rice created the Project to cut through all the bullshit."

"See, that's why Elizabeth and Rice want you to run things with Steph. You understand the dynamics, how things work behind the scenes."

"There's a lot I don't know."

"Nobody knows it all, not Elizabeth either. What's really bothering you?"

"You want the truth? What if I make the wrong call and someone gets killed?"

"Do you really need me to tell you there aren't any guarantees?"

He looked at his empty glass. "What if you get killed? Because of one of my decisions?"

It was out in the open.

"Oh, Nick. You can't make me the reason to take this on or not. Elizabeth said something to me a while back, about feelings. About how we have to put them aside. Does it really make any difference, in the end? Did it make any difference in Argentina, or in Tibet?"

"No. But I think about it."

"You wouldn't be who you are if you didn't think about it. You're not like Lodge, or one of those Pentagon types. That's why you're the right person for the job. I trust you. We all do. Besides, it's my choice to stay. I know what I'm up against. I'll deal with it. And so will you."

"So, you think we should take this on?"

"We?"

"You're on the team. You're part of the decision."

"Would it make a difference, you think? What we'd be doing?" Her voice was light, but Nick heard a deeper question in her words.

We.

"It could," he said.

"Then let's do it."

NEW RELEASES

Be the first to know when I have a new book coming out by subscribing to my newsletter. No spam or busy emails, only a brief announcement now and then. Just click on the link below. You can unsubscribe at any time...

http://alexlukeman.com/contact.html#newsletter

You can contact me at: **alex@alexlukeman.com.** I promise to get back to you.

My website is: **www.alexlukeman.com**

The Project Series:

White Jade
The Lance
The Seventh Pillar
Black Harvest
The Tesla Secret
The Nostradamus File
The Ajax Protocol
The Eye of Shiva
Black Rose
The Solomon Scroll
The Russian Deception
The Atlantis Stone

AUTHOR'S NOTES

I always research my books carefully and this one is no exception. The internet is an amazing tool, though you have to separate the wheat from the chaff. There are millions of pages about Nazis like Himmler. Here's what is true and what isn't, to the best of my knowledge.

Himmler was indeed in Alsace-Lorraine on his private train in December of 1944, where he had been sent to oversee "Operation North Wind", his first and only command in the field. He failed miserably.

The Grand Council of Knights is real. It consisted of Himmler as Grand Master and twelve senior SS Generals. Some reports say more were involved. It was modeled on King Arthur's Round Table. He would meet with his Generals in the "Generals' Hall" of his castle in Westphalia. That room has been restored, including the Black Sun inlaid on the floor, along with the "Hall of Heroes" below. After the war had been won by Germany, it was supposed to become a shrine. There is a central circle with provision for an "eternal flame" in the center, with twelve plinths arranged around it that were to hold the ashes of his so-called Knights. It was never finished.

I've often wondered why anyone bothered to restore it. Today it is a tourist attraction. You can see these places for yourself, if you really want to. You might find the atmosphere a bit...oppressing. Evil lingers for a long time.

Himmler had big plans for his castle grounds, including a war college for SS officers, formal gardens, etc., etc. The plans still exist. Everything was shaped like a spear, with the castle (which is three-sided) at the point.

Himmler created the *Ahnerabe*, a special SS branch devoted to "racial research" and searching worldwide for important relics, particularly the Holy Grail. He sent teams abroad as far as Tibet seeking secrets of magical power. This is true.

One of the first things Hitler did when he entered Austria in 1938 was to send a special SS detachment to secure the Vienna Lance. It was taken to Nuremberg and recovered by Patton's army in 1945. It was returned to Vienna, where it can be seen today as part of the Hapsburg Imperial Regalia.

The legend of the Lance is as stated in the book. The technology did not exist in 1938 to accurately date the relic. More recently, the Vienna Lance has been proven to be no older than the sixth or seventh century CE.

Rumors have persisted since the end of the war that the Lance recovered by Patton is a forgery and that the Nazis hid the real one. There is no doubt at all that Hitler viewed it as a divine and magical object offering power to the one who held it. Himmler had a copy that he used for his rituals. That is also documented, although no one knows what those rituals were. What if Himmler had the real thing and Hitler had the copy?

It is said that Reinhardt Heydrich was the one person who fully understood the power of the Lance. He was the true architect of the "Final Solution". A genuine sociopathic narcissist who believed himself beloved by the Czech people he brutally oppressed, Heydrich was number two in the SS hierarchy after Himmler. The tide turned against the Nazis in 1942, about the same time Heydrich was killed by Czech partisans. If he was able to invoke some occult power from the Lance and no one else knew how, that would explain a lot, wouldn't it? If so, it's a damn good thing they killed him. It's a good thing anyway.

The secret Antarctica base has never been found, but it's another of those rumors that just won't go away. The internet is full of things like drawings purporting to be plans of Nazi flying saucers and secret weapons, supposedly built there. Admiral Doenitz did actually refer to an invincible fortress in the Antarctic.

After WWII a large military expedition code named Operation Highjump was launched by the United States, Britain and Australia, under command of Admiral Byrd, partly to try and find this base. They searched on the western side of Antarctica, which has much better weather than the eastern side where I put it. Nobody really knows what else the military was doing there, but the operation did take place.

There is a German Antarctic research station near the Fenris Mountains named Neumayer III. I modeled my station after that one. You can find a picture of it on the internet.

Type IXD U-boats existed as described, likewise the D2s. The last known D2 was number 884. Early in the war the numbers were removed from the U-Boats and badges like the one I have described were used to identify boat and crew.

For more about runes, Elder Futhark and translation, visit this great website about runes; http://www.vikingrune.com/rune-converter/. Someone has gone to a lot of trouble to make this happen. Thank you!

ACKNOWLEDGEMENTS

Thanks to Gayle, Greg, JJ, Glenn, Ron, Noah, Ger. Others, who encouraged me. No one writes alone.

ABOUT THE AUTHOR

Alex Lukeman writes action/adventure thrillers featuring a covert intelligence unit called the PROJECT. He is the author of the award-winning Amazon best seller, *The Tesla Secret*. Alex is a former Marine and psychotherapist and uses his experience of the military and human nature to inform his work. He likes riding old, fast motorcycles and playing guitar, usually not at the same time.

Made in the USA
San Bernardino, CA
09 June 2020